BOOK FOUR: THE WEIR CHRONICLES

STACK A DECK

OTHER BOOKS BY SUE DUFF

The Weir Chronicles
Fade to Black
Masks and Mirrors
Sleight of Hand
Stack a Deck
Dim the Lights
(available February 2018)

Short Stories
"Duo'vr"
a short story in the anthology
TICK TOCK: Seven Tales of Time

"A Mistake"
a short story in the anthology
OFF BEAT: Nine Spins on Song

BOOK FOUR: THE WEIR CHRONICLES

STACK A DECK

SUE DUFF

For my sisters, Margaret, Joan, TeeCee, Barb & Mary

You are the ground beneath my feet,
and the rainbow after a storm

DETOUR

Is it possible to truly know thyself? Isn't man like a pebble upon the shore, forever battered by the waves, nurtured by the warmth of the sun and polished smooth by the forces of nature, destined to be a prisoner of constant change?

Mankind is more fluid than solid. We are permeable and molded by what intersects with us throughout our lives. How can I truly know myself when what I am today, may be different tomorrow, based on what I experience with every passing moment.

The Pur Heir, Book of the Weir, Vol. II

PART
ONE

The line between good and evil became blurred.

ONE

Ian shyfted to the alley behind the market and pressed against the wall. He pushed his sunglasses higher on his nose and lowered the brim on his baseball cap, then listened for any sign of presence nearby, fearful the emerald shimmer of his corona might have been spotted in spite of the midday sun. The tiny heartbeats and scurry of startled rats feasting on decaying scraps reassured Ian they were the sole witnesses. He inhaled the cumin, tarragon, and mint that drifted out of the bustling market of Calle Pastor y Landero on the other side of the building while the heat of late May formed bands of sweat beneath his cap.

Gothic spires rose above the nearby buildings. Roman, Muslim and Castilian influences eclipsed the city of Seville, Spain. The historical aspects of the city intrigued Ian, but his curiosity would have to wait. He wasn't here for a vacation. He came in search of Milo.

He slipped into the market with its rows of tip-to-tip makeshift tables and pushed between the packed bodies of tourists buying trinkets and souvenirs, they stood out among natives purchasing the evening's dinner supplies or restocking pantries with fresh spices. The local merchants sold their wares on plywood tables held up by sawhorses covered in thin, colorful tablecloths. It was difficult to see the sellers sitting or standing behind their tables unless you were directly in front of their booths. Ian's instinct was to flee. Why had Milo gone against protocol and insisted on such a public rendezvous?

He peeked around strings of garlic to find a merchant no more than ten or twelve years of age. A few adults sat in the back of the stall enjoying a simple midday meal. An elderly man gave Ian a sideways glance then returned to his sandwich. A young girl smiled up at Ian with huge milk-chocolate eyes and extended two arms loaded with beaded necklaces.

Ian returned the smile, then continued through the packed crowd in the suffocating heat. The bakery at the tip of the third lane was his destination. Ian turned keen ears and furtive glances to the clusters of strangers surrounding him, mindful of anything that might indicate he was being followed. He wasn't about to give the Pur Syndrion army an excuse to arrest Milo and toss him in a cell. Ian had hurt his loved ones enough by aligning with the rebel Jaered, but was desperate to know what the Syndrion was up to. Thankfully, the old caretaker still had Pur Weir friends scattered across the globe who would keep his secrets.

He pushed his way through the crowd and paused a few feet from the bakery stand. The chalky scrawl of Milo's handwriting on the overhead sign was a beacon of hope that the old caretaker was well and remained beyond the reach of the Pur army.

Two brown-robed monks stood behind piles of rolls and loaves of every shape and size. A hint of a smile spread across Ian's lips. Milo must be in his element among the monks of St. Basil's, at least where his baking skills were concerned. Did the old caretaker miss his ice cream binges and his detective novels while hiding among the cloistered?

One last check, but no erratic or racing heartbeats. No Pur guard appeared to be lying in wait, so he approached the stockier monk and picked up a loaf. "I'd like a baker's dozen of these."

The monk peered up from beneath his hood. A clamp gripped Ian's heart when a stranger's face stared back. The man's shoulders were relaxed but his eyes widened. Was it fear, or confusion? The monk glanced around, then grabbed an already filled sack from the back of the stand. He tossed it at Ian, as if coming any closer would be death itself.

Ian caught the sack with one hand and pulled out his wallet with the other. "How much?" he asked. This wasn't going according to Milo's instructions. What had happened to Milo?

The stranger remained mute but thrust an opened palm at Ian. He didn't have any European currency and handed the monk a ten-dollar bill. The man snatched it and then, without taking the time to put it in their money tin, scrambled out of the market leaving the other monk to the baked goods. The man gave him a subtle backhanded wave to leave.

He made his way up and down one row after another, searching for the scared man. He spied a monk with the same build and matching robe, but when Ian grabbed him and turned him around, it was yet another stranger. Further search yielded nothing. Self-conscious and vulnerable in the public market, he returned to the alley. Confusion morphed into concern. What had happened since Milo sent word last night? Ian looked down at the bag of rolls. How could he leave Seville without knowing the old caretaker was safe?

Creak. A back door opened onto the alley and Ian jerked back. A grimy man, not much older than Ian, entered the alley carrying a large metal trash can overflowing with food scraps. He dumped its contents into the alley without acknowledging Ian. A couple of nearby trash mounds moved, then bulged. Rats migrated toward the newest banquet as the man returned to the building. The door slammed behind him.

Ian decided to return to the market and question the remaining monk, but when he turned, a tall, broad man entered the alley and strolled toward him.

Ian shyfted and reappeared in the middle of the auditorium, but dropped to his knees as crushing pressure deep within his chest robbed him of breath. The bag of rolls slipped from his arms. He collapsed on all fours and gasped for air. Shuffling and dragging feet faded, and the pressure soon lifted. Ian sat on the gym floor and watched as Jaered dropped a doubled over, groaning Patrick into a seat at the end of the auditorium.

"Why are you back so soon?" Jaered shouted.

"Something's wrong. He wasn't there." Ian scooped up the rolls and shoved them into the bag, then got to his feet. "A Pur guard cornered me in the alley."

"A little warning would have been nice," Jaered yelled.

Ian tightened his fists to ward off the core blasts that itched to form. "You're right. Next time I'll tell the Sar assassin that I have to send a text before he can fling a core blast at my head!"

Jaered grunted then grabbed Patrick by the arm and jerked him to his feet. Patrick kept his hand pressed to his chest and looked like he might puke. Ian's friend wasn't used to his newborn core, or the effects of the Curse.

"Are you okay?" Ian directed at Patrick.

Patrick nodded. "What about Milo and Tara?" He rubbed his chest.

"I don't know," Ian said. He headed for the expansive kitchen at the rear of the auditorium and set the bag of rolls on the stainless steel counter. Was it all a trap, to lure him there? Ian recalled Milo's handwriting on the sign, but the text message from the previous night could have been anyone using Milo's phone.

It had been a week filled with revelations about the darker side of the Pur Weir: heartache at his inability to return to the only home he'd ever known, and discovering that the Primary had denied Ian access to his mother, his entire life. He flexed his stiff shoulders from the physical and mental training at the hands of the rebel drill sergeant. Ian didn't trust Jaered, or the band of rebels. He went along with everything for Patrick's sake—and Rayne's. Jaered knew where she was and Ian needed him. Jaered claimed she was safe as long as their common enemy, Aeros, remained on Earth. But Ian wasn't sure who the enemies were any longer. Trust hadn't developed as fast as the sore, stiff muscles.

The trio had endured several contentious days cooped up in the isolated auditorium in Greenland. Today was the first time in a week that Ian had seen another living soul besides Jaered and Patrick. Where was Milo? Was he safe? What had become of Tara? Was Saxon with her? Ian had left to get answers about his loved ones, but returned only with questions and a churning stomach.

When Ian turned away, the bag toppled over and a few of the baker's dozen escaped across the shiny counter. One dropped onto the floor. Ian snatched it up and with a shout that did little to purge his frustration, he threw it against the wall. The roll burst and crumbs sprayed across the counter. A sizable chunk revealed a sliver of paper. Ian pulverized the piece in his fist and discovered a handwritten word. SYNDRION. It was in Milo's scrawl.

He grabbed a roll off the counter and tore it apart to find another word. MISSING. By the time he'd uncovered the rest of the puzzle pieces, Jaered had appeared in the doorway.

"And here I thought you brought us a snack." Jaered approached the counter and picked up one of the larger pieces of bread, then leaned his back against the counter, tossed it into the air, and caught it in his mouth. "Thanks for not taking this out on us," he mumbled.

Ian arranged the scraps of paper. SYNDRION, MISSING, TOOK, HUNTING, ALL, TARA, TOGETHER, SAXON, CAN'T, SAFE, SEEN, STAY, BE, US. Arranging the words in his head got him nowhere, and Ian went about switching the scraps of words in different order.

"It could be more than one cryptic phrase," Jaered said with his elbow propped on the counter. He reached for the closest word, but Ian snatched it away.

A few seconds later, Ian leaned back. TARA MISSING TOOK SAXON. SYNDRION HUNTING US ALL. CAN'T BE SEEN TOGETHER. STAY SAFE. Ian's breaths quickened the longer he stared at the message.

"You don't know if that's right," Jaered said. He rearranged a few of the words. "What if it's, Saxon missing. Syndrion took Tara. Can't be seen together. Hunting us all."

Ian shook his head. "That's not right," he snapped and put the words back in his order. "The Syndrion didn't take Tara." But was it wishful thinking?

Jaered touched his ear. "He wants to talk to you." He pulled an earbud out of his pocket and set it on the counter.

The tiny electronic device had been the lifeline between Ian and Patrick these past few days. Forced to stay apart or be dropped by the Curse, it'd become a symbol of the chasm between them. The Pur and Duach cannot unite. They must stay apart. The childhood lesson had come true in the most painful of ways. He and his only true friend would never be able to come within thirty feet of each other. Ian picked up the earbud and pushed it into his ear. "Patrick."

"Ian, what's wron? Has something happened to Milo?" His voice softened. "Tara?"

"I don't know. He wasn't at the rendezvous. He left me notes in the rolls. It's not safe for any of us."

"What about Tara?" Patrick said.

Ian didn't answer right away. "According to Milo, she's missing."

"Or the Syndrion has her," Jaered said a little too loud.

"The Syndrion has her?"

The panic in Patrick's voice fueled Ian's. "I'm guessing that she took off. She was pissed that I left her behind." Ian clung to that belief. Taking Saxon would have been the best way to find him.

"Where would she go?" Patrick asked.

"I don't know." Ian looked at Jaered. "You're the only one who can find her, Patrick. Milo and I are the ones the Pur are hunting. Keep her safe until I get back with Rayne."

"We can't go looking for her," Jaered said. "Patrick's not developing his powers fast enough. He's not ready."

"You don't know how they feel about each other," Ian said. "Hell, I don't think they even know. He won't rest until she's safe. The sooner you find her, the more focused he'll be. Besides, Tara can help you train him."

"I'll deal with him." Jaered pushed away from the counter. "I heard from Eve. We've run out of time. You need to leave for Thrae today."

Ian wasn't about to argue. The sooner he retrieved Rayne from Earth's alternate universe, the sooner he could cut ties with Jaered and figure things out for himself. He stared at the two pieces of paper: Tara missing.

A chill ran its finger down Ian's spine. From what Jaered described, standing on the mountain of ice was nothing compared to the frigid parashyft ahead of him.

"You need to shyft to the estate's northern vortex first," Jaered said. "Then parashyft to Thrae from there."

"Aeros can detect parashyfting?" Ian said.

"Aeros and the Primary," Jaered added.

"This is where she is?" Ian asked, studying the black-and-white snapshot of a small storage room.

"It's the compound where I took her," Jaered said with an edge to his voice. "If she's not there, they can tell you where they're hiding her. Find Gwynn. She'll help."

The idea of meeting his mother on Thrae had Ian unnerved more than he could voice.

Jaered looked concerned at Ian's hesitation. "She'll be able to answer any questions you have."

"Why is Aeros after Rayne?" Ian asked. He hated how Jaered kept information from him and was convinced that the rebel enjoyed being in control. Ever since Ian was brought to the isolated auditorium at the edge of nowhere, he'd gotten most of his information from Patrick. But Ian's friend knew very little.

"Be ready for the intense cold during the parashyft," Jaered said, ignoring Ian's question for what had to be the hundredth time. Ian stared at his feet, kicking at an ice chunk with the toe of his boot. "I wouldn't have to break Weir law and go get her if you hadn't interfered in our lives," Ian snapped, but Jaered's brooding silence didn't hold a hint of smugness. Did he feel guilt at stranding Rayne on Thrae?

"Once you leave, you're on the clock," Jaered said. "Your parashyft will draw Aeros's attention. It won't be long before he follows you to Thrae."

This was the first Ian had heard of this. What else was Jaered withholding? "Then maybe she's better off where she is for now. Perhaps we shouldn't draw attention to her," Ian said.

"Would you rather him hunt her down in secret?" Jaered said. "You can't defeat him, not alone. Stay one step ahead of him. Find her before he does, then return to the coordinates I gave you. She'll be safe there."

The receiver in Ian's ear came to life. "Be careful. Rayne's the only souvenir I want from Thrae."

Ian leaned over the precipice and waved to his friend far below. He turned to Jaered and pressed the off switch on the earbud, then handed it to the rebel. When Jaered went to take it, Ian grabbed his wrist and got in his face. "If any harm comes to Patrick while I'm gone, you won't be able to hide from me . . . on either planet."

"If we're going to defeat Aeros as a team," Jaered said, "you have to learn to trust me."

"When hell freezes over." Ian let go of Jaered's arm and stepped back.

Darkness clouded Jaered's features. "That's exactly where you're going."

TWO

Jaered waited five minutes after Ian shyfted to the estate, then appeared outside the northern vortex building just as a bright flash lit up the hall inside. Jaered hunched down next to the front door, determined to buy Ian as much of a head start as he could.

A moment later, the shimmering, opaque cloud formed. The second his father's image solidified, Jaered jumped to his feet and rushed toward Aeros with raised palms. "Wait!"

"Insolent bastard!" his father roared. He flicked his wrist and Jaered lifted from the ground, then slammed against the building.

He slumped in a heap on the concrete step. A muffled moan escaped. "It wasn't me," Jaered croaked.

"The variation in the earth's field. A parashyft." Aeros grabbed Jaered by his hair and dragged him away from the building. "Only you would be so bold!"

Jaered held tight to his father's wrist to prevent his hair from being ripped out. He scrambled to get to his feet, but his father jerked him about and kept him off balance.

With a final shake, Aeros let go and Jaered ended up in a pile of pine needles, flat on his back. The stabbing pain in his side was nothing compared to the pounding at his scalp.

"Open your goddamn eyes. I'm here, it wasn't me!" Jaered shouted.

Aeros stilled. He gazed at Jaered with crimson flames for eyes. "Who?"

"Ever since the Heir disappeared, I've been trying to track him down." Jaered got to his feet. "I caught up with him at a market in Seville today. But I lost him. I came back here to search for more clues when I saw him enter the building. A few seconds later, there was a stutter in the vortex."

"Why would he dare Weir law and parashyft? Which dimension did he go to?"

"I'm not a damn mind reader." Jaered rubbed his scalp. "As far as I know he's never left Earth before."

"My brother forbids all Weir to parashyft under penalty of death." Aeros grew still.

"Apparently, the Heir thinks himself above the Primary's laws." Jaered couldn't recall ever seeing his father so rattled. He fought to keep the satisfaction off his face as he got to his knees. "Looks like your brother's influence with Earth's Heir has fizzled."

A dark storm filled Aeros's features. Jaered knew that look all too well.

"My brother's hold over the Pur Weir is crumbling. I'll show the Weir who's really in charge," Aeros hissed.

"There's a handful of possible dimensions," Jaered said. "And they're big worlds."

"Not for me." A blinding light and a deafening sonic boom. Aeros was gone.

Jaered's core absorbed the energy of his father's parashyft, and the ache in his side lessened. The ringing in his ears took a few seconds to subside. His ability to store tremendous amounts of energy had saved him countless times from his father's power.

Once he'd recovered, Jaered shyfted to the gym just as Patrick groaned, "Four." He then stretched it out to, "Forty-nine." The Duach Heir was in the middle of doing chin-ups on the raised bar. Had he sensed Jaered's return? If so, he'd made progress in reading the subtle energy changes in his newborn core.

Patrick's next chin touch was counted off at fifty. Jaered rolled his eyes. He hadn't seen the Duach Heir do more than eight or ten in the past week. The guy wasn't breaking a sweat.

Patrick dropped to his feet, then glanced over his shoulder. He feigned surprise at Jaered standing in the middle of the gym. "Where'd you go?"

Jaered hadn't told Patrick that Earth's greatest threat was his father. He wondered how long he could keep that bomb from exploding. "I had an errand to run."

"Where?"

"You ask too many questions." Jaered turned away. The comment brought back memories of working with Vael. Jaered didn't know if his friend was in a Pur prison, or dead. He shook off the flicker of melancholy like he had so many other losses in the battle to defeat his father. "I'm stepping up our timetable," Jaered said. He pulled his T-shirt off and tossed it to the side.

Patrick's brow lifted. "What happened to you?"

The concrete step had left an elongated bruise across Jaered's side, and already it was turning from red to deep purple. "I slipped." Jaered fell to his hip and swung his feet around. Patrick hit the floor with a resounding *Splat!*

"Ugh! Stop doing that!" Patrick yelled.

"Your enemy will catch you by surprise every chance," Jaered said. He pinned Patrick to the floor before he could regroup and held him down with the weight of his body. "If they won't offer you mercy, why should I?"

Jaered didn't roll off of Patrick until he relented and his face took on an ugly shade of pink. He headed toward the weapons cabinet with coughs and gasps in his wake.

"We need to find Tara," Patrick rasped.

"You're not ready to take on the Pur army," Jaered tossed over his shoulder. He chose broad swords. It was time to add some weight to their sparring.

"We won't have to worry about them," Patrick said, resting on his knees. "The Syndrion is looking for Ian and Milo. Not me. Ian said so."

"This isn't about you or your girlfriend," Jaered snarled. This is about defeating Aeros and saving not one, but two planets!" Jaered approached Patrick with determined steps. "Get up!" he shouted.

Patrick rose to his feet. "Tara can help us. We need her."

Jaered tossed the sword at Patrick, but the skittish imbecile danced back, allowing the precision weapon to drop to the floor. Jaered clenched his jaw and took three quick breaths to steady his temper. The Duach Heir's training had made scant progress and they were wasting precious time, something his home world of Thrae, and Earth, didn't have.

The need to defeat his father became more compelling with every encounter. Jaered paused in midstride and grabbed his aching side. Patrick and Ian didn't have history with Aeros, not like Jaered did. Could he blame them for not grasping how brutal the man could be, that he can destroy entire planets? If Ian didn't find Rayne fast, he was about to learn firsthand. Jaered counted on him surviving. They needed the Pur Heir.

THREE

The tremendous energy surge of the parashyft ignited every nerve in Ian's body, but Jaered had failed to mention the need to take a deep breath before parashyfting. Ian appeared in the storage room gulping air.

His inaugural trip to a new planet had left him dazed, while his core and muscles felt lighter. Was the gravity different on Thrae? Ian took a moment to adjust to the changes in his body and was comforted when he could draw warmth from the surrounding air into his core. His shivering lessened, but the chattering teeth took their time to ease.

He tested his powers by forming a core blast in his open palm. It stuttered at first, but then came to life. He snuffed it out, then used his keen sight to study the dim surroundings. The lone, upper window was covered in what looked like cardboard. Wide tape held it in place. Long wooden crates were piled from floor to ceiling along the perimeter. An amber light peered from beneath the steel door. It flashed on and off to a rhythmic beat.

A faint whiff of burnt flesh made him pause. It seemed a lifetime ago when Ian flung the core blast at Jaered, the night he kidnapped Rayne. Was this the very spot where Jaered had parashyfted both of them? If so, Ian was in the right place.

A sound of running footsteps, then a metallic *click* and the door opened. A tall, wiry man stood in the doorway. He wore a plain tunic and loose, thin fabric pants. The stranger blinked with wide eyes, then glanced around the room. "Who are you?"

"I need to meet with Gwynn. Jaered sent me."

Alarm contorted the man's face. He rushed in, grabbed Ian by the arm, and ushered him out of the room, then paused long enough to lock the metal door. He pressed a button. The flashing amber light stopped. The stranger gestured to follow and led Ian down a dark corridor.

Lights blinked on as they approached, then off a few feet behind them. In spite of the rustic appearance of the storage room and hallway, the motion sensors gave Ian the impression of modern technology.

The man stopped at a single panel door, identical to all the others they had passed. He knocked twice, hesitated, then once again. A second later, the door opened with a jerk.

"Is Mother Gwynn back yet?" the escort asked.

"No," the middle-aged woman said. She peered at Ian with a mix of curiosity and concern. "She didn't know when she and Liem would return."

The man glanced at Ian from over his shoulder. "He claims our Heir sent him."

Heir? Jaered was Ian's counterpart on Thrae. Ian took a moment to ponder this new revelation. "I'm here for someone. Her name is Rayne."

The woman scrutinized him. "Who are you?"

"My name's Ian. Ian Black."

She gasped. "Forgive me, Your Highness." She dropped to both knees with clasped hands and hung her head. "I am Catherine. This is Sven." The man fell to one knee and bowed.

Stunned, Ian took the woman's elbow and helped her to her feet. "Who do you think I am?" he asked.

"Aren't you Earth's Heir? The one our Mother told us about?"

"Whose mother?" Ian asked.

"Gwynn. Mother-to-us-all," the woman said.

Ian's questions would have to wait. This confusion wasted precious time. "We need to hurry. I have to find Rayne. Do you know who she is? Where she might be?"

"Of course." Catherine came alive. She grabbed Ian's arm and dragged him into a small, sparsely furnished apartment, then addressed the man in the hall. "Sound the alarm. Make sure everyone knows this isn't a drill. Aeros is coming." She slammed the door.

How did these people know to expect the threat? The woman led Ian through the small kitchen toward a narrow door. It opened to a pantry filled with spices and grains. A few jars with handwritten labels were stacked on shelves and a couple of canvas bags were propped just beyond Ian's feet.

Shoved from behind, he entered but soon stopped in front of the pantry wall. The woman reached up and pushed on an upper corner of the wall, and then pressed the toe of her shoe against a lower corner. It opened to what appeared to be a hand-carved dirt tunnel. Ian couldn't see but a few feet ahead.

Catherine pressed up against him from behind, but he didn't budge. "Where are you taking me?" he said.

"Your Highness, please. Unless you're ready to confront Aeros, you'll do as I say or you'll get us both killed. In all likelihood, more than just us." This time the woman gave him a forceful nudge, and he entered the tunnel with cautious steps.

She withdrew a straw cloak from a hook and wrapped it around Ian's shoulders. The smell reminded him of freshly mown alfalfa. She led him down a descending tunnel where the air soon cooled and the walls grew damp. He caught the sound of distant rushing water.

Catherine stopped at a wooden-planked door embedded in a rock wall, put an ear to it, then knocked. A metallic scrape and the door opened to a massive cavern with stone walls and natural rock benches. From the looks of it, more than a hundred people of all ages had gathered.

A bright light illuminated the room. It came from a wide column of energy that rose from the dirt base, then disappeared into the rocky ceiling. The energy pulsed to a rhythm all its own and lit up the people in a strobing glow. Stalagmites and stalactites were scattered throughout the space. Moisture filled the air and drips pooled at the base of the stalagmites next to Ian. A few of the people sat with dangling legs on overhead ledges. Everyone was eerily silent. Those closest caught sight of Ian and fingers or chins soon pointed in his direction.

Ian searched the faces for Rayne, but she wasn't among the gathered.

The core deep in Ian's chest adopted the pulse of the column of energy. Mesmerized, he approached with slow steps as the gathered bodies parted. Many faces regarded him with curiosity, others with suspicion. A few stared at him with nothing short of awe.

The closer he drew, the more intensely his core beat, matching the column's rhythm. He stopped and reached toward it, but it vibrated in a shuddering beat that repeated itself in Ian's chest. A man grabbed Ian from behind, pinning his arms to his sides. "Stay still," he hissed at Ian's ear.

Ian took in those closest to him. Everyone was frozen in place. Some had lowered their faces to their laps and thrown their arms over their heads.

In an instant he understood the dread surrounding him. Aeros was here.

FOUR

The man released him and sat down in silence. Ian tuned into the heartbeats around him and was shocked to find that his was the only one drumming in panic. He focused on quieting his heart and backed away from the column to soothe his core.

Questions swarmed about Ian's thoughts as he studied their faces. These people were accustomed to hiding from Aeros. Earth wasn't the only planet the megalomaniac had laid siege to.

Ian didn't know how long they sat unmoving with shallow breaths. It felt like an hour or more before the brilliant column of energy shuddered once again. No one moved for several more minutes.

Catherine was the first to stand. At her gesture, the crowd stood while children dropped from the ledges into waiting arms.

"Why did Aeros return?" a man called out from the edge of the crowd. He pointed at Ian. "Did he follow you?"

Catherine stepped onto a nearby rock. "This is one of Earth's Heirs and he deserves more than pointed fingers and disrespect," Catherine said with a raised chin.

Whispers and gasps filled the cave. Everyone fell to one or both knees and bowed their heads.

"He is here for our Sun," Catherine announced.

I'm here for Rayne, Ian kept to himself. His powers might be developing further, but he'd never be able to harness the sun. "Please, stand," Ian said. The crowd did his bidding as if one.

"Who was it this time?" The voice came from the back of the cavern.

"Aeros never comes without taking a life," an older woman said. Desperate voices and fearful glances rose from the gathered crowd.

"You ask what I cannot answer," Catherine replied in a voice tinged in frustration. "You know the drill. In Mother's absence, report back to me if you find something amiss."

"When will Mother return?" someone shouted.

"I don't know," Catherine said. "Go, do some good instead of griping and moaning about what we have no control over."

The bodies filed out a handful of doors in an orderly fashion. Ian returned to the column of energy. With each step, his core absorbed the power and every nerve in his body tingled as if struck by lightning. "What will happen if I touch it?" he asked.

"I wouldn't know," Catherine said. "Our Heir is the only one who has."

If Jaered could touch it . . . Ian extended his hand. The column pulsed toward him like a greeting and met the tips of his fingers. A surge of electromagnetic energy ripped through his body while deep in his chest, his core absorbed it like a ravenous predator. With an upheld palm, he walked around the column, relishing in the concentrated energy.

"This amount of power must be coming from the planet's core. How did you contain it?"

"I don't have the information you seek." A tremendous sigh came from the small woman and it echoed about the cavern. "I'm sorry, Your Highness. Mother Gwynn is typically in charge." Catherine wandered over and sat on one of the rock outcroppings. "I'm not a leader, not like our Mother."

"Where is she?" Ian said. He found it difficult to pull his attention away from the column. "You must know where she took Rayne."

"You are referring to our Sun," Catherine said.

"Why do you refer to her as that?" Ian asked.

Catherine indicated the wall behind him. A towering triangle with a sun at its center had been carved into the sheer rock. It was identical to the Seal on Ian's chest, and the one that both Jaered and Patrick shared.

"She is the sun that binds the three Heirs and gives you tremendous power," Catherine said. "She must be protected at all cost in our fight against Aeros."

Ian had searched for answers most of his life. He'd never imagined that he'd find them on Thrae. Was this why the Primary had forbidden all of Earth's Weir to come here, because they'd learn the truth? "As long as I'm here, there is a risk Aeros might return," he said. "I need to find her soon so your Heir and I can keep her safe."

"No one knows where she was taken. It was to protect her, and us," Catherine said.

"There must be someone who has a clue, a starting point."

"There is . . . one." Catherine stood and led Ian out of the cavern and then through the tunnels. They returned to the back of her pantry.

He hung up the straw cloak and closed the pantry's back wall. When he stepped out, Catherine spoke in hushed voices with Sven. The look on their faces gave Ian pause. "What is it?" he said.

The tall, wiry man hurried out of the apartment. Catherine bit her lip. The worrisome gesture reminded Ian of Rayne.

"Aeros has left a message," Catherine said in choked words. "For you."

On the way to the control room, Catherine filled Ian in on what she referred to as the heartbeat of their compound. It housed all the controls for the settlement. Water filtration, air circulation, and something called the dome, were monitored and adjusted from the single room.

They both froze at the threshold, as though to take a step into such horror would make it real. To call the scene a bloodbath wouldn't begin to describe the mutilation. The poor woman gasped and turned away from the sight. Instead of an efficient technological center, it resembled a meat-packing warehouse. Blood had sprayed the walls like an uncorked, shaken champagne bottle. Chunks of flesh and brain matter littered the controls, chairs, and floors. Scraps of clothing were ripped to shreds along with what was left of bone and tissue. From where Ian stood, it was impossible to guess how many bodies perished in the massacre.

What possible power did Aeros possess that could rip humans apart like this? Ian swallowed, but a lump of guilt caught in his throat.

"Aeros never comes without taking a life." The technician looked like he was about to hurl. With a shaky finger, he pointed at the far wall.

WHEN I RETURN GIVE ME EARTH'S HEIR OR MORE WILL DIE. It was written in blood.

It took a few seconds for Ian to find his voice. "What happened?"

"I went to the bathroom," the technician said. "I was about to open the door and return, when I heard shouting. I realized it had to be Aeros, and . . ." He dropped his face. "I was too afraid to come out."

"If you had, you'd be among them," Ian said.

The technician grabbed Catherine's arm so tight that the woman winced. "Why did he come here? The control room has always been off-limits. We were promised we'd be safe!"

"What did Aeros say?" she asked.

"He kept shouting for the Heir." The technician swiped at his cheek, and his hand left a bloody smear.

Terror lifted Catherine's features. "They didn't tell him about the tunnels, did they?"

The technician shook his head. "He tortured each one. I heard Wendel's screams . . . then Barrons . . . Dunlap . . ." He gazed upon what was left of his comrades with a quivering lip. "No one gave in, not one."

Catherine's tears dampened both cheeks. "They gave their lives for us all." She gestured to two men standing nearby. "Do what you can. I'll send more to help."

Ian stared at the tortured remains while nausea rose and bile burned his throat. He gagged and turned away. They died because of his defiance of the Primary's order not to leave Earth. Ian had brought this upon the innocent people of Thrae.

A few weeks earlier, the Primary had his Elite guard slaughter factory workers in Germany, just to send a message to Eve. But this carnage put that scene to shame. Aeros's tyranny was insurmountable compared to his brother's. "I'm so sorry," Ian choked and inwardly vowed to make Aeros pay. The technician collapsed to his knees and dropped his head, releasing what he couldn't hold back any longer.

Catherine took Ian's arm and led him away in silence. He had no words to ease her sorrow, nothing to lessen his guilt. "Aeros has done this before?" he asked, trying to wrap his head around such a monster.

"Too many times," Catherine paused in the middle of the hall. "Has he treated Earth as he's done to Thrae?"

"On Earth, he's gathering an army of the most ruthless Weir. To what end, I still don't know."

"He will steal Earth's energy and change its landscape forever," Catherine said. "If he hasn't already begun."

"No Weir is capable of that," Ian said. "We can only draw upon the energy. Too much, and it would kill any one of us."

"He's not just anyone." She led him farther down the corridor, then paused at a fork. "I will show you what he's capable of." She took the left tunnel, led him to a massive door, and unlatched it. When Catherine pushed her shoulder against it, the door swung wide, washing the hallway in a blood-red light.

Ian stepped out into what appeared to be the surface of the planet, but threw his arm up and squinted at the penetrating glare surrounding them. The gigantic, clear dome overhead reflected the crimson sky, which swirled as though turbulent wind drove it. "What is this?" he asked.

Catherine stepped next to him with her attention above. "It is a methane cloud, our inner atmosphere poisoned by the changes Aeros has made to Thrae."

Ian scrutinized what was left of the city buildings. They were nothing but forgotten relics, crumbling and decaying beneath the dome. The air was fresh, but in an antiseptic way. A few burnt-orange vines, more weeds than healthy plants, had carved and twisted their trail on the surface of the buildings. The only form of life down the wide, crumbling, vacant street. "No one lives above ground?" he said.

"We do what we can to grow a few crops upside," Catherine said. "Miraculously, a few smaller animals survived. But we use hydroponics below for most of our food."

"Where's the sun?" Ian asked.

"Usually hidden by the methane cloud that hovers over our northern colony. We rarely see it." Catherine walked toward the closest building and touched the rusted metal of an exposed beam. "My memories of our above-ground existence are fading faster than my health."

"How long has it been like this?" Ian's gut twisted. Thrae was supposed to be the mirror image of Earth, but instead, was the polar opposite of his home world. A foreign, disturbing wasteland. "Does the entire planet look like this?"

"Once the air became polluted, a few brave souls attempted to find survivors. They never returned. Gwynn is the only one. We fight to live the best we can with what's left."

"Did Gwynn take Rayne beyond the dome?"

"I believe so," Catherine said.

Ian stared at the desolation. "Take me to whoever can help me."

The woman opened the door and disappeared inside. He shut the door, leaving the bleak world on the other side. Jaered was right. Ian was in hell.

FIVE

A woman stood at the fork in the tunnel and stared at him with eyes as crystal blue as Rayne's. Everything about her face conveyed a life filled with strife, yet she was stunning. The shape of her mouth, her jawline, was familiar.

She addressed Catherine in a voice dipped in sorrow. "The technicians."

"He is hunting Earth's Heir," Catherine said from beneath a lowered face. "We kept him safe in the cavern. Jaered sent him."

At the mention of Jaered, tears veiled the woman's eyes. "I am Sophenna," she said and clasped Ian's hand tight.

"Ian. I am in search of Gwynn. Can you help me find where she is hiding Rayne?"

Sophenna cringed. "Come to my quarters where we can talk."

"Are you all right?" Catherine asked. "Did that monster . . ."

"No," Sophenna said. "I was spared." She put a reassuring hand on Catherine's arm. "Their bravery and sacrifice will be remembered by all."

"Till my dying breath," Catherine whispered. She left Ian and Sophenna, headed for the control room. Bulbs blinked on and off, lighting her mournful journey.

Sophenna peered past Ian at the outside door. "Catherine showed you."

Ian nodded. "I got a glimpse of what Aeros has done to Thrae."

"A glimpse is not enough," Sophenna said in a steeled voice. She turned and Ian followed her through the tunnel. "You must understand why."

"My battle is with Aeros," Ian said. "I understand that now."

"You understand very little," Sophenna said and led him down the corridor. "But it is not your fault. The Primary denied you the truth." Her shoulders were pulled back and she held her head high, yet her steps dragged. Ian wondered if she was ill. She stopped at a door, wider than others they had passed along the way.

Visions of the Thraens hiding in the cavern and the carnage he'd witnessed in the control room filled his thoughts. "I want to know . . . everything," he said.

Sophenna gave him a weak smile, then opened the door. She stepped into an apartment filled with countless antiques and curio cabinets crowded with trinkets. Larger than

Catherine's apartment, Sophenna's resembled a museum rather than living quarters. The woman stood just inside the doorway, as Ian wandered about the displays.

"I am the Keeper of Thrae," she announced, then shut the door and joined him. "Many of these were salvaged in the aftermath of Aeros's reign. Some from crumbling museums, others from . . . the ruins."

Most of the items were identical, or at least similar, to objects in Earth's past. Antiquities that would readily be found in antique stores across the United States. A rusted cast iron skillet, a scattering of jewelry, belt buckles, and pieces of clothing. An old plow was propped in a corner next to a straw broom. Some of her furniture was made of hand-carved wood, upholstered in needlepoint tapestry.

Sophenna opened one of the cabinets and removed a music box. "I gave this to Kyre, Jaered's wife, on their wedding day."

Jaered—married? Sophenna wound the box and it began to play an unfamiliar tune. The ballerina danced in an arrhythmic circle, with its gears slipping along its track. He knew so little about Jaered, other than he was in league with Eve and her band of rebels fighting Aeros on Earth, and had hailed from Thrae. The revelation that the rebel had a normal life gave Ian pause. What took him away from home to fight Aeros on a foreign planet?

"I'm Jaered's mother," Sophenna said. The music stopped in mid-tune and the ballerina froze in place. Sophenna returned the precious item to its showcase, then closed the door. "I need to show you something."

She opened a door leading to a bedroom. Sophenna indicated pictures on a dresser. Ian approached the photos, while disbelief slowed every step. He picked up one of the framed photos depicting Jaered in a wide smile. The remarkable change in a man always serious, and stoic wasn't what turned Ian's pulse to ice. Rayne was in the pictures.

"That is Kyre, Jaered's wife," Sophenna said.

"I know her as Rayne." Ian set it down and studied the others from afar, unable to make sense of what he saw.

"There are incidences of parals, genetic doubles, between dimensions. They are rare, but do happen." She ran her finger along the top of the wedding picture. "How old is Rayne?"

"She's twenty-one," he responded.

"Jaered is twenty-seven. Kyre was twenty-five," she said.

"Was?" Ian stared at a picture of her.

"Aeros murdered her and their unborn child." Sophenna's voice cracked. She turned and walked away. "To punish my son."

Jaered's obsession with Rayne these past months on Earth now made sense. Ian wasn't sure if this revelation comforted him, or frightened him. "Is that why Jaered is bent on defeating Aeros?"

"Jaered couldn't save his planet. Our Heir was born too late to make a difference. Aeros had already sucked too much of Thrae's core energy. Because of that, Thrae lags five days' time behind Earth. Our oceans have shrunk. Our landmass has been permanently altered."

"How can one Weir suck so much energy from a planet and not die?"

"He's not a Weir. He's a god," Sophenna hissed. "He and his brother are the fathers of all Weir."

"You mean the Primary." It hadn't come as a surprise when Patrick told him about the Ancients and who the Primary really was. Ian had discovered the dark side to the man who had raised Ian as his own son.

"Aeros ruled Thrae," Sophenna said. "Johann, the man you know as the Primary, ruled Earth."

The Primary had only disdain for Aeros whenever he spoke of him. Was it because Aeros invaded the Primary's territory? Lessons from Ian's past swirled in his thoughts. The Duach broke away from the Pur during the Dark Ages. Is that when Aeros first arrived to insinuate himself on Earth and form his Duach legion? Did the Weir that remained loyal to the Primary come to be called Pur? Ian had been taught that Aeros was some kind of fanatic prophet. Both Aeros and the Primary—were so much more. "The Primary threatened me not to pursue Aeros."

Unbridled emotion deepened the creases in Sophenna's face. "The Primary has his own agenda for Earth. I suspect that the two of them came to an . . . understanding."

The Primary is working with Aeros? Unbelievable as it seemed, it explained so much. "The Primary forbade me to track down Eve and the rebels."

"He and Aeros have a reason to fear my sisters and me," Sophenna said.

"Because you, too, are Ancients."

"From what we know, the Ancients are interconnected." Sophenna sat on the edge of the bed. "My sisters and I have tried, and failed, to stop Aeros here on Thrae. Earth is the new battleground. If we aren't victorious there, planets in other dimensions will crumble beneath him."

"To what end?" Ian said. "What can he hope to gain by destroying planets?"

"At first, he sought nothing but power, growing stronger, closer to invincible with each century. The more energy he drew from Thrae, the more destructive he became, until the environmental damage was irreversible. That is when he turned his attention to Earth. But in the past century, he's been fighting to regain what he lost. What we all lost." Sophenna stood and faced Ian. "The five of us: Aeros, Johann, Eve, Gwynn and I thought we were immortal. We'd lived for thousands upon thousands of years. Seen our Weir offspring be born and die. But in the past fifty years, everything changed. We began to grow old." Her voice took on an edge. "Aeros isn't ready to die."

"He's counting on absorbing enough energy to regain his immortality," Ian said.

"But now that the three Heirs have connected, along with the Sun, you can defeat him." Sophenna clasped her hands and brought them to her chest as if in supplication.

"But if the Ancients are interconnected . . ."

"We have a plan," she said. "One that will succeed."

Ian took her hands into his. "How can you be so sure?"

"Because my sisters and I wrote the Book of the Weir. We foresaw this and were shown the way."

"You're clairvoyant," Ian said.

"To defeat Aeros, we had to bear our sons from his seed."

Ian's skin turned clammy. "What?" He dropped her hands and stepped back.

"Who better to combat Aeros, then his offspring?" she said.

Jaered swung around and with everything he had, came down hard on Patrick's sword knocking him onto his back. The guy's head wasn't in the moment while sparring, he would have lost various appendages had Jaered removed their protective shields. As far as Jaered knew, growing back limbs was not among the Weir powers.

"Get up!" Jaered shouted. His patience had fizzled an hour ago and he couldn't contain himself much longer.

Patrick dropped his head back and closed his eyes. The Duach Heir's chest heaved with every gasp. "No," he coughed. "Enough."

"It'll be enough when we defeat Aeros," Jaered snarled and ripped off the shield on his saber. He rested the tip against Patrick's throat and, tempted to penetrate his skin, but Jaered held his anger at bay, at a loss how to get across to Patrick how serious this was. He stepped away. Eve would question him drawing blood. Or would she?

"Have you heard from Ian?" Patrick asked, wiping his face with his hands.

"We can't communicate between dimensions," Jaered said. "He's on his own."

"Tara deserves answers," Patrick said.

Jaered grabbed Patrick's saber and stored the weapons in the cabinet at the far end of the gymnasium. His disgust in finding the Duach Heir so ill prepared, mentally and physically, fed his defeat. He'd been mulling over a new tactic. "On one condition," Jaered said.

Patrick rose to his knees faster than Jaered thought him capable. "Name it."

"You do as I say. If we compromise ourselves, we abandon the search. We'll be lucky not to bring the entire Pur army down on us."

"Agreed." Patrick headed for the doors.

"Where are you going?" Jaered said.

"I need a shower." He disappeared into the hall.

"Fuck!" Jaered spat. He hated that Ian was right. The lovesick puppy had to clean up for her.

Patrick had no choice but for Jaered to call the shots. The rebel shyfted them to the Seville alley coordinates that Ian had followed earlier that day. It was the only clue they had for Milo, and the old caretaker was their best bet for finding Tara. Patrick shuddered; the effects of the shyft chilled him to his bones.

"Draw energy into your core like I taught you," Jaered said.

Patrick put his palm against his chest. He took a deep breath, and warmth returned to his face and arms. He relaxed. "That's getting easier," he said with immense satisfaction.

"That's a drop compared to what you still have to learn," Jaered snapped. He stepped out of the alley and into the street. Patrick followed. Vendors were packing their unsold wares into boxes and crates, then loading them into trucks or cars. A few vehicles sat idling.

"Did Ian mention where Milo's booth was?" Jaered asked.

"No." Patrick peered over his shoulder.

Jaered headed for the farthest row. "Whistle if you spot him."

"I can't whistle, so you better listen for slobbering shrieks." Patrick made his way up and down the dismantled rows, pushing past men and women carrying boxes or sawhorses. One row over, a colorful tablecloth whipped in front of Jaered and he paused as if about to lash out. The woman gave him no mind and shook it out, then folded it and put it on top of a crate loaded with hand-painted vases.

Patrick spied familiar handwriting on a chalkboard being loaded into a weather-beaten pickup truck by a brown-robed monk. He headed for it at top speed when the monk got inside and revved the engine.

He stuck his fingers in his mouth and as predicted, slobbering shrieks came out. "Waaait!" Patrick screamed and waved his arms. "Stop!"

Jaered was faster. He reached the driver's side of the truck before Patrick could exit the row. Whatever he said to the driver worked, because the brake lights came on and the truck jerked to a stop. Patrick met up with them and propped himself against the door to catch his breath.

"He claims he doesn't know anyone by the name of Milo," Jaered said. From the look on his face, Jaered was skeptical.

"Ask him if he knows Milonius," Patrick said. Jaered asked, but the monk shook his head and shrugged his shoulders.

Patrick held his hand up. "*Uno momento.*" He walked to the rear of the truck and lifted the chalkboard out of the back. He brought it over and turned it toward the monk, pointing. "The man who wrote this. Where can we find him?"

When the monk didn't respond, Jaered translated. He nodded and cut the engine, then got out and pointed to the chalkboard. "*Sí, Senor M.*"

"You know him as Mr. M?" Jaered asked.

"*Sí.*" He rattled on in Spanish, not stopping for a breath, holding a conversation with Jaered, while pointing toward the mountains in the distance. Jaered thanked him, shaking hands. The monk turned toward Patrick, but instead of taking his extended hand, he gave Patrick a bear of a hug as if given by Milo himself. The monk returned to the truck and, with a wave, drove off. The evening lights flickered on as dusk melted into the horizon.

"He knows where Milo is?" Patrick asked.

"No, but he had an idea where he might have gone." Jaered headed for the main street and it took some effort for Patrick to keep up. The guy had a long stride and it was impossible to walk side by side with him.

"After what Ian said about the monks being so skittish, I'm surprised he opened up," Patrick said. "I thought you'd have to beat it out of him."

Jaered scoffed. "You watch too many movies."

"TV shows, really." Patrick grabbed Jaered's arm and stopped him. "What else did he say?"

"That the men following Ian took off after he shyfted and never returned to the market. Milo had left instructions in case Ian returned. We showed up instead. At first I didn't think he was going to cooperate, but then, he seemed to recognize you."

"Me? How would the monk know me?"

"He didn't say." Jaered looked up and down the street. "We need a car."

Patrick pulled out his wallet and removed a credit card. "I can help with that."

Jaered snatched the card out of his hand, took the wallet, and waved them both in front of Patrick's face. "You have a lot to learn about keeping under the radar."

"Add it to the list." Patrick stared Jaered down, all the while hoping he hid his shaking knees. Another excruciating second and Jaered's intense gaze softened. Was that a smirk, or a hint of a smile? Patrick chose the smile. "I'm guessing you've been at this a lot longer than I have," Patrick said.

"All my life," Jaered muttered.

"It's been about seven days for me." Patrick offered him a knuckle punch. "I'll try harder, if you don't give up on me." Jaered stared at his fist. "Come on, don't leave me hanging." Jaered grabbed his fist in a vice of a grip and Patrick fought not to flinch.

"If you can't do this, everything, everyone, including this girlfriend of yours, will die." Jaered leaned closer. "It won't be quick, or painless."

Sorrow flickered in Jaered's gaze, and then it was replaced by the hardened look that had haunted Patrick's dreams this past week. He nodded and Jaered let go.

"Now, we need to find a car without leaving a trail of our own." He bent Patrick's credit card back and forth until it broke in two, then handed the pieces to Patrick.

"I don't have enough cash on me." Patrick flexed his hand.

"Who said we needed money." Jaered strolled along the street, cat-like, and tried the door handles of the vehicles while studying the people around them.

"You can't steal a car," Patrick hushed. "It'll be reported and we'll get caught."

"Eve will take care of it," Jaered said.

"My mom doesn't have any pull with police in Spain," Patrick said.

Jaered paused when a handle gave and the passenger's side door opened. It was a weathered four-door sedan, circa 1990's. To Patrick's relief, the dome light was out.

Jaered got in and scooted across the bench seat. Then his head disappeared under the console. Patrick joined him, shut the door, and felt around at the ignition. A set of keys jingled.

"I don't think you have to hotwire the car." Patrick smirked.

"Fuck you," Jaered said. He started the car and pulled away from the curb.

For being so stealthy, Jaered sure had a short fuse. Patrick studied the crowd for the car's owner among the packing vendors, but no one seemed to notice their departure. He stared at the city lights streaming by in a hypnotic daze. How much sleep did he get last night? This past week? Was it exhaustion or lack of food that turned his muscles to putty and weighed upon his eyelids? Patrick couldn't remember the last real meal they'd had. His mother was the rebel leader Eve. Patrick was the Duach Heir. He'd been on a collision course since birth, but kept in the dark, unable to see it coming until it was too late.

"Why are you so resistant to develop your powers?"

The rebel's question pulled Patrick out of his pondering and he sat up. They had left the city behind, but small bungalows were scattered off the road, many windows lit in candlelight or low-watt bulbs. He rubbed his face. "I wasn't born into this like you," Patrick said.

Jaered's jaw bulged at Patrick's comment. "You don't know anything about me," he grumbled.

"Excuse me for not grasping your life in a handful of days," Patrick shot back.

Jaered drove in silence but as time wore on, color returned to his knuckles gripping the steering wheel. "Your mother told me something once, the day she recruited me," Jaered said. "That loss is but a beginning."

"A beginning of what?" Patrick mumbled.

"Purpose." Jaered glanced in the rearview mirror.

Patrick didn't respond and watched the fields go by.

"Stop fighting it and get with the program, before it's too late." Jaered stole a glance over his shoulder at a car approaching from behind. He leaned forward, peering out the windshield in all directions.

"Trouble?" Patrick asked, eyeing the vehicle through the back window.

"Maybe." Jaered swerved off onto a dirt road, while the other car continued onward down the road, ignoring their turnoff. He threw the car in park but kept it idling, got out, and wandered away with the door propped open. Jaered stepped off to the side of the isolated road, pulled a cell out of his pocket, and pressed buttons. He held it next to his ear.

Patrick had known he'd talked with Eve a few times this past week. Never anyone else. He exited the car and walked up to Jaered with his hand out. "I want to talk to her."

Jaered grunted in response to whatever Eve was saying. He glared at Patrick when he poked Jaered's chest with his index finger. A second later, he handed Patrick his phone.

"Ian went to Thrae to get Rayne," Patrick said.

"I know," his mother said without a lick of emotion.

"We're trying to find Tara," he added and steeled himself against the inevitable repercussions, but she was silent. "I need to find her."

"So I've been told," his mother said.

"You're not going to try and stop me?" It wasn't like her to give him free reign. Especially now.

"Patrick, you have to understand. We are on a very strict timetable. It's against my better judgment, but perhaps you'll progress more if we throw you into the field."

"I just need to know that she's safe," he said.

"I have made inquiries," his mother said. "I don't know where Tara is, but she is not in a Pur prison. That, I can assure you. Milo is doing a good job at keeping himself hidden."

"Once I find her, I promise to continue training, harder than ever," Patrick said. "I understand why everyone is so impatient."

"This isn't about you, Patrick. Never forget that," his mother said. "Find Tara and get back to work."

"And Saxon," Patrick said, but his mother cut off the call. He didn't miss the tension in Jaered's shoulders at mention of the wolf. Was Jaered not an animal lover, or was it something else? His mother's acquiescence was better than Patrick could have hoped for, so why was he so apprehensive? What wasn't he seeing? He handed Jaered the phone. "You convinced her, didn't you?"

Jaered pocketed the phone, then brushed by Patrick, headed for the car. "You say it like I care. I don't."

Patrick returned to the passenger seat with apprehension seeping out of every pore. What was he missing?

SEVEN

atrick dozed on and off as Jaered drove them by olive groves with their moonlit fruit hanging from branches. The Spanish countryside offered rolling hills with a splash of wide open fields as far as he could see. The rural setting lent to Patrick's calm, and he struggled not to drift into a deep sleep.

When they passed an ox-drawn cart making its way home after a long day in the fields, Patrick grew pensive. It reminded him of being kidnapped and taken to Greece where he discovered he had powers, and that his mother was the rebel leader, Eve. Was that only a week ago? How everything had changed.

Jaered pulled onto a dirt road that soon turned into a rising web of cobbled streets lined on both sides with single and two-story buildings, shops, and cafés. Patrick's stomach growled and he licked his lips, but Jaered didn't pull to a stop until he'd made his way deeper into the town.

"Where are we?" Patrick asked.

"Osuna, Spain." Jaered looked around but didn't budge.

Patrick rolled down his window. "Is this where Milo might be hiding out?"

"It's our best chance to find him, but I can't go until tomorrow," Jaered said.

"You mean we," Patrick said.

"Duach Sars and Pur Sars don't exactly mix," Jaered said.

"But he knows you as an enemy," Patrick said. "He won't let you near him."

"Then between now and tomorrow, you better come up with something I can tell him that will convince him otherwise. Or this is all a stupid-as-hell waste of our time."

"Give me your phone, I'll find a good place to eat," Patrick said. "My treat."

"We're staying there tonight." Jaered's chin jerked toward a run-down hotel across the street. "We'll go to where the monk suggested in the morning. I will find a market that's still open and bring food back to the room. Under the radar, remember?"

"It's late. This town isn't a crawling metropolis. You won't find a market open at this hour." Patrick studied their surroundings. "Did anyone follow us?"

"No," Jaered said.

"Then no one knows we're here. I've never been to Spain before, so I won't be recognized by anyone." Patrick got out of the car, then stuck his head in the open door. "Are you concerned someone might recognize you?"

"Very few people know who I am," Jaered said.

"Then unless you intend to throw me over your shoulder and carry me into that hellhole, I'm going to sniff out a decent meal before I sleep with the cockroaches." Patrick shut the car door and headed down the street. When he didn't hear steps behind him, he peered over his shoulder. From what he could tell, Jaered wasn't in the car, but hadn't followed, either. Patrick paused at the corner, concerned that the rebel might have deserted him. He sniffed the air. The most fragrant of meals wafted toward Patrick and his stomach lurched.

"It does smell good," Jaered said from behind.

Patrick jumped. "Don't sneak up on me like that!"

"The fluctuation in your core energy should have signaled my shyft," Jaered said. "You have better hearing than most. Start tuning into your senses."

Patrick faced him. "I am. My stomach is screaming *feed me*."

"You have American currency on you. It'll red flag us," Jaered said.

"We're tourists, too stupid to get it exchanged." Patrick had thought it through. At least to that point. "How were you going to pay for the room?"

"Eve took care of it."

"I'm not shocked that she'd spring for a mouse-infested place for me to stay," Patrick said. He followed his nose down the street. "Punishment for not cooperating."

"Low profile," Jaered countered.

"I'm getting a cerveza, ice cold with a lime," Patrick groaned. "Or maybe a grande margarita."

"How does any of that align with your training?" Jaered stopped Patrick before he could step out onto the corner. "Learn." He glanced around the corner of the building, then signaled it was clear to continue.

"That's not suspicious," Patrick muttered under his breath.

"You can't be too careful," Jaered said.

"We're tourists, remember?" Patrick shook his head. "Have you ever let loose in your life?"

"I prefer to stay alive." Jaered strolled up the street toward a café where patrons sat at tables outside; laughter and conversation drifted toward them. Guitar music emanated from speakers. For the first time, Patrick wondered what the guy's past was like for him to be so angry and bitter . . . so driven.

He met up with Jaered at the entrance, still panting at the uphill trek, but relieved when a waitress set plates of steamy food in front of a couple. "They're still serving," he said at Jaered's back.

"We'll sit there." Jaered indicated a corner booth at the rear of the café, next to the kitchen.

"It'll be cooler if we take that last table outside," Patrick said. Jaered grabbed a couple of menus and took up residence in the booth. Patrick slipped in across from him. "You don't play well with others, do you?"

Jaered didn't look up from reading the menu. "The patio is too exposed and we'd be noticed."

"As long as we're noticed by the waitress, that's all I care about." Patrick glanced over his shoulder to find her out on the patio, replenishing water glasses.

"What do you see?" Jaered asked.

"Dinner," Patrick licked his lips at a massive plate passing them on top of another waiter's tray.

"There's twelve seated patrons, another one sitting at the bar, a bartender, two waiters, one waitress and by the sound of it, two cooks inside the kitchen," Jaered rattled off. "Most of the patrons are local but four are teenage tourists, probably staying at the hostel we passed on the way here." He set his menu down.

"Okay," Patrick said, not sure where he was going with that.

"Always be aware of your surroundings, learn to read people at a glance. It just might save your life." Jaered signaled and the closest waiter set down his tray of dirty dishes. He came over with his notepad out and a pencil at the ready. "Do you speak English?" Jaered asked.

The waiter nodded. "*Poquito*," while holding up his fingers to indicate a little.

Jaered pointed to his chest. "The *gambas al ajillo* and he wants the *cochinillo asado*."

"*Aperitivo?*" the waiter asked.

"No appetizer," Jaered responded.

"Guacamole," Patrick said.

"Gazpacho," Jaered amended

The waiter pocketed his pad and pencil. "I get *agua* for you. *Mas* drinks?"

"Cervezas, por favor," Patrick blurted before Jaered could deny him. He held up two fingers. But the waiter stared at him as if confused.

"*Dos Alhambra Mezquita*," Jaered said.

"*Bueno*." The waiter left.

Jaered tossed Patrick a smirk. "I could take some lessons from you."

"Lessons about what?" Patrick said.

"You do dumb tourist like a pro." Jaered leaned back.

"You could have let me order for myself," Patrick said.

"I'm betting you couldn't read the menu," Jaered said. "Don't worry, I ordered you something good."

Patrick wasn't about to admit that Jaered was right on all counts. "I'm shocked you allowed the beer."

"I do let loose, here and there," Jaered said.

Patrick smiled. "You are human after all."

The creases at the corners of Jaered's eyes deepened. "You shouldn't mock what you don't understand."

Patrick leaned closer. "Then enlighten me."

"You come from privilege, wanting for nothing." Jaered picked up his knife and ran his finger across the dull edge. "How can you possibly fathom what strife is?"

"I know that it means to fight, struggle," Patrick said.

Jaered pushed the knife's dull tip against his palm. "Knowing the dictionary meaning is not the same as living it," he said.

"Then teach me, or show me," Patrick said.

"That would mean taking you to Thrae, and that's not going to happen."

"Yet you sent Ian there. Was that why you stranded Rayne on Thrae, for some kind of twisted lesson?"

"I don't have to explain my actions to you or anyone else," Jaered snarled. He put the knife down. The waiter stepped up and set the beers in front of them. "To lessons learned." Jaered clinked his bottle against Patrick's, then took a long, drawn-out swig, emptying half of it before setting it down. He inhaled deep and then belched. He gazed across the room with sad eyes at the laughing and relaxed patrons. The music turned soulful.

The waiter returned with their plates and they dug into their meals in silence. The cooked pig was incredibly tender and it hit the spot with each bite melting in Patrick's mouth. The meal was so grand, Patrick wasn't sure he could finish it all. But he forced himself anyway, unsure when they might eat again. Jaered devoured his giant prawns down to the last strip of lettuce, then sat back with a satisfied sigh.

"So what's the plan?" Patrick said, lowering his voice as the waiter approached. Jaered looked down at his empty plate and nodded when the waiter asked if he was done. The man removed everything, including the drained bottles.

"We sleep with the cockroaches." Jaered drank the remaining water in his glass. "In the morning, I'll head to the monastery in time to catch one of their tours."

"Is that where Milo is?" Patrick said. "Another monastery?"

"Why do you ask when you know as much as I do?" Jaered peered at him as if he was curious, without a hint of sarcasm. "Vael asked questions all the time. It got on my nerves."

You aren't exactly forthcoming, Patrick thought. Ian had told Patrick that Vael and Jaered had worked together for the rebels. Jaered's tone told Patrick they were friends as well. "Do you know what happened to Vael, after the Pur soldiers attacked the rebel ship?"

"How did you know about that?" Jaered asked.

"Ian told me. He witnessed the slaughter. Dr. Mac had operated on him . . . and on Vael."

"Eve tried," Jaered said. "But couldn't find anything out."

"They threw Vael's father, Marcus, in a Pur prison." Patrick leaned back and sighed. "That's what Ian thought, anyway. His only crime was to help Ian in his search for the truth about the Weir."

"The Primary's secrets run deep," Jaered muttered. "And he'll do the unthinkable to keep them that way." Jaered dropped his head, and by the feel of it, his defenses.

Patrick wasn't sure if he'd gotten drunk on a single beer, or if exhaustion had set in. Perhaps it was a willingness to open up. He wasn't about to ignore the rare opportunity. "My mother told me that the Primary is one of the five Ancients. That he came to earth thousands of years ago and that Aeros is his brother."

A spark of surprise came and went in Jaered's eyes. He stared at Patrick. "She told you more than I would have guessed." He leaned his forearms on the table. "Did you know we're related?"

"Our mothers are sisters. That makes us cousins," Patrick said. "Ian, too."

"We're closer than that," Jaered said, but he didn't elaborate. He slipped out of the booth. "Thanks for dinner. Can I trust you to not get into any trouble while I hit the bathroom?"

"I can take care of a check," Patrick grumbled. Jaered crossed the room and disappeared down a back hallway. The waiter set the check down and Patrick motioned for him to wait, then put on his tourist persona and pulled out American currency. The waiter gave him an obligatory grimace, but nodded and disappeared toward the cash register at the end of the bar counter. Patrick figured they'd convert whichever way they chose, regardless of the current banking recommendations. He leaned back and rubbed his abdomen with sheer satisfaction that he'd at least got a decent meal. A lull in the patrons conversation caught his ear. Movement came at the corner of his eye.

A Pur guard stood at the entrance to the café, and peered inside. Patrick would have recognized the uniform anywhere. He slid deeper into the booth's shadow, then half turned and wiped off the used knife blade. Patrick positioned it to see over his shoulder. The man didn't step inside, but returned to the sidewalk and closely regarded the patrons sitting on the patio. Patrick knelt on the bench and peered over the top of the booth. Another guard from across the street ran up and they studied the crowd further. Then the men turned and wandered off toward the street corner. Patrick pressed his forehead against the booth and drew a deep breath, letting it out in a gradual stream.

"We're out of here, now!" Jaered grabbed Patrick's arm and dragged him out of the booth just as the waiter appeared with Patrick's change on a black plastic tray. Jaered grabbed it and led Patrick by the elbow to the bathroom.

"I thought we were leaving," Patrick said.

Jaered closed the door, grabbed Patrick's shoulder, and shyfted.

They appeared in a darkened bedroom with flowery cloth curtains drawn three-quarters shut. Two twin beds were up against one wall. The TV in the corner was a big fat box. Cigarette smoke permeated the room. The bed linens were worn, but appeared clean.

Patrick shook off the frigid effect of the shyft and sat on the closest bed. "This is where we're spending the night?"

"We're not staying." Jaered pulled out his cell.

Alarm lifted Patrick off the bed and he grabbed Jaered's wrist. "Don't call her."

"We need an exit," Jaered said.

"She put me in the field with you for a reason." Patrick let go. "Don't save me. Teach me."

Jaered stared at Patrick for a few seconds, then stuck the phone back in his pocket.

"How did they find us?" Patrick asked.

"They might have intercepted the police call about the stolen car before Eve's contacts could." Jaered walked over to the curtains and peeked outside. "I was going to desert the car in the next town. That's why I came to check out the room first.

"So you had a place to shyft back to." Patrick knew that's how shyfting worked. He'd yet to master it.

"But you kept walking down the goddamn street, and I made the call to stick with you instead of covering our tracks," Jaered said.

Guilt sagged Patrick's back. "So they found the stolen car outside."

"Probably checked the hotel first. That's what I would have done. When they couldn't verify we were checked in, they assumed we were still in the area, on foot." Jaered held his vigil at the window.

"Do they know it's us?" Patrick drew the latch on the door, but knew it wouldn't detain anyone wanting in.

"The monk would have left before they discovered the stolen car," Jaered said. "So probably not."

"They might think it's Ian," Patrick said.

"By now, the Primary knows Ian's off world." Jaered slid down the wall and settled in a crouch near the floor. "If it was the monk who alerted them to check here, we can't afford to look for Milo tomorrow."

"But," Patrick said.

"I'm trying to protect Milo, too, not just us," Jaered shot back.

"If they are looking for Milo, who better to protect him than us?" Patrick said. Jaered glared up at him. "Don't pass up a teachable moment," he added, and tossed Jaered a knowing look.

"Keeping you alive will get me killed," Jaered said. He stood and checked the outside street again through the slit in the curtain. "Just because they didn't find anything suspicious here, doesn't mean they won't return."

"So we're going back to the auditorium," Patrick said.

"You begged to be put in the field." Jaered reached for Patrick. "So the field it is."

"Blast," Patrick said and braced himself for the shyft.

EIGHT

Sophenna insisted on making tea for them. All Ian could think about was that Aeros would be back, but every time Ian asked about it, she changed the subject.

The tea smelled of licorice and orange. "This is unlike anything I've ever tasted," Ian said, relishing in the aroma and savoring the citric aftertaste in his mouth.

"It is an herb that grows above ground." Sophenna handed him a hard biscuit. "I can be quite handy. I used to make my own honey, before we lost the bees."

Ian couldn't begin to imagine the number of species lost to this world. "Are there any animals or insect life left?"

"Some. I am amazed with what has survived above ground. Larger species were taken to the preserve in what you would know as lower Africa."

He set the teacup down. "There are other protected areas?"

"Yes, to my knowledge, there are five," she said.

"What about the methane cloud? Are they all encased in domes such as this one?" Ian asked.

"I believe so, but Gwynn is the one to ask such . questions. She shared that there are more methane clouds that float across the planet, threatening the other colonies. There were six colonies, but one had a catastrophe and everyone perished. That was several years ago. Gwynn hinted that it may have been sabotage."

"Aeros?" Ian asked.

"I know only what Gwynn shares. She is the one who travels from colony to colony."

"Can she shyft?" Ian asked

"Heavens, no," Sophenna chuckled. "We do not have cores like you men. But we do possess ingenuity." She smoothed her loose gown across her lap. "For us, that has been enough."

"I fear for you and what Aeros will do to you in my absence."

"We have weathered Aeros's vengeance for centuries," she whispered. "When he turned his attention to Earth, it gave us the opportunity to build tunnels where we could hide most of the colony whenever he returned. We will continue to survive, long after you've left."

"If we're successful," Ian said.

"When you're successful," Sophenna corrected.

"I promise to get all of you to Earth," he said.

Sophenna patted Ian's hand. "You are such a child of the universe. So much holds you back, yet you continue to reach for the stars." She picked up her teacup and took a delicate sip. "First things, first. Now eat the measly offerings I have, and then we'll get you on your way."

The rushing water Ian had heard while navigating the tunnels with Catherine earlier turned out to be an underground river. The tremendous force of the massive, natural aqueduct had Ian cautious. If a human was caught in the current, they'd drown for sure.

Sophenna stood on the ledge, gazing across the water. The river's path disappeared into the shadows at a curve several yards away.

"Gwynn is the only one who has used this?" Ian asked, placing the supplies in a rowboat that creaked and scraped against the rock's edge, held in place by a thick rope latched to an iron ring hanging from the wall.

"When the earlier explorers didn't return, it was discouraged. Gwynn is the only one who has ventured out, and returned." Sophenna said. "She is the explorer in us all."

Ian's mother was a risk taker. The more he learned about her, the more eager he was to meet her.

Sophenna handed Ian a bag. He opened it and discovered a suit and helmet.

"What's this for?" he asked.

"Not all of your journey will be underground. You'll need this to protect yourself from the methane cloud should you encounter it." She placed her hand on the duffle bag slung over his shoulder. "Inside is a map that Gwynn created."

He set the suit bag in the boat with the other supplies, then removed the paper and unfolded it. It was a hand-drawn map of Thrae. Five circles were scattered across the globe. A sixth one, where Australia would have been on Earth, was crossed out.

"We are here." Sophenna pointed to a circle in the region of the California-Arizona border. "If I've guessed right, Gwynn will have taken Rayne here." She indicated the lower region of South America.

"Why there?" Ian said.

"It's the most brutal colony on the planet. Aeros would not guess that anyone would travel there."

"Brutal?" Ian folded the map.

"It is where the Primary sends his political prisoners."

Marcus had told Ian that the Primary had a prison on Thrae and that no one ventured there. Ian was about to find out firsthand how the Primary treated his prisoners.

"It's going to take me days, maybe weeks to get there," Ian said.

"The river only goes as far as here." Sophenna pointed to a spot down near the Mexico-Central America border. "According to my sister's accounts, there's transportation when you emerge that will take you the rest of the way. You should be there in about a week, maybe a little longer." She squeezed Ian's arm. "Be careful, the trip is arduous.

Creatures dwell in the underground caverns. Do your powers work, here on Thrae?"

"I tested them when I first arrived. It appears that they do," Ian said.

"You'll need them." Sophenna gathered Ian up in her arms and held him tight. She sniffled with her face pressed against his chest. "I am so thankful that we had this opportunity to meet. I wish it had been under better circumstances."

Ian returned the heartfelt embrace. "I'll bring them back. Then we'll get you to Earth."

She pulled away and swiped at a tear. "My place is here on Thrae. No matter what happens."

His aunt turned and disappeared through the rock crevice that had led them to the underground grotto. Ian stared at the opening, committing her to memory. The longer he'd been in her presence, the more his feud with Jaered had turned frivolous. The rebel fought for more than Earth's survival. His battle was for all of his people, but especially for his mother and her love of Thrae.

It had to be torturous whenever Jaered was near Rayne. Or had he already replaced his deceased wife with Rayne? A spike pierced Ian's heart that he might be fighting a losing battle to keep Rayne's affection.

He untied the rope. It took two hands to steady the boat and Ian slipped in with less grace than he planned as the thick-planked rowboat smashed against the rocky edge. Its oars were in good shape and made of solid wood. He grabbed them and steered into the center of the raging river. It taxed his muscles to veer around the sharp turn ahead, but he managed to keep some distance between him and the jagged wall.

The water was fierce, splashing into the boat and pooling at Ian's feet. His boots were soaked, but he didn't dare let go of the oars to remove them. If it hadn't been for the light strapped to his forehead and his keen eyesight, he'd have been scalped by the jagged rocks overhead. More than once, he had to crouch down in the boat when the ceiling lowered but the water did not.

At one point, the sound of rushing water increased. Around the next bend, Ian was drenched from an overhead waterfall. He shook it off like a wet dog and kept his grip on the oars, fearful that if he let go, he'd crash against the rock wall.

Several miles later, and unsure if he could take much more, the current slowed and he leaned back in exhaustion. The boat glided into a wide cavern with a high-arched ceiling. A narrow ray of natural light streamed from a sizeable crevice overhead. The striations across the rock walls took Ian's breath away and he yearned for better light to view them in all their splendor. The wall depicting the planet's evolutionary story, displaying various crust layers rising high above his head.

Bump! One of the paddles slipped out of Ian's hand and he scrambled to retrieve it before it floated away. He slid the handle back into the iron ring that rose from the side of the boat and breathed a sigh of relief. Droplets, either from sweat or from his wet hair, plopped onto his cheek, and he used his forearm to swipe his forehead. *Bump!*

The rowboat swished sideways in the water. It hadn't been diverted by an underwater rock. The motion felt more like a nudge.

A water creature swam beneath him. Was it playing with him, or was the gesture a warning?

In order to conjure a core blast, Ian would have to let go of one of the oars. If he pulled it into the boat, he'd be unable to steer.

The creature's back broke the surface on the port side. It was about seven feet long and covered in thick scales, each one the size of Ian's hand. Phosphorescent algae grew between the curved scales, outlining them in an emerald glow. Ian leaned over the side of the boat as the creature dove beneath and disappeared into the murky depths. He had no idea how deep the water was in the cavern, but from what he could tell, it was enough deep for this creature to have grown to the size of a small car.

He searched for a ledge, anything he could paddle over to so he could be better prepared if the creature returned. Nothing but sheer rock walls surrounded him.

The sounds of the gentle lapping water kept his breaths company, yet were unable to sooth his pulse.

When the creature didn't return after a couple of minutes, Ian dipped the oars into the water with the merest of sound and pulled back with gentle force, headed for the mouth of the cave several yards ahead. Ian passed under a stream of natural light, and was blinded for a few seconds.

He cocked his ear at a change in the surface of the water from behind. The creature was on a direct path toward him. Ian pulled the oar in his left hand with everything he had but it wasn't enough to skirt the oncoming blitz. The creature lifted the back end of the boat out of the water and sent Ian lunging to the side.

He face-planted on the surface, and then was pulled under the water.

NINE

The creature's teeth caught on Ian's pants and grazed his hip. Blood seeped into the water and the fish flew into a frenzy. He banged his fists between the creature's eyes but only succeeded in aggravating it further. It chomped at Ian with razor-sharp teeth. He managed to keep his leg out of the slashing jowls, but they caught his pant leg again. The creature slit a gash down his thigh.

"Agh!" Ian let off a primal scream and river water filled his mouth and throat as the piranha-like creature swished him back and forth. A core blast sputtered inside his fist, unable to form. He fought not to lose his concentration while struggling to draw enough energy to shyft back into the boat, but his core stuttered and failed to ignite.

A gigantic, dark shadow approached in the water. If two of them intended to fight over Ian, he didn't have a chance.

With everything he had, he shoved against the slippery fish and tore his pants free from the creature's razor teeth in time to kick the newest arrival in the snout.

The second creature backed off and swam away, but then turned and crashed head-first into the side of the piranha-like fish. It opened its mouth in protest and buckled in the middle. Ian swam for the surface, but the strap on his boot caught on the gigantic piranha's teeth.

The two fish snapped at each other with the snagged Ian caught in the middle. He dodged the larger fish's jaws by using the piranha's body as a shield. With his free hand, Ian pulled a knife out of the sheath strapped to his calf. A bon voyage present from Sophenna. He stuck the blade between his boot and strap, and with a powerful swipe, he cut himself free. He then pumped his arms for the surface at the same moment the larger fish took a bite out of the piranha's head.

With a massive kick, he broke the surface and sucked air while the light on his forehead cast bobbing streams across the cave walls. The rowboat remained afloat, but was on a beeline path for the mouth of the cave where the river narrowed and the current picked up speed. Unable to draw enough energy to shyft, Ian swam with everything he had. The boat sideswiped the mouth of the cave and the current jammed it against the cave wall. But to Ian's horror, its front tip turned toward the opening in the quickening current.

Ian lunged and grabbed the trailing rope just as the boat sped off through the mouth of the cave. The rope jerked in Ian's hands, and he was dragged through the water. Inch by inch Ian pulled himself toward the boat while choking on mouthfuls of river water. He grabbed the back edge and managed to drag himself inside. From the looks of it, all of Ian's other supplies had slid under the seat at the front of the rowboat.

A smaller piranha had snagged on his pants. He shook it off and it plopped about at his feet. He ignored the snapping jaws of chiseled teeth and searched for the oars. One had been caught in the same current as the boat and slid alongside. He scooped it out of the water and secured it in the iron ring, but the other had been swept against the wall of the narrowing cave on a parallel course with the rowboat. Too far away to grab, Ian drew every bit of energy he could from the surrounding energy fields and extended his hand. Try as he might, he couldn't conjure the oar.

A sharp stab in his toe. The uninvited guest had bitten down on Ian's boot. He pried it loose with his free hand and tossed the fish over the side. It left a slimy film on Ian's palm that soon turned into burning, rising welts.

Ian had never had a reaction to anything natural on Earth. He was immune to all of nature. Why now? It looked like his hand had been stung by a swarm of bees.

He brushed the pain aside and used both hands to steer with the lone paddle, keeping one eye on its escaped partner while navigating the raging river. At another curve in the river bed, Ian held steady and reached out with his sore hand to grab the paddle, but the flat blade caught on an edge of rock protruding from the wall and it swung out of Ian's reach at the last second.

An unfamiliar sound pricked Ian's ears. It came from farther up the river. He adjusted his headlamp and discovered that the river split in two, by a narrow break in the wall directing separate streams to either side.

The bag holding the map was wedged up underneath the front seat and he couldn't reach it. He extended his foot and it took three tries to snag the strap with the toe of his boot. He opened the bag at his feet and rummaged around for his mother's map. He couldn't unfold it with one hand, and he was forced to stick the paddle under his arm, holding it in place against his torso. The river depicted on the map didn't indicate a fork. Ian tried to judge if the line went in a particular direction, but it was straight down.

The intersection was fast approaching. He turned a keen ear to the cave and stilled his heart. Which one, which one, repeated in his thoughts. He caught the sound of a massive amount of rushing water to the right. A waterfall!

Ian grabbed the oar and dug his heels against the bottom of the rowboat. He pulled back on the oar with a groan, holding the makeshift rudder deep in the water, but the stronger current headed toward the waterfall tunnel.

"Ahhh," he groaned as the raging river swirled and separated, pinning the side of the boat against the divide and trapping the oar against the rocks. Ian held steadfast in spite of every muscle in his arms and legs being depleted. At the last second, the boat swung to the left and turned around, caught in the correct current. The second paddle headed down the opposite tunnel and disappeared.

He lay panting with the beat of his heart threatening to break his ribs, but he had to gain control of the boat. He sat up with the paddle still in his grip and took heed of his injury. The welts had burst open, seeping a yellow pus in thick streams along the edge of his hand. He sniffed. The pus had an acrid odor to it. A few drops of the pus fell into the bottom of the boat. Small puffs of steamy gas rose wherever they made contact with the water.

Ian scooted back. Sulfur oxide. What the hell? That came from volcanic activity, not fish. The throbbing pain in his foot threatened to split his boot apart and he struggled with removing it one-handed. Ian wedged the heel in the missing slat between the seat and the inner edge of the boat, and leveraged himself using the iron ring of the paddle. The boot slid off, but the burning scrapes elicited another scream. He pulled off the sock and stared at the pustules covering what formerly made up his foot. He'd never get his boot back on. He propped his foot up on the edge of the boat to keep it away from the water under his seat. Otherwise he might pass out from sulfuric acid searing his lungs. Sophenna hadn't packed meds.

The river slowed to a steady stream and Ian rigged the paddle to steer in the middle of the current. He coasted along in a daze. Whatever the poison, it played with his senses. He could have sworn that poppies were blooming nearby, their fragrance overwhelming.

The river widened into a gentle flow and Ian drifted in and out of consciousness. When lucid, he watched his headlamp play with the shadows across the ceiling of the aqueduct. The motion of the rowboat often lulled him to sleep and he dreamed of the estate . . . walks with Rayne . . . the taste of Milo's lasagna . . . sparring with Tara in the gym. The applause of the audience reminded him that not too long ago, he'd been an illusionist. A life left behind for the sake of duty, but never forgotten. The rush of adrenaline whenever he imagined his illusions kept him alert and he recounted his favorite ones, describing them in painstaking detail to his only companion, the oar tied above him.

His stomach stopped growling and protesting hours ago. He licked his lips, cracked and bleeding, a conundrum when he was surrounded by so much water. Ian swung his arm out and snagged one of the bags. By the time he brought it to his chest, he couldn't remember why he wanted it, but rummaged around in it with his good hand. It rested upon a water bottle and Ian put the lid in his mouth to loosen it when he couldn't open it otherwise. He spit the lid off to the side and gulped the refreshing, lifesaving fluid, then cradled the bottle against his chest and dropped his head back. The lamp at his forehead flickered, sending faint streaks across the ceiling. Ian set the water bottle down and turned the lamp off, thankful for the coherent moment.

Afraid to look at his injured hand or foot, there wasn't anything he could do. The infectious slime and bite appeared to be made of the same chemical makeup. He wondered what it could be and recalled his knowledge of chemistry and all natural substances. No surprise that he drifted in and out—it was the periodic table after all—but he remembered where he left off whenever he aroused, at least he thought he did.

The current picked up speed and the makeshift rudder strained to stay on course. The front of the boat skidded along the rocky wall in the narrowing channel. Ian fought to get up, but his clothes were soaked from the water in the bottom of the boat and felt like they weighed a ton. His foot slipped and upon impact with the bottom, he let out a horrific scream while the searing pain crept up his leg as high as his hip. Sulfuric acid pooled in the middle of the boat. Ian turned his back to it and hid his face in his bent arm.

"You owe me!" he screamed at the top of his lungs, to no one but the universe itself. "I ask nothing for myself. I only want to make a difference. But I can't if you don't keep me here!" Driven by his rage, he pulled himself onto the seat and stuck the oar handle under his arm, untying it with fingers and teeth. He grabbed it and wiped the sweat from his eyes with his forearm. "I'm not done!" he said, his voice getting stronger. "I'm not done."

He swung the oar to the side of the boat and steered until his lids grew heavy, but had the forethought to pull the lone oar into the boat before the darkness enveloped him.

TEN

Jaered awakened from the restless sleep with a start and sat up, blinking. He rubbed his face and took a deep breath, welcoming the fresh air. At the sound of voices, he peered through the grove of olive trees and spied the orchard workers in the distance.

"Wake up." He nudged Patrick next to him and was greeted with a moan. He shoved Patrick. "Come on, we're about to be spotted."

Patrick sat up, rubbed his eyes, and stretched his arms. "That was unpleasant."

"You're lucky we didn't sleep in an alley." Jaered regarded the overhead trees and inhaled the scent of the olive branches. It reminded him of his childhood meals with his mother. He pushed the rising melancholy to the side.

"So you've spent time in an alley or two." Patrick rose to his knees.

Jaered got to his feet and swiped at his jeans. "We don't have time for a sharing moment. Let's move." He offered Patrick his hand.

"Where?" Patrick grabbed it and got to his feet.

He looked around. It was open space between the orchard and the edge of town. "We can't walk back to town. We'd be too exposed."

"So where are you shyfting us?" Patrick said.

"Not me, you," Jaered said.

Patrick chuckled, then sobered. "You can't be serious. I haven't been able to shyft with just me, much less two of us."

Jaered gestured toward the workers making their way deeper into the orchard. "Then you better figure it out. Fast."

"Where?"

From the tone in Patrick's voice, Jaered wasn't sure if this would work. "Are you hungry?"

"Sorta," Patrick said.

"Then remember the restaurant from last night and take us to the bathroom." Patrick closed his eyes but nothing happened. Jaered grabbed his shoulder. "Pull energy into your core. Feel it tingle as the cold seeps into your limbs." Patrick stiffened and tightened his fists, but Jaered didn't feel the energy coursing through him. The orchard workers were closing in. "The odors of food spilling into the room. The sound of laughter in the distance. The low-watt light overhead," Jaered coaxed. "You were full from the meal." Then he put himself in Patrick's head. "Freaked out by the Pur soldiers looking for us."

Patrick shivered. They appeared in the restaurant bathroom. He kept shivering, even when he opened his eyes. "I did it!" He looked equally shocked and elated. "Wow!"

A toilet flushed behind them. The stall door opened and a man stepped out, looked between Jaered and Patrick, then dropped his head and left without washing his hands.

"I hope he isn't the cook," Patrick said.

"Let's celebrate over breakfast." Jaered swung the door open. "Your treat."

Patrick had a hard time suppressing his excitement at shyfting for the first time, and Jaered had to shush him countless times as they walked the streets of Osuna, keeping to the shadows and cutting down alleyways. They found a small café several blocks from the other restaurant and this time, Patrick chose an inside table in the back. They ate a simple meal and lingered at the table, forming a plan for connecting with Milo.

Jaered pulled out his cell, checked it. "I missed a text from Eve."

"What time is the tour?" Patrick asked.

He silently read her message. "She said there didn't appear to be one. She suggests going there and ringing the bell." Jaered put his cell away. "The question is, what to do with you in the meantime."

"I can practice my shyfting." Patrick said, not holding back his enthusiasm.

"I'd rather you work on your conjuring. Less likely to mess up." Jaered pushed his chair back. "We'll head to the monastery on foot. The Pur guard might have given up last night. But my gut tells me they're still in the area, especially if there aren't any new reports of stolen cars. The local taxi service will be the next thing they check," Jaered said. "Caps and sunglasses will help us look like every other tourist."

Patrick stood and dropped the money on the table. "We need a map of the city. And I'll take lots of pictures with my phone." His confidence was at an all-time high. Tourist he could do.

Jaered headed out of the café. "At this rate your cash won't last the day. All I want is for this escapade to end so we can get back to training in Greenland."

The duo found a small tourist shop down the street and picked out some glasses. Patrick chose aviator reflective ones, but Jaered removed them and handed him darker ones. "These cover your face more."

Patrick tried to convince Jaered to wear the Osuna, Spain cap with a huge olive on it, but Jaered chose a simple, nondescript navy one. Patrick picked out a black cap with the flag of Spain on the front, admired himself in the small rectangle mirror, and then purchased everything. They stepped out onto the sidewalk and opened the city map that they'd probably never fold so neat and compactly again.

"This is where we're headed." Jaered pointed to a blue dot with the number five inside.

Patrick referred to the legend at the bottom of the map. The Monastery of la Encarnacion. Jaered got his bearings from the street sign on the corner and he cringed. They would have an uphill trek.

Jaered returned to the cashier inside, and in fluent Spanish spoke with the woman. She gestured, speaking rapidly.

Patrick stood on the sidewalk and raised his face to the heat of the day. Ian could speak six or seven languages. He wondered how many Jaered spoke and chastised himself for paying more attention to his high school French teacher than his class work. Jaered returned a couple of minutes later.

"What was that about?" Patrick said.

"I wanted the best route to take on foot to get to the monastery." Jaered folded the map. "I'm channeling my tourist side."

Patrick huffed and puffed to catch up at almost every corner, and it took a while to reach the monastery. He was equally shocked and embarrassed at how out of shape he was. At one corner Jaered threw him a scowl.

"I get it. I need to be more serious about using the gym, and to work harder at everything," Patrick panted.

"Wait there," Jaered said and pointed to a bench, just inside a barbershop. There were a handful of men waiting for their turn. "I'll go the rest of the way."

"Be careful," Patrick said. "I just want to know he's safe and how to find Tara."

"If I don't return within two hours, contact your mother," Jaered said before the door swung shut.

Patrick took a seat next to a man who needed a trim. Patrick removed his hat, reached up, and ran his fingers through his own hair. If he had two hours to kill, this looked like a good place to hang out. He was thankful that Jaered seemed to know what to do every step of the way. Patrick perused the reading material on the seat next to him and discovered that the magazines and newspaper were in Spanish. It would be a long two hours.

Jaered walked the rest of the way up the cobbled street, then paused when he saw a single car parked in the lot. He stopped at the door at the Monastery of la Encarnacion, rang the bell, then turned a keen ear to the sounds beyond, but all was silent. He studied the architecture, a mix of adobe and hand-carved bricks. Additions had been built over the centuries with a two-story building attached and tiled roof off to the side. The wrought iron gate appeared to have received a new coat of black paint. Jaered rang the bell again. The street was quiet. A dog barked in the distance.

Footsteps. A petite, crape-paper-faced nun in a long robe opened the door. Tufts of her white hair stuck out beneath her capped veil.

"I'm trying to visit as many monasteries as I can. I'd love a tour," Jaered said in Spanish. "Would you be so kind?"

She nodded and showed Jaered into the vestibule, but held her hand up as if telling him to wait. Then disappeared through a side archway. A moment later, a much younger nun approached Jaered from a rear door. "I can give you a tour," she announced in Spanish.

Jaered met up with her. "Thank you. I heard that you have a lovely garden in the back. Would I be able to see that, too?"

She smiled and gestured around the vestibule, then slipped into her well-rehearsed litany. "The monastery was erected in 1547. Located in the Plaza del la Encarnacion, just below the Collegiate Church. It is of the Baroque style. The main altarpiece . . ."

Jaered nodded often to appear engaged, but was on the alert for any sign of Milo. He remarked on a few of the exquisite artifacts in the chapel and on the collection of small Christ dolls with their elaborate, embroidered wardrobes displayed in little chests. While the tour pressed on, he caught a whiff of baked bread and commented on the wonderful aroma. The nun smiled wide and told him that they baked rolls at the monastery. With a twinkle in her eye, she added that he could buy them at the end of the tour.

When she finished, Jaered was shown into the back room where they displayed their rolls on tables and religious knick-knacks on the surrounding shelves. He asked again about seeing the garden, but the nun smiled and gestured to the rolls as if that wasn't an option. He hung around the baked goods and tried to come up with a new plan.

"Is Mr. M. working today?" he asked the elderly nun behind the cash register.

She gave him a confused expression and shrugged. "I don't know anyone by that name," she said.

What did Patrick call him? Jaered racked his brain. "Milonius?" he asked, but the vacant expression didn't change. He remembered the rolls Ian brought back and picked one up. "Maybe he helps bake in your kitchen?"

The nun shook her head no. He wasn't sure if she understood, or just took pity on him, but she guided him to the kitchen and opened the door.

A blast of heat hit Jaered in the face and the amazing smell of baking bread calmed his impatience. A handful of nuns were kneading dough or pulling trays of bread out of the old oven. Across the kitchen, a robust man washed dishes at a long sink. His back was to Jaered.

The nun smiled at Jaered and held her hand up to wait, then approached the man. He half-turned to her. She said something to him, that was difficult to make out with the chatter and tin pans clanking in the small space. The man followed the nun's pointed finger and he locked eyes with Jaered. Disbelief raised the features on Milo's face. Then the old caretaker took off at full run, headed for the back door.

ELEVEN

The nuns gasped. Jaered's escort gave him a disapproving stare as though he'd disturbed their well-oiled workplace. He took off after Milo, hampered by the tight aisles around the large center island. His escort planted herself in the way, ready to defend the dishwasher. Jaered grabbed her by the shoulders, lifted her, then repositioned her off to the side.

He reached the back door and banged it open before it latched shut, but he took a second to glance back into the kitchen. The nuns threw a few rolls at him and one bounced off his shoulder. Jaered shook a finger at one nun who clearly had decided that cussing was not a sin within kitchen walls.

Confident he could catch up to the old man, Jaered stepped out, but the intense sun blinded him and it took a couple of seconds for his eyes to adjust. He found himself in a back alley filled with trash cans and discarded wooden crates. Strong arms grabbed Jaered from behind and a kitchen knife was held to his throat. Suds dripped from Milo's arm.

"You're supposed to be dead!" Milo growled at Jaered's ear. "Perhaps I can make that a permanent thing this time."

Jaered held his hands up in surrender. "But then you won't have a clue how to connect with Patrick, who very much wants to talk to you."

Milo scoffed. "Nice try, but the last time I saw you, you were kidnapping him."

"Patrick has answers for you, and a bunch of questions about Tara." Jaered didn't have to tune into the man's heartbeat; it pumped with vigor against Jaered's back.

"Where's Ian?" Milo hissed.

"He's on Thrae, rescuing Rayne." The knife at Jaered's throat sagged.

"He wouldn't dare, it's forbidden," Milo said. "The Primary told us that Earth would self-destruct if Ian left."

"That's only one of his countless lies," Jaered said.

The knife pressed harder against Jaered's throat. "You're the one I don't trust."

"Then why are you hiding? It's obvious you no longer trust the Primary," Jaered said.

"That doesn't mean that I trust you," Milo said, but his tone was no longer hostile.

Jaered half-turned to look up at him. "Patrick said that his favorite meal of yours is paella."

"So?" Milo shot back. "You could have found that out torturing him."

Jaered chuckled, but it came out like a snort. "Why would I torture him for his favorite meal? He also said that whenever you cleaned his room, you'd leave at least one shirt on the floor. Why's that?"

"To get him to pick up something." Milo grunted. "You would have me believe that the two of you are buddies."

"Ian, too," Jaered said. "I'm not here for a fight. Just to connect you and Patrick."

Milo lowered the knife but kept it at the ready. "So where is he?"

"Down the street inside the barbershop on the corner."

"Why didn't he come?" Milo said.

"We think the Pur guard are onto us. We didn't want to draw attention to you," Jaered figured half a lie was better than the truth.

"I'm not going anywhere with you," Milo snarled.

"You don't have to." Jaered stuck his hand in his pocket and withdrew an earbud. He tossed it to Milo who caught it in his free hand. "He really wants to talk to you. He's worried about Tara." Jaered backed up. When the old caretaker didn't lunge, he turned and walked away.

The barber used the towel from over his shoulder to swipe the hair off his chair. Then with a wide smile, he gestured for Patrick to take a seat. He stood, but the crackle in his ear stopped him cold. He gestured to a local who'd come in after him to take his turn. Patrick sat down at the end of the row to the surprise of the other waiting patrons.

He turned his head away and covered his ear. "Milo?

"Is that you, boy?"

"Yeah, it's really me," Patrick said and leaned against the wall. "I'm glad you're safe."

"What the hell are you doing, running with that rebel?" Milo said.

His parental tone brought warmth to Patrick's core. "You need to talk to Dr. Mac, Milo. He can fill you in on what's happening with Ian and me."

Milo muttered something under his breath. Patrick didn't have to hear it clearly to know the old caretaker was cussing a mile a minute. "I knew Mac was in league with that Eve!"

"Please, Milo, you've got to trust us. If you can't, then trust Dr. Mac." Milo didn't respond. "Milo, we need to find Tara. Where could she have gone with Saxon?"

"I don't know . . ." Milo said. "I'm still not sure I trust the rebels, and I don't want her to fall into the Primary's hands."

"You have to trust someone." Patrick closed his eyes, hoping the tone of his voice was enough. "No one cares more about her than me," he said. "You know that's true."

"You're more afraid of her than anything." Milo muttered.

"Let me keep her safe," Patrick hated that his tone came across as pleading.

"You catch up with her," Milo said. "And it'll be the other way around, for sure." The old caretaker grew serious. "If she doesn't kill Jaered, first. I hope you know what you're doing running with that group."

Patrick ached that he couldn't tell Milo everything, but if they survived the Primary and his army, he hoped to get the chance.

Jaered came up short of the barbershop door when Patrick bolted out like a kid on a sugar high, but then caught himself and paused to take heed of their surroundings. His mother was right, Jaered thought. Eve was always right. Patrick would learn everything faster if he was in the thick of things.

"God, it was good to hear his voice," Patrick said. "He's moving to a new city. If we could find him, so could the Pur guard."

"Did you get what you needed?" Jaered asked.

"He suspects Tara went in search of Joule."

Jaered hadn't anticipated that. "Why the geophysicist?"

"Because Ian had made her a promise before he disappeared. Tara intended to make good on it."

"So you know that she's safe and on her own," Jaered said. "Time to get back to Greenland."

Panic widened Patrick's eyes. "Whoa, no, we're going after her."

Jaered clenched his fists. "That wasn't the deal. The longer we stay out in the open, the better the chance we'll be caught by the Pur guard."

"But she deserves to know the truth," Patrick said. "I need to see her and tell her what's going on. All she knows is that I disappeared and Ian left her behind to go find me. That's not fair, not to her."

Jaered got in his face, but Patrick didn't back down. He had grown a backbone in the past twenty-four hours. Jaered weighed the risk of continuing this pursuit. "What happens when you find her?"

"I'll tell her whatever it takes, anything for her to trust us enough to come with us."

A dark SUV turned the corner. Jaered pulled Patrick away from the street and up against the building, under the shadows. "And if she rejects you?" He threw his arm around Patrick to look like they were a couple.

Patrick shook his head. "Why would she do that?"

"Because when Vael and I kidnapped you, you were a friend." The SUV went by at a crawl. Jaered followed its reflection in the barbershop window. He lowered the edge of Patrick's cap.

Patrick pushed his brim back to where it'd been, as though oblivious to Jaered's concern. "I still am her friend."

"No, you're a Duach," Jaered countered. "One of her natural enemies." He stepped away from the building, stuck his hands in his pockets, and watched the SUV up the street disappear around the corner. "Do you really believe this will be a happy reunion?" he tossed over his shoulder.

Patrick didn't respond.

TWELVE

A brilliant white light formed in the center of the storage room. Sophenna's vigil had come to an end. She got to her feet and stood firm, not about to let Aeros see her flinch. His image solidified, then he hesitated, facing her.

"Are you here to stop me from exacting my punishment?" he said with a smug expression.

"I am here to tell you that you are wasting your time," she said. "Earth's Heir is not within your reach."

He scoffed. "Everything is within my reach."

"The boy had a right to learn about his heritage, his family. Johann was wrong to keep the truth from him."

"I know that you and your sisters are plotting against me," he said. "Is Earth's Heir coming to Thrae part of that plan?"

"We have fought you for centuries. Yet, you remain a god and we, your servants." Sophenna stepped close. "Go, wreak havoc on Earth. There is nothing left for you on Thrae."

"You're wrong," he said. "You're here."

She raised her chin along with her shoulders. "Wielding power over others will not make me love you."

Flames replaced his irises. "You are stubborn to the end," he snarled.

"As are you," she whispered.

He grabbed her by the shoulders and squeezed so hard she grimaced, yet held his stare and didn't let him see her crumble. "Go, Aeros. The Heir will return to Earth, soon."

"I punish those who have colluded against me," he said and gave her a murderous glare. "To quench their boldness."

"Then I am the one you want," she said. "For it is I, and no one else who has sent him on his journey."

His eyes scanned her body, and he let her go with a shove. "I can still hurt you."

"Everyone is gone. There is no one left to hunt," she said, and crossed her arms.

"In your tunnels, your caves?" He smirked. "I know they exist. It's the only explanation for such massive disappearances whenever I come calling."

Sophenna grabbed the folds of her clothes. "Then do what you must. Whatever it will take for you to leave us alone."

Aeros dragged her out of the storage room. "I think above ground this time, don't you? Amidst the ruins that used to be our love."

"You can't claim what you've never had," Sophenna said.

Aeros swept her up into his arms. "Then this will not be pleasant."

THIRTEEN

Patrick almost asked how Jaered knew where the Willoughsby research camp was located, but every question earned him a scowl. By standing his ground and insisting that they continue their search for Tara, Patrick was in Jaered's crosshairs.

The sweltering heat of the Congo swarmed around Patrick the second they appeared. At least Spain had a much drier heat.

"Where to now?" Patrick said.

"Down there." Jaered indicated a camp at the base of the hill.

A few people wandered around the clearing carrying boxes or sacks. Jaered exited the rock outcropping they had shyfted to and followed a narrow car path.

Patrick ran to keep up. They walked in silence for about a quarter mile. The quiet turned unbearable. "Have you met Joule before?"

"No," Jaered said.

"Then how do you know about her research camp?" Jaered threw the predicted scowl at Patrick and picked up his pace. Patrick paused mid-step. "You were following Ian."

"Willoughsby had worked for the Primary for a while," Jaered said. "But at the end, his work was commissioned by Eve."

"What kind of work?" Patrick said.

"The science-based kind I'm not privy to," Jaered snapped. "All I know is that he was helping the rebels. If the Primary suspected his collusion with us, Dr. Willoughsby probably disappeared when he could." A Jeep headed up the road. Jaered grabbed Patrick's arm and pulled them down into a gulley along the road. Jaered landed on top of him.

"Joule knows me. We don't have to be so stealthy," Patrick said.

"You might trust her, but we can't trust other Sars that might be here," Jaered hissed.

Patrick nodded, it was all he could do with Jaered crushing the breath out of him.

Jaered rolled off the second the Jeep passed by. "It might be safer to wait until nightfall."

"We need to get out of this heat," Patrick said. "I didn't think to bring water."

Jaered held out his hand. A canteen appeared. He unscrewed it and inspected the contents, then looked baffled.

"You can conjure a container, but not the water to go in it." Patrick pursed his lips. "Some teacher you are."

"Fuck you." Jaered kept low and continued down the hill, using the gulley for a path.

Patrick grabbed the back of his shirt and pulled them both down when the grind of two car engines approached. "It sounds like they are packing up and leaving. We might not have till nightfall."

"Agreed," Jaered said. "They're headed for the vortex field above. That means . . ."

"A Pur Sar will be up there, shyfting supplies away, not down in the camp," Patrick said. "It's clear sailing below."

"Provided there's only one Pur Sar with them," Jaered said.

"Guess we'll find out." Patrick pushed ahead. A couple of heartbeats later, Jaered followed.

By the time they reached the edge of the encampment, Patrick's clothes were soaked and he hated how sticky he felt. When he looked around, Jaered was gone. "What a stealth-wad," Patrick griped under his breath.

A handful of minutes later, Jaered returned with a dripping canteen. "Here, don't pass out on me."

Patrick gulped down half the water without pausing. He put the top back on and passed it to Jaered. "Thanks."

"They are breaking down the outer tents. Three are still standing in the middle. Joule's is untouched, so it looks like she'll be one of the last to go." Jaered put a hand on Patrick's shoulder.

They appeared inside a sizeable canvas tent, high enough for people to walk inside. At one end sat a makeshift desk held up between sawhorses. A two-way radio crackled but no voices came out of the box. Papers and printouts of graphs and columns were scattered across the desk. A cot was at the opposite side of the tent; a plump pillow and sleeping bag lay on top.

No sign of the scientist, or Tara.

Patrick stepped away, but banged his forehead on an oil lamp that hung next to the center pole. "Ow. They're not here."

"Duh," Jaered said.

Patrick rubbed his forehead and wandered over to the desk. He picked up one of the printouts and absorbed what he could. "I thought she was studying lightning," he said. "This looks like something else."

Jaered snatched it from him. "It's a seismic graph. There's a lot of activity going on."

"Who the hell are you?" They held up their hands and turned around. Joule Willoughsby stood glaring at them. Her face lit up when she recognized Patrick and she ran over, throwing her arms around him. "Oh my god, where have you been?" She pulled away and froze at the sight of Jaered. "You!" She shoved Jaered and he stumbled back against the edge of the desk. "What did you do with Rayne? Is she alive?"

"She's on Thrae. Ian went to retrieve her," Jaered said.

Perplexed, Joule looked between Patrick and Jaered. "What the hell's going on?"

"We're trying to find Tara. Do you know where she is?" Patrick said. "Is Saxon with her?"

"She visited me a couple days ago. The wolf was with her. Said she was trying to find my father. She thought that if she found him, she might find Ian."

"Why?" Jaered asked.

"Because she believes my father was working for the rebels." Joule glared at Jaered. "She's right, isn't she?" Jaered didn't answer her.

"But she's not here now." Patrick sat on the edge of the cot.

"She and I were to meet up in London, tomorrow," Joule said. "I had to stay and see to the move."

"What do you mean were?" Patrick asked. "Where are you going?"

"Home." She turned away. "I've lost everything. My permits, my funding. My assistant and two others died when poachers attacked our camp."

"Right after your father went missing." Jaered looked pensive. "What happened to Bhutto?"

His question left Joule stunned. "How do you know him?"

"Because my boss was the one who funded your father's research," Jaered said. "Bhutto was our contact."

"He went with Tara. They're working together to find him," Joule said.

"Then we're headed to London," Jaered announced.

"Do you know where Tara and Bhutto were staying?" Patrick asked.

"They were going to my father's flat." She got out a pen and wrote the address on the edge of one of the graphs, then tore it off and handed it to Patrick.

He hugged her. "Are you sure you're all right? Is there anything we can do for you?"

"I'm fine," she mumbled at his shoulder. "I'll see you in London, tomorrow evening."

Patrick stared at the address on the sheet. "Ready?" he said to Jaered.

"Not here," Jaered said and gave Joule a sideways glance. He grabbed the paper from Patrick, looked at it, then put his hand on Patrick's shoulder.

They appeared in a bright, open-space modern loft with wide overstuffed furniture and stainless steel fixtures. Patrick shivered and shook his hands. He wandered around the flat. "I never met the man, but from what Joule told me about her father, this doesn't strike me as Dr. Willoughsby's style."

"It's not his place. It's one of your mother's safe houses in London." Jaered walked into the kitchen beyond and opened the refrigerator. He pulled out a bottle of water and tossed one to Patrick."

"We're going to Dr. Willoughsby's though. Right?" Patrick said.

Jaered opened a cabinet and pulled out a box of crackers. He tossed one in the air and caught it in his mouth. His speech came out garbled. "Take a shower, everything you'll need is upstairs. We're going to make a plan. No more driving blind."

Patrick took a cautious whiff under his arm. "A shower won't make much difference if I put these back on."

"There are some clothes in the closet. I'm sure there's something that will fit you." Jaered plopped down on the couch and threw an arm over his face. "Take your time. I'm going to grab some sleep."

Patrick went upstairs and found a small guest bedroom and a larger master bedroom, each with their own bathrooms. He peered over the side of the balcony and found that Jaered had indeed drifted off with the box of crackers lying on his chest. The view from the flat was breathtaking. They were in a high-rise building towering over London. The London Eye, one of the largest Ferris wheels in the world, rose above the Thames in the distance. Patrick couldn't remember the last time he was in London and pondered it while the water grew hot.

The soothing shower was the perfect remedy for his sore muscles. He turned on the massage nozzle to work out some kinks in his back and shoulders, lingering reminders of his orchard bedroom the previous night.

Tara had told Patrick that shyfting could be disorienting, and often get your internal clock out of sync. They'd spent the night in a Spanish orchard, visited the heart of the Congo, and were now in London all within a few hours of each other. Disoriented didn't begin to describe how Patrick felt.

The master closet offered shirts and pants of multiple sizes, colors, and styles, complete with attached store tags. The underwear drawer had an equally large selection, everything still in retail packages. Patrick discovered a plastic bin under the bathroom sink with individually packed toothbrushes and travel size toothpaste. The safe house was certainly prepared for the occasional drop-in guests.

Once he felt human again, he lay down on the bed and fell into a troubled sleep. Jaered had a point. How would Tara receive him, knowing who—what—he now was?

FOURTEEN

Patrick stood in the dimly lit hallway and leaned in, peering through the peephole. He couldn't see a thing beyond the thick, wooden door that boasted several coats of paint. The number five was brass plated, and dulled from wear.

Jaered was downstairs, across the street. The one thing they could agree on was that Tara was going to be shocked, and Jaered didn't need to complicate things further. He also mumbled something about him and the wolf not being the best of friends.

Patrick clanged the brass loop that surrounded the apartment number. Footsteps. A deadbolt clicked and the door opened. Tara stood, frozen in place. Her long white hair hung loose around her shoulders. Tears collected in her eyes and she reached for Patrick. He swept her up in his arms and buried his face in her neck, then inhaled her scent to convince himself the reunion was real. Her embrace was full of warmth and love.

"Where? How?" was all she could voice between sobs. She pulled back and swiped at the tears snaking down her cheeks. "Ian?"

"He's good," Patrick said. "He's on Thrae."

Startled, she shook her head. "What?"

"He went to retrieve Rayne." Patrick grabbed her hands. "Tara, there's so much I need to tell you." He stepped into the apartment and closed the door with furtive glances. "Where's Bhutto?"

"He went to meet with a few of Dr. Willoughsby's associates," she said. "I've been searching his paperwork but can't seem to find anything useful."

Patrick stepped around stacks of books. The apartment was in direct contrast to the safe house. Dr. Willoughsby preferred dark wood furniture and thick curtains that blocked out the light. Patrick sneezed from the dust. "Ian's mother is on Thrae. The Primary isn't who you think he is. He and Aeros are brothers."

Tara's face scrunched in disbelief. "The rebels, they've brainwashed you." She pressed her palm to his chest. "Patrick you need to . . ." Tara's concern faded and she turned her focus to his torso. "No," she whispered. She jerked her hand away and took a couple of steps back. "It can't be. You have a core." He heard a whimper from the other side of the couch. Saxon lifted his furry head above the back, then plodded over to Tara's hip. He growled, low and deep, baring his fangs.

It was as if Patrick had been shot in the back. "It's more than that," he said, ready to come clean, to bare all.

"They made you a Duach Sar." Tara held her palm toward him. "I can feel your negative energy."

"Tara, I can explain." Patrick took a step toward her.

"You're not Patrick," she said. "You can't be." She leapt across the couch and in one fluid motion, withdrew her gun from the holster lying on the table, then swung around and pointed it at him. At the same time, Saxon sprang at Patrick digging his teeth into his neck. The wolf's jaws were massive, crushing bone as they dug deeper, ripping Patrick's throat. Blood spurted everywhere and blinded him as his world faded into darkness.

Patrick jolted up in the bed. He rubbed his neck, but it felt intact. His chest heaved and he gulped for air while his pulse took its time to slow.

"What's with you?" Jaered held a gun next to his face and peered at Patrick from the doorway. He entered the bedroom, gun first, and poked his head into the open closet, then the bathroom. "Why'd you scream?"

"Bad dream." Patrick got off the bed and went to the bathroom sink. He splashed water on his face and hung his head, dripping.

"You scream like a girl." Jaered lowered the gun. He studied Patrick in the bathroom mirror. "You still want to do this?"

Patrick's heartbeat wouldn't stop racing.

FIFTEEN

Sophenna lay still on the concrete slab. Aeros hadn't been that violent in a long time. He'd bitten her shoulders and breasts, drawing blood and then smearing it across her face and into her mouth between his slobbering kisses. The concrete block that he'd chosen as their bed dug into her back, leaving raw and bleeding scrapes. She was numb, but the pain would soon come. She welcomed it, a reminder that she was still alive.

Sophenna hadn't uttered a sound, enraging Aeros that much more. He had whispered his love as he bit her ear, thrusting himself deep. Her insides throbbed in beat with her heart.

She closed her eyes, recalling the earlier days. Long before the solar wave had changed their DNA and created gods out of children. If it hadn't been for her sisters,

Sophenna would have gone mad. Perhaps she already was, and they were too kind, unwilling to tell her the truth.

He'd wandered off after purging his rage with her, and she caught his footsteps in the distance. He often came above ground after having his way with Sophenna, surveying the evidence of his power over a planet. The destruction made him feel invincible, and he'd boast about it whenever he returned to her apartment. But over the past decade, he'd become pensive and somber.

Aeros returned, and kicked away a chunk of concrete at his feet. He sat on the edge of the slab and stared at her, brushing her hair off her face. He used the edge of his sleeve to wipe at the blood but soon gave up and tucked the bloody smear inside his sleeve. "If you didn't resist me, it could be so much more," he said gently.

Sophenna turned her face from him, but he cupped her cheek in his hand and forced her to look at him. "Am I such a tyrant?" He whispered behind unshed tears.

"You surveyed all that you have done, and you still ask me that?" she said.

"Come to Earth." He scooped her up in his arms and rocked her. His tears wet her cheek. "There is nothing left for you here. I can give you the universe."

"You take what's not yours. You promise what isn't yours to give." She looked up at him. "You have only power, yet nothing else. How lonely you must be."

Enraged, Aeros bolted to his feet. He turned from her, roaring with raised fists, turning his power against Thrae.

The shell of a building shook and dust, chunks of concrete and debris rained down. Sophenna brought her legs up to her chest and bent over, covering her head with her arms, ignoring the shooting pain in her body. She thought of the colony, deep underground, hiding in the cavern.

"Stop!" she shouted.

Aeros turned on her. "Perhaps if there was truly nothing left here, you would have no choice but to follow me."

"You will only kill everyone, including me." Sophenna stood on rickety legs. She pressed her hand to her abdomen, and although it did not ease the spikes of pain, she stood tall. "What would happen if you kill me, Aeros?" He looked away. "You don't know, none of us do. My sisters and I may not have powers, but we're all connected." She turned his chin to face her. "Are you ready to take that chance?"

"The day will come when we find out, I promise you that," he sneered.

"Until then, go back to Earth." She wobbled toward the tunnel door. "Get your sadistic pleasure somewhere else."

"Why did Ian defy everything he was taught . . . and come here?" Aeros called out to her. She did not answer, focused on taking one step after another. "I think it has something to do with whoever our son brought with him, on his last visit to Thrae."

Sophenna stopped dead in her tracks. "I have no idea what you're talking about."

Aeros stepped ahead and blocked her path. "I know Jaered brought someone to Thrae," He leaned in and hissed at her ear. "You're not rid of me. Not yet. I have unfinished business."

"Jaered was attacked, burned alive. The human tried to help and got caught in his corona." She wobbled on her feet. "It was an accident."

"I can't believe anything that spills from your mouth," he snarled. His irises burst into flames. "I will hunt the human down and have my fun. Then I will take Ian back to Earth and make sure he never sets foot on this dead planet again." He backed away from her.

Sophenna's knees threatened to give out but she stayed on her feet. It wasn't until Aeros disappeared, that she collapsed on the ground.

SIXTEEN

Dr. Willoughsby's address wasn't a flat inside an apartment building, but a row house on a quaint cobbled street. Gone were the dimly lit hall and dull brass knocker on the door of Patrick's nightmare.

If there were stars overhead, they weren't visible. Clouds had rolled in late afternoon and by nightfall, a steady drizzle had swept across London. Everyone walked by with heads down and shoulders hunched. No one gave Patrick and Jaered so much as a glance as they stood inside an unlit doorway across from Dr. Willoughsby's house.

"Well," Jaered said, rubbing his hands. "What now?"

"It's dark, no one's there," Patrick said.

Jaered pressed his ear to the door. "Probably picking Joule up at the airport."

"I don't know what I'm doing," Patrick admitted.

"Then thanks for dragging me along for the ride." Jaered gave him a severe glance. "I vote we return to the auditorium and get down to business." He stepped down from the stoop.

"Wait," Patrick said. "We can at least rummage around inside. Find out what they know."

"She's in London. Now, so are we. We'll connect later." Jaered reached the small wrought iron gate and opened it, but paused on the sidewalk. "Come on, already. Stop wasting precious time."

Patrick stared at the front door of Dr. Willoughsby's flat. Drew energy—tingling. He shyfted in front of Dr. Willoughsby's door. He was tired of the ache, not knowing if everyone in his life was gone, including Tara who might still reject him.

Jaered looked both ways, crossed the street in three strides, and pushed Patrick up against the door. "What the hell are you doing, shyfting like that? I could see your red corona from over there!"

"I have to know." Patrick turned and knocked with forceful knuckles on the door. Silence. "Is anyone there?" he called through the door.

A second later, scrapes approached along the floor, and then a forceful *thud* came from higher at the door.

"Saxon, is that you?" Patrick called out.

"No one's there. We gotta go," Jaered hissed.

The wolf whimpered, and sniffs mixed with snorts came from the bottom edge of the door. "Saxon, I'll be back," Patrick said. "I'll see you soon." He grabbed Jaered's arm from behind and they appeared in the safe house.

"What the hell!" Jaered said, and punched Patrick in the arm.

"No fun when there's no warning, huh?" Patrick said.

"At least this hasn't been a total waste. I can report to Eve that you have your shyfting down."

"We're going back, in a couple of hours," Patrick said.

"Whatever." Jaered stepped over the top of the couch and sat cross-legged. He grabbed the remote and turned on the television. An emergency newscast was in progress.

"Authorities are still trying to find out who's responsible for the bombing at Heathrow, a mere thirty minutes ago. There are multiple casualties, but it's unclear how many perished in what people are calling one of the worse terrorist attacks in years." Fire trucks obliterated the front of the airport and police waved their arms, directing traffic and scrambling pedestrians from behind the newscaster. The woman reporter standing amidst the melee pressed her fingers to her ear, then raised the microphone to her face. "Karl, I've been told by our people in the airport terminal that the blast originated from an aircraft that had just pulled up to its gate." The newscaster turned toward the screen. "Willa, do we know where the flight came from?"

She nodded but there was a few-second delay. "I don't have a departure city yet, Karl, but it's our understanding that it came from Central Africa."

Stunned, Patrick collapsed onto the couch.

"We're out of here," Jaered said. He stood and turned off the television.

"We've got to find out if it was Joule's flight. If Tara and Bhutto were waiting for her, they might have gotten caught in the blast."

Jaered pulled out his cell, punched two buttons, and wandered off into the kitchen. A moment later, he was in a debate with whoever was on the other end. Patrick figured it had to be his mother.

He stood and closed his eyes, recalling the bedlam at the airport, the fire engines, and the police cars. It was too chaotic for him to be noticed, he reasoned. Patrick shyfted.

A fireman ran by Patrick just as he appeared next to the truck. The airport was lit up from inside and by the looks of it, the police weren't allowing anyone to exit. Helicopters circled overhead, lighting up the airport in all directions and skirting the roof.

Patrick grabbed a reflective vest that had been discarded on the side of the fire truck. He donned the vest to resemble someone who belonged there and ran alongside the airport until he found a way to look inside without being noticed. A window into a deserted office looked promising. He glanced about and confirmed that no one was paying attention to him; then he shyfted inside. The office contained a couple of walkie-talkies lying on a credenza. Patrick grabbed one and let himself out, stepping into a hallway. Then he slipped by the frantic voices talking on phones and television watchers in the front lobby. It took a couple of wrong turns, but he finally reached the main terminal. If Tara and Bhutto were waiting for Joule, this is where they'd be. A group of boisterous rugby players walked past Patrick, and he fell into step with them. The men towered over him.

The guy next to him eyed his walkie-talkie. "Hey, you hear anything, yet? What happened? They won't let us out of here."

Patrick shrugged. "I'll be the last to know. Still investigating, I figure."

"You're not from around here. You have an American accent." The guy slapped Patrick on his back and gripped the back of his neck. He stumbled, but stayed on his feet. "I'm with NATO," Patrick said, improvising. "I'm here as a consultant, nothing more."

"A real diplomat, whad'ya know! Hey, you ever met the mum?"

Patrick gave him a quizzical look.

"The Queen Mum, you know," the guy said.

Patrick fingered the on button and turned the volume up high. Static crackled and muted voices came out. He held it to his ear and looked over his shoulder, then waved the walkie-talkie above the men's heads. "Sorry, I'm being hailed. Good luck getting out of here soon."

He headed for a large group of people detained in the center of the terminal. Most were seated but a few stood talking to one another, or were hunched over on their cell phones. Patrick froze in his tracks. A tall young woman with long, snowy hair stood next to a towering man. Ian had described Bhutto as tall as a telephone pole. Two policemen were asking him questions.

Patrick was a few feet away when Tara glanced over her shoulder. Her eyes grew as wide as an owl's, and she turned to face him with the slow, deliberate grace that he remembered so well. She stared at him with concern, unmoving.

He took a couple of steps, but stopped when she crossed her arms and gave him a subtle shake of her head. When he tossed her a questioning look, her head cocked to the side and her eyes darted to the left, and then back to him. He dropped his face and brought the walkie-talkie to his ear. With a swivel on the ball of his shoe, he strolled across the terminal to the overflowing bar, keeping his back to the rest of the terminal.

The Pur guard were there. They must be watching Tara.

It wasn't until he was deep inside the bar that he paused. It took perseverance to make his way to the counter and gain the bartender's attention. Then he ordered a beer. The guy gave him a curious look, and it was in that moment that Patrick realized he wore the reflector vest and had the walkie-talkie in his hand. He changed his order to a glass of water. What he would have given to have an airline-size bottle of bourbon to pour into it.

The bartender set it down and Patrick took a generous sip. He turned around, perusing the crowd, but didn't recognize any faces except the rugby team who had claimed the back corner for themselves. His buddy wormed his way through the crowd, no small feat considering how broad the guy was. He spied Patrick and worked his way to him. "Hey, you taking a break?"

"Yeah, but don't worry," he held up his half-empty glass, "it's just water."

The rugby player had no difficulty getting the bartender's attention, and he ordered a couple of pitchers of beer, ready to party his detention away. A moment later, he grabbed the pitchers of beer in each hand and, sloshing the foam onto himself, gestured for Patrick to follow. The guy made a perfect shield, and Patrick crossed to the opposite end of the bar without incident.

The empty barstool was the perfect height for surveillance. "Mind if I sit?" Patrick asked his newfound friend. "I've been on my feet all day. And it's going to be a long night."

Without hesitation, the guy grabbed Patrick under his arms and plopped him onto the stool. "Hey guys, this is . . ." he slapped his forehead and leaned toward Patrick, "I never got your name."

"I'm Joseph Gordon," Patrick said, not sure why he was channeling Joseph Gordon Levitt at that moment.

"Hey, this is my buddy Joe!" The rugby player shouted. His teammates raised their filled glasses and yelled, "Joe!" in unison. One of them passed Patrick a topped-off glass.

The clinking of beer glasses went on forever. Patrick peered over the guy's shoulder and tried to locate Tara or Bhutto in the distance. They weren't to be found. Deflated, Patrick nodded when someone said something to him; he couldn't make it out because the guy's dialect was so strong.

A flitter of white between bodies. Patrick sat up and searched for a clear image. Tara had worked her way into the middle of the bar.

She turned toward the bar. Patrick cut off his shout and melted below the rugby player's shoulder. A Pur guard had followed Tara inside while another one stood vigil at the entrance.

Tara didn't approach the bar and stood as if in a quandary.

Patrick grabbed a napkin and pulled out a pen from the passing waitress's tray. By the time he finished the note, Tara was facing the bar. He grabbed the rugby player's shoulder. "I need a favor. Would you get this note to someone across the bar? I'm too embarrassed to do it myself."

The guy smiled from ear to ear. "I'm your wingman, bro." He took the note without looking at it and turned to face the other patrons. "Point me in the right direction."

Patrick described Tara and the guy nodded. He handed his drink to Patrick, then closed the distance in record time. He didn't approach her at first, but seemed to be sizing her up. Then he tapped her on the shoulder, leaned in and whispered something, and slipped her the note. She shook her head, then pulled back, slapped him, and stormed out of the bar.

"Wha the . . ." Patrick ran his fingers through his short-cropped hair. When the guy returned, he grabbed his glass from Patrick. "What did you say to her?"

"That she had a secret admirer, but if she wanted a real party animal, she had to look no further than yours truly." He slapped his chest.

"What happened to having my back?" Patrick said.

"All's fair in love and . . . RUGBY!" he shouted and held his glass high. Hoots and hollers came from his teammates.

The Pur guard disappeared once Tara left the bar. Patrick said his goodbyes, at least a couple of times over, but they wouldn't let him leave until they made him an honorary team member and asked for him to take a bunch of pictures of the group.

He paused at the entrance to the bar but didn't see Tara, Bhutto, or the Pur guards anywhere in the terminal. He slipped into a nearby bathroom and locked the stall door. Tingling. He appeared in the living room of the safe house. His corona dispersed in an instant.

His mother stood at the windows. Although she didn't turn around, it was impossible to miss her reflected scowl.

SEVENTEEN

Patrick walked into the kitchen and opened cupboards until he found a bottle of whiskey. He got out two tumblers and poured himself a stiff drink. "Want one?" he called out, but he got the cold shoulder from his mother. He poured her one anyway and handed it to her, then stood gazing out at the lights of London.

"You think this a game," she grumbled.

"Before I commit my life to the earth, I need to get my affairs in order."

She turned away from the picture- perfect view and took a swig of her drink. "Getting your affairs in order means wills, contracts, paying bills, closing out accounts. It doesn't mean exposing yourself for a love interest."

"I thought you approved of my bringing Tara into this," he said.

"I approved of you searching for her. Not to getting yourself caught on television."

He gave her a blank stare. "What are you talking about?"

She picked up the remote and hit a button. The television played a recording. There was Patrick, running toward the entrance to the airport in his reflective vest. He'd passed right behind a reporter and her crew while filming.

Patrick downed his drink. "I got a message to Tara. She's to meet me at the Eye in an hour."

"The Ferris wheel?" Eve returned to the window. "As if you can get any more public."

Patrick watched a speedboat navigate the Thames. At night it wasn't hard to spot the amusement ride. Tonight it was lit up in dazzling strawberry.

"How do you plan to stay under the Pur guard's radar once the ride is over?" She took a sip of her drink.

"We won't be getting off," Patrick said.

Eve nodded. "You can't shyft from inside a packed gondola with all those witnesses."

Patrick went to pour himself another drink. He was going to need it to convince his mother his plan would work.

The summer heat radiated from the concrete below Patrick's feet, but the air was cooled by the breeze coming off the

Thames. There were two main lines, one for the poor souls who didn't plan ahead and get their tickets online, and the other for the ones who thought themselves smart and did, only to have to stand in another long line.

Patrick fingered his ticket deep in his jacket pocket. He had left the one for Tara hidden behind the ticket office. He had feared that the bombing at Heathrow would have prompted authorities to shut down the ride, but the middle of tourist season was not to be ignored. From the looks of it, they must have doubled the police guards, though. Patrick saw that in their favor if the Pur guard made a move against them.

He had no doubt that his mother had her own rebels in place since she left him nursing his celebratory drink and closed herself up in the master bedroom earlier. Her muffled voice drifted down via the balcony for better than a quarter-hour. Jaered drove Patrick to the Eye, then sped off. Patrick didn't know if it was to find a parking spot, or a different agenda. Either way, Patrick stood in the line alone. The ticket booth sign switched to a later boarding time. They had sold out of Patrick's boarding.

Out of the corner of his eye, he spotted milky white. Tara strolled toward the ticket booth. Confused, Patrick thought that she hadn't read his message all the way through. His answer arrived a couple of minutes later when the same Pur guard that had tailed her at the airport approached. They saw her purchasing a ticket for a later time.

Tara stepped away with ticket in hand, then wandered around the booth. One of the Pur guards went inside the ticket office, while the other followed Tara. He disappeared around the building a few seconds before Tara emerged at the opposite end of the ticket office wearing a different colored jacket and her signature hair stuffed into a hat. She joined a group of teenagers a few people ahead in Patrick's line, and with a smile, struck up a conversation with them as they made their way toward the entrance to the ride.

"You alone?" a middle-aged woman asked Patrick from behind.

"Uh, sort of," he said.

"You're American, aren't you?" She batted her artificial lashes at him. "Your first time to London?"

"Uh, no. I was here a few years ago." Patrick craned his neck to confirm that Tara remained ahead of him. Each car held close to twenty or more people and he calculated whether she would end up on the same gondola as him.

"I'm here with my daughter. We do this a couple times a year." She tugged on a ringlet of hair cascading over her shoulder and positioned her daughter between them.

"Sorry," her daughter said. She turned to her mother. "Stop trying to set me up with every bloke you see."

"Well, you ain't no spring chicken," her mother shot back.

They fell behind Patrick and he kept his head down, trying to make himself as invisible as possible. When a policeman approached them, they quieted but kept throwing verbal jabs at each other under their breath. When Patrick stepped through the entrance, Tara was on the gondola.

A moment later, he was admitted and stood behind her. She didn't turn around. "God, I've got so many questions," she said for Patrick's ears only. "It's killing me I can't throw my arms around you right now." She glanced over her shoulder and gave him a weak smile.

The Pur guard rushed up, but the waiting patrons grabbed their sleeves and distracted them enough that the ride clerk admitted one last group. Then he hooked the chain across.

Everything Patrick had rehearsed didn't make it to his lips. He was afraid to touch Tara, as though she'd know his secret right then and there.

"You okay?" Tara said. "Patrick?"

Their guide shouted announcements about what they could and couldn't do and finished with, "Enjoy your ride." The door shut and the gondola rose above the Thames River. The passengers pressed toward the windows surrounding the car and Patrick leaned in to take advantage of the private moment, ready to confess his love for her.

Tara turned around. "Did Ian find you? Is he all right?"

The opportunity, the desire was gone. Patrick nodded.

"Tell me everything you can. There isn't much time." She kept her voice low and her eyes darted every which way, taking in the passengers. "The guards will be waiting for me at the end."

"They haven't hurt you," Patrick said.

"No, but they caught up with me here in London." She met Patrick's gaze. "How did you find me?"

"Milo. He suggested I start with Joule. She told me where you were."

She swiped a tear from her cheek. "Joule never arrived."

"Was she caught in the blast?" A blood vessel throbbed at his neck. Was the Primary really as ruthless as his brother?

"It went off before her flight was set to arrive," Tara said. "I don't think it was related. But if they diverted her flight after the bomb, she never called, and she isn't answering her cell."

"I have to get you off of this ride," he said.

Her chuckle brought back such wonderful memories. "How do you intend to do that?" she said. Their gondola rose faster than Patrick had predicted, and they were already above many of the downtown buildings. The crimson lights of the ride swept in, setting each rider's face in an intense glow.

Patrick grabbed her hands and looked around the car to determine if he'd been right. Everyone was gazing out the windows. The gondola reached its pinnacle and the passengers leaned closer to see the sights of London.

He drew the earth's energy into his core, and the magnetic tingling excited every nerve in his body. Tara's eyes widened as she, too, felt his power. Shock painted her face, and her mouth sagged. "Patrick," she whispered.

They shyfted.

EIGHTEEN

They appeared in his mother's safe house. Tara pushed away from Patrick and stumbled backward.

"How the hell did you get a core!" Tara shouted. Tears streamed down her face.

"I'm a Sar, like Ian," Patrick said, but when he drew closer, she stepped back.

"You're not Pur," she said. "You're a Duach!"

"Patrick and Ian are both Heirs of Earth." Patrick's mother sat in the chair across from the couch. At her nod, he pulled up his shirt, exposing the Seal on his chest.

Tara gasped.

His mother scooted to the edge of the chair and poured brewed tea into three cups. She stood and offered the steaming beverage to Tara.

"This isn't a social event, JoAnna." Tara glanced over her shoulder at the door. "What's going on here?" Tara looked between Patrick and his mother.

"You have only known me as JoAnna Langtree," she said. "But I am someone much more than that."

"When Jaered kidnapped me," Patrick said. "I found out that my mother is the rebel leader."

"You're . . . Eve?" A shiver racked Tara's body and her breaths turned shallow and rapid. She took a step toward the door. Patrick's heartbeat pounded. His mother would never allow Tara to leave after what she'd just learned.

"If you're the rebel leader, then you know where Ian is," Tara said in a voice edged in battle

"Ian's fine. He's been with me, and Jaered, this past week," Patrick said. "We've been working together." Patrick pressed a fist to his chest. "He's been helping me to learn how to use my powers."

"Where is he?!" she blurted.

"He's on Thrae," Eve said.

Tara looked at them like they were insane. "You lie. He can't leave Earth. It will self-destruct."

"The Primary has fed Ian and all Pur nothing but lies," Eve said.

"I know you have doubts about the Primary," Patrick said. "I—" He gestured between his mother and himself. "*We* have answers. The truth about the Weir. About Aeros and the Primary's connection to him."

Eve regarded Tara with a keen eye, yet a gentle expression. "My dear, are you ready to hear it?"

Tara sprinted for the door and grabbed the handle.

"Wait!" Patrick screamed. Tara hesitated, then pressed her forehead against the door. He rushed over and put his hands on her shoulders. "Don't go. Please. I can't lose you again."

"This is too much," Tara said on choked words. "I've lost so much."

"Sometimes, loss is but a beginning," Patrick said and whispered at her ear, "Give me a chance. Let's begin again."

It had taken most of the night to convince Tara that they were not the enemy. His mother shared the history of the Weir with her, and Tara kept nodding, or gasping.

Patrick was shocked when Tara so easily accepted that the Primary and Aeros were related. She admitted she had doubts about the rift between the Pur and Duach for a while. Hardest for her was accepting that Patrick, her only human friend and colleague, was a Duach Heir. All her life, she'd been taught the Duach were her sworn enemy. He often caught her staring at him with apprehension tinged in awe. More than once, he noticed her glances fell to his chest.

Patrick knew that one of Tara's passions was history, and she took full advantage of picking his mother's brain about all that she had seen and lived through. He'd drifted off to sleep on the couch as they talked about the Renaissance period while they made pancakes in the middle of the night.

Patrick rolled over onto his back and discovered that one of the women had covered him with a blanket.

The morning sun filled the safe house with light and promise. He rubbed his face and squinted at the glare streaming into the flat, then he rose and shuffled into the kitchen. The coffee pot still had about a single mug's worth in it. He flipped open the top and sniffed. Good enough, he thought, and pressed the button to warm it up. He searched for a mug.

Patrick was heading back to the couch with the steaming brew when Jaered shyfted right in front of him. Patrick stumbled back. "Hey!"

Jaered grunted. "Now you know why it can be dangerous to shyft into a blind spot." He grabbed the mug of coffee from Patrick's hand. "Thanks." He took a sip.

Patrick growled and returned to the pot to rinse it out and make more. Jaered rummaged around the cupboards, then opened the refrigerator.

"Where'd you go last night?" Patrick asked.

"Bhutto and I interrogated the two Pur guards that were following Tara," he said.

Patrick noticed the bruised and scraped knuckles on Jaered's hand and wondered if he could ever be desperate enough to beat up a man for information. "Joule is missing." Patrick found the scoop but paused. He couldn't remember how many to put in.

"I know," Jaered said, grabbing a banana out of a basket. "The Primary had her kidnapped, hoping to draw her father out of hiding."

"Another victim of this senseless battle," Tara said from the bottom of the staircase. She glared at Jaered.

An unchewed bite of banana bulged out his cheek. "I'm not the enemy," he said.

"I don't trust you, no matter what everyone tells me." Tara regarded Patrick. "But I want to trust you."

Patrick gave her a tight-lipped grin. "It's good to have you back."

"Now we just need Ian," Tara said. "And to retrieve Saxon from Willoughsby's flat."

At the mention of the wolf, Jaered stiffened.

"What's with you?" Tara said.

"The wolf and I don't exactly get along," Jaered muttered.

"He's one smart animal." Tara headed up the stairs.

"I'm glad she's on our side," Jaered said. He tossed the banana peel in the trash and washed his hands. "I need to debrief with Eve. I'll be back."

"What did you do with the Pur guard you interrogated?" Patrick asked, but Jaered dried his hands and tossed the towel to Patrick. He stepped into the middle of the room and shyfted without responding, leaving Patrick with a feeling of dread.

Patrick shyfted Jaered and Tara to Dr. Willoughsby's address in the middle of a downpour. His crimson corona was reflected by hundreds of prisms from the water droplets. Patrick beamed with pride.

"Look at you!" Tara said. "You've really mastered shyfting. When did you do it for the first time?"

"When we were tracking down the old caretaker," Jaered said.

"I wasn't talking to you," Tara's tone was icy. Jaered turned his back to her and looked up and down the street. As hoped, everyone was inside, out of the storm.

"About forty-eight hours ago," Patrick said. Scratches came from the other side of the door.

Tara used Joule's key to unlock the door to the row house and poked her head inside. "Bhutto, it's Tara."

Saxon headed for the open doorway. Patrick reached out to give Saxon a huge rubdown, but instead, the wolf rushed past him and leapt at Jaered, knocking him down. Saxon's powerful jaws snapped, trying to reach Jaered's neck.

"Saxon, stop!" Tara yelled, "We need him to find Ian!"

Jaered grabbed Saxon by the neck and pushed against his belly with his boots, keeping the animal at bay.

The wolf had never worn a collar, and Patrick and Tara could only grab handfuls of his snowy coat. Bhutto ran out and wrapped his long, lanky arms around the wolf's body.

No one wanted to get near Saxon's neck. It took a few seconds for Tara to convince the wolf to back down.

Patrick and Bhutto helped Jaered to his feet, but he jerked his arm away. "I'm staying put. Keep a muzzle on that thing," he said, glaring at the wolf. Saxon bared his teeth and with a snort, turned and trotted back into the row house.

The wolf settled under a small folding table off to one side of the living room. Stacks of towering notebooks and charts covered almost every inch of the table and the surrounding floor. Bhutto had been busy. He walked over and grabbed a notebook on top of one stack.

"I think Dr. Willoughsby is somewhere in southern Africa." Bhutto opened the notebook and flipped through pages.

"What makes you think that?" Tara tilted her head to see the page he indicated with a finger.

"From what I've read in his log, he traveled there frequently during our research expeditions. He never told us where he went, and didn't take anyone with him. At first, I thought he was just getting supplies, but he never came back with anything—other than a suitcase full of bottles of rare Scotch."

Tara's face lit up. "When we were searching for Patrick, Ian checked out a Scotch company by the name of Dambrin, in Wales." She regarded Patrick. "It was owned by your mom."

"My mother?" he said. "It doesn't sound familiar, but my parents have lots of interests across the world."

"Bhutto, what was the brand, do you remember?" Tara asked.

"It was a green label with gold lettering . . ." He placed a finger to his lip, pensive. "It had a strange name that started with a C."

"Could it be Coedhir?' Tara asked.

Bhutto nodded. "Yes, I do believe that was it."

Patrick pulled his cell out of his back pocket, but Tara grabbed his arm. "Wait, we don't know if the Pur guard are monitoring your calls." He stuck it back in his pocket and opened the door. From the corner of his eye, he caught movement. Saxon had lifted his head and his ears perked up. Patrick slipped out and shut the door before the wolf could have another go at Jaered.

Jaered flexed his shoulder near the sidewalk gate. "Anything useful?"

"You need to contact my mother and find out if there is a particular place in south Africa where she ships the Coedhir."

"What's Coedhir?" Jaered pulled out his cell and punched the two-button code. He held the phone to his ear.

"If Bhutto's right, Dr. Willoughsby has a place there," Patrick said. "If we can find out where he purchases the Scotch . . ."

"It might lead us to Willoughsby." Jaered turned away and talked to Eve.

NINETEEN

The rush of water. Parrots chattering in the distance. Plopping drips. The river had transported Ian and the rowboat to the unknown. He lay on something soft and flat underneath. From the feel of it, his body had regained its land legs long before he woke.

Parched, Ian licked his lips and fought to open his eyes, aware of a heavy dampness in the air. When his lids released their hold, he sat up, and discovered that he was in a huge cave. Its wide mouth revealed an expansive rainforest beyond. The massive river had widened as it emerged from its underground lair, ending in a waterfall several feet beyond the cave.

An attempt to speak came out like a croak. Ian cleared his throat. "Hello?" he called out, but his weak voice was unable to carry far.

Beside him, water sat in a hollowed-out reed, about three inches wide and five or six inches high. He reached for it and discovered his injured hand was wrapped in some kind of broad tropical leaf held together with a thin strip of vine, as was his infected foot. The battered rowboat had been pulled up onto the shore, just inside the mouth of the cave. Ian drank the gift of water, gulping it down and relishing in how it both numbed and refreshed his throat.

It took some effort, but he managed to rise on one foot and hop toward the mouth of the cave, using the rocky wall for stability. By the time he reached the exposed ledge, he was breathless. He raised his arm at the bright sun as his eyes took their time to adjust. The river continued to cut a path through the valley for a few miles, then disappeared in the thick trees at the far tip.

A few minutes later, a small man wearing a loin cloth tied at his waste approached along a path leading up to the cave. His leathery skin hung loose on his body. He wore a wide beaded collar around his wrinkled, thin neck and his earlobes sagged from the weight of his earrings. A small bone protruded clear through the bridge of his nose. He held onto hooved legs while carrying a dead animal on his back. The man didn't look up, but kept his attention on the path, swinging his walking stick in beat with his steps as though he hadn't a care in the world.

A few yards from the cave, he glanced up, and stopped. He smiled at Ian, then spoke in a language similar to Portuguese.

"*Obrigado*," Ian thanked him, and pressed his fist to his chest with a bow.

The man touched his chin with his fingers and then touched his chest. The gesture was unfamiliar to Ian, but the smile on the man's face didn't fade. When he entered the cave, Ian noticed that the man had trapped a small wild pig. After storing his walking stick, the man dropped the pig onto a stained rock at the edge of the river and retrieved a knife from a hand-woven basket. He proceeded to chop off the pig's head and then skin its torso.

The overwhelming smell of blood turned Ian's stomach. How many days, weeks, had he drifted on the river? He sat next to the man and placed his palm on his chest. "Ian," he said.

The man paused and imitated Ian's gesture. "Ilyak."

Ian pointed at the boat and then at Ilyak. "You pulled me out?" he said in Portuguese, then held up his bandaged hand. "And took care of me?"

Ilyak nodded. "*Peixe*." He pointed the tip of the knife at Ian's wrapped hand.

"A *peixe* did this," Ian said. He thought back to the underwater battle with the mother of all fish and shuddered. He never got a good look at the larger fish that inadvertently rescued him, and wondered what it was called. "*A gigante peixe*." Ian spread his hands wide.

"*Bebe peixe*," Ilyak said. He held his hands close.

The baby is the poisonous one. Ian nodded. He'd only sustained the pustule injuries from the baby, where the gigantic one had ripped his clothes and taken a couple of scrapes out of Ian's leg, nothing more. Ian watched Ilyak in silence while he deboned the pig like a network chef. His thoughts wandered, wishing Milo were there to see the master at work.

The pork was undercooked but Ian was too ravenous to care. He figured if salmonella was going to set in, Ilyak would have a remedy. They ate with their hands and Ilyak cleaned off the rock with the river water. He was quiet, moving about the cave like he was used to being alone.

Ian learned much from the man while he went about crushing the pestles of tropical flowers and mixing them with river water. The salve rapidly healed Ian's wounds and after another day, he could bend his fingers and bear weight on his foot with minimal discomfort.

It felt good to walk again, and Ian followed Ilyak into the forest collecting berries, seeds and the healing flowers. They trapped another small pig, and he taught Ian how to prepare it by rubbing salt into the meat to cure it. Ian wondered if there were other valleys such as Ilyak's that offered a respite from the harsh elements of Thrae. But Ilyak didn't seem aware of others and had never ventured out of his lush valley.

In spite of Ian's limited Portuguese, their communication had earned him some good news. Ilyak confirmed that Rayne and his mother had passed through, but Ian couldn't decipher how far ahead they were. The man didn't seem to measure time in days. If he understood Ilyak, the man was alone in this small rainforest-like valley. He'd lost his wife and child to what he called the red storm. Ian wondered if the methane cloud that hovered over much of North America had swept through Ilyak's valley.

Sophenna mentioned that Ian would find transportation when he emerged from the underground river. Was this the place, or did he have to get back in the boat and travel farther downstream? The stronger he felt physically, the more anxious he grew, desperate to find Rayne and his mother. He didn't know if he'd made good time getting this far, or wasted precious time because of his injuries.

At the end of the third day, Ian stood at the mouth of the cave and mellowed to the sun's rays fading into muted grays. He'd decided to pack up the boat with some provisions the next morning and continue downstream.

Ilyak joined him, puffing on his reed pipe and carrying a lit torch. The pipe made Ian think of Milo and how the two of them would enjoy each other's company, confident that the old caretaker could have worked through the language barrier. Ilyak took a long draw and released it in a steady, cloudy stream. He then handed the torch to Ian and pulled out a long reed with holes, like a flute.

Ilyak stepped to the edge of the cave and blew into the reed. If it emitted sound it was too high-pitched for human ears, yet Ian swore he caught something with his keen hearing. Ilyak returned the instrument to his pocket. Several minutes passed, yet Ilyak continued to watch at the horizon, as though waiting for something to happen.

An hour had passed and then another. Darkness filled the sky with a thousand or more stars blinking out of sync overhead. Ready to abandon his vigil and return to the cave, Ilyak stopped Ian and pointed at a small image, darker than the sky, appearing at the horizon.

Ilyak cupped his hands around his mouth. "*Cawcaw-ooo-caw*," he yelled at the top of lungs, followed with an, "*ooocaaaw!*" It echoed through the valley and gained intensity.

The approaching creature was more wide than tall and moved like a bird in flight. It sailed upon the rising air, drawing closer and closer. When it reached midway in the valley, Ian could make out its long tail with a spearhead for a tip and a lengthy snout. Horns rose from each eyebrow and pointed ears stuck out beside them.

His mind told him that they didn't exist but Ian couldn't deny what flew toward him.

It was a dragon.

TWENTY

The creature's shadow flitted across the mouth of the cave, then landed at the rocky ledge with one foot planted in the water. Its talons were the length of Ian's arms. It leaned down and lapped at the river, its tongue long and forked at the tip. Scales as large as Ian's head covered the beast, they were the same shade as the rocks surrounding it. Its breath had the odor of sulfur and Ian's hand twitched at the memory of his injuries, now nothing more than blemishes on his skin.

Points of long, chiseled teeth poked out between the dragon's lips.

Ilyak reached up and the dragon lowered its head. The man made cooing sounds and the dragon responded with what sounded like purring. Its gray irises had vertical slits as long as Ian's torso, and it regarded Ian with an intense stare, yet was more curious than hostile.

"*Dragao*," Ian said.

Ilyak touched the dragon while addressing Ian. "*Oocaw*."

"*Oocaw*," Ian repeated the dragon's name.

He reached out at Ilyak's invite and stroked the creature with boyish excitement, running his hand over the rough scales along its snout while he took in the size of the wing joint that towered above its body. Its wings were folded back, but Ian calculated that they each had a span of twenty feet or more. The animal appeared to be female.

"Is this my ride?" Ian asked Ilyak. The man patted the dragon without answering.

Ian wandered back toward the tail, taking in every inch of the magnificent creature. From where he stood there didn't appear to be any saddle-like contraption. If this was his ride, how would he steer? How would the creature know where to go? How would Ian? His mother's map wasn't detailed enough to follow from the sky.

Ilyak brought Ian his supplies. His friend had repacked and laced everything together like saddlebags.

He took them, but set them on the ground with a lump lodged in his throat at the thought of leaving. The man had rescued him and nursed him back to health. He regretted that he'd never be able to express his gratitude and hoped that Ilyak somehow knew. "*Obrigado*."

Unsure if hugs were part of his tradition, Ian chanced it and embraced Ilyak tight. The man patted Ian's back without a word. Ian picked up the supplies and looked up at the dragon, confused.

Ilyak laughed at Ian's hesitation. He gripped the edge of a scale and demonstrated where to plant the toes on the narrow curves in the sides of the scales. Ian sat on the ground, removed his boots, and stuffed them along with his socks in one of the sacks. He flung the supplies over his shoulder, and traversed the dragon like free-climbing a granite wall, reaching the creature's back at the base of her neck. The wide, bony area was a natural saddle. Ian laid the supplies across it, then straddled the dragon.

He leaned over and waved to Ilyak. The man held up his hand while puffing on his pipe, then said something to the dragon that Ian couldn't make out. Oocaw spread its wings and flapped. Ian gripped the scales at the back of Oocaw's neck, and with a tremendous downward thrust of her wings, the dragon took to the skies.

They rose higher and higher, then settled above the clouds. Ian adjusted to the thin air, thankful that he stored large amounts of oxygen in his blood compared to humans. Was dragon flight one of the reasons that Weir had that ability? He took a moment to see everything through Rayne's eyes and regretted they hadn't experienced this together. With each leg of his journey, more and more questions arose. He had no idea where Oocaw was taking him, but Ilyak must have known.

His newfound friend had been a rare respite along the hazardous travels of Thrae. Ian wondered if he would encounter others like Ilyak.

The chilly air bit into his muscles, cramping them. Ian removed his boots and socks from the bag, and put them on.

Ilyak had thrown in one of his blankets and Ian wrapped it around himself. The graceful sweep of the dragon's wings was calming, and in his struggles to stay awake, Ian pondered why he couldn't draw energy from Thrae like he could on Earth. Did the column of energy that he saw in the cavern have anything to do with it? Should he not have touched it?

He pulled out his mother's map, but the stars didn't provide enough light to see its details. Ian fished out his headlamp, but when he turned it on, it flickered for a moment, then shut off for good. The batteries had died. He stuffed everything into the bag and sat back, absorbing Thrae's universe overhead. What had Sophenna said? Aeros had pulled so much energy from the planet that he'd disrupted the planet's rotation. How long were the days? Their weeks, years? Ian's thoughts jockeyed with a myriad of environmental changes.

Golden streaks lit the upper atmosphere. Most of the meteorites snuffed out but one punched through, descending at a severe angle and disappearing into a cloud in the distance. A tremendous explosion lit up the cloud from underneath and it sparkled with a golden firework. Even from here, Ian felt the energy emitted from the impact. He leaned over, but poor visibility prevented him from seeing below.

He grabbed Oocaw's neck and pushed to one side, trying to steer the creature toward the event, but his efforts didn't make a dent in the dragon's direction. "Oocaw!" Ian shouted over and over, but the wind stole his voice. He tried kicking and patting the side of her neck, then punching, but nothing that Ian did got the creature's attention.

He gave up and leaned against Oocaw's neck. He focused on channeling, connecting his thoughts with the dragon's like he could with Saxon. *Oocaw, can you hear me?*

The dragon snorted. *Of course, you are her son.*

He straightened up. *Whose son?*

Mother-to-us-all.

Gwynn could channel with the dragon! *Are you taking me to mother?*

That is my journey.

A fireball hit the planet just now, Ian channeled. *Will you take me to where it struck?*

Mother is not where fireball is, the dragon responded.

I wish to see what fireball did to the planet, Ian urged.

The dragon stopped flapping its wings and made a severe downward tilt. Ian was thrown off his perch on top of the supplies and slid down the side, headed for the dragon's wing. He clawed and tried to get a foothold but kept sliding. He snagged the edge of a scale with one hand and hung on as the dragon dropped out of the clouds and descended toward the ground.

Smoke filled the air and Ian blinked to combat the burning in his eyes. Gusts of heated wind swept over Ian as he clung to the dragon. After a swoop of her powerful wings, Oocaw landed on the ground with a tremendous *thud*. Ian let go and slid the rest of the way, coming to an abrupt stop at the edge of the wing.

Oocaw lay down and snorted.

Ian was relieved to discover that the event had not occurred in a populated area. The ground had been stripped of any vegetation and the surrounding land was scorched. Chunks of burning had been stripped of any vegetation and the surrounding land was scorched. Chunks of burning rock had been scattered everywhere. Ian found the point of impact and surveyed the small crater. The meteorite had been whittled down by the atmosphere to a rock the size of Ian's fist; it was searing hot. He wandered about but in the dim light of dawn, it appeared he was surrounded by barren, flat land as far as he could see. No rock outcroppings, no trees—nothing. If Ian remembered the map correctly, they had to be somewhere in northern South America, an area that on Earth was rich in vegetation and mountains. It shouldn't resemble a wasteland.

Ian ventured toward the horizon, searching for answers to questions he couldn't voice. As a boy, he'd visited other meteorite impact sites on earth, yet there was something different about this one. He found his answer a few yards ahead. Another impact crater, slightly larger than the other one. An ebony, jagged rock the size of a Ping-Pong ball lay at its center.

He tried to calculate the odds of more than one meteorite landing in the same immediate area.

Oocaw bolted to her feet and stomped as if agitated. Her bellow was deafening.

Ian rushed back. *What is it?* he channeled.

The dragon raised her wings and snorted a stream of fire. *Father!*

TWENTY-ONE

It took a full second for the dragon's words to register. Ian ran toward Oocaw and was tossed upward by her wing. He landed at her spine and scrambled on all fours along her back toward his perch.

Energy strong, Oocaw channeled. *Hide!*

Ian grabbed his provisions and slid to the ground, but the heel of his boot snagged on one of Oocaw's scales and he fell the rest of the way, landing in a roll. An intense, white light grew near Oocaw's head. The dragon scooped him and his things up with its wing, tucking him underneath, against her breast.

Through the narrow slit that was Ian's vantage point, a man's image solidified. He wore an off-white robe with its hood drawn up. Confused, Ian didn't know if it was Aeros, or the Primary.

Oocaw.

The dragon's name pierced Ian's mind. Aeros could channel with Oocaw, yet their communication resonated in Ian's thoughts. He could listen to their channeling.

Where is your mate? Aeros asked.

One with Thrae, the dragon responded.

He never recovered from our battle? Aeros asked. *Such a gift of his spirit to the planet, but those left on Thrae have lost a mighty warrior.*

Oocaw did not respond to Aeros's taunt. *Why are you here?* the dragon asked. *Father-of-us-all has not ventured this far south in quite some time.*

Aeros's shadow passed by the slit in the wing as he strolled around the dragon. Ian held his breath and stilled his pulse in spite of the dragon's heartbeat pressing against him. He marveled at how steady it was compared to his.

"I am searching for my son," Aeros said aloud. "I know he is on Thrae."

Thrae's Heir has not humbled me with his presence, Oocaw channeled.

"It's not Jaered I am looking for," Aeros barked. "It is Earth's Heir that I seek."

Oocaw bent its neck, blocking most of Ian's view. *My eyes have not lain on him. How might I know of whom you speak?*

"He looks like the Mother-to-us-all," Aeros said. He stepped up and placed a hand at the base of Oocaw's neck, inches from Ian's hiding spot, and ran his finger over her side. When he lifted it, it was red. Ian's heel had ripped back the scale. *This looks fresh,* Aeros channeled.

I am often hunted.

"I suppose you would feed an entire colony, wouldn't you?" Aeros said.

Oocaw bent her head to the side and extended her long, snake-like tongue. It brushed Aeros away and she licked the wound, then snorted and laid her head on the ground.

What is wrong with your wing? Aeros turned toward Ian's hiding place.

Oocaw's wing muscles shuddered, knocking Ian off balance, but he leaned into her side, burying himself so deep that her scales scraped his cheek *You injured me, when I tried to save my mate.*

That was such a fierce battle . . . Aeros channeled.

Ian still couldn't get a clear look at his father. Aeros wandered toward her head. *Why are you here, Oocaw?*

The energies of Thrae are dying with her, the dragon responded. *I need to absorb whatever I can find.*

The meteorite strike was a blessing then, was it not? Aeros channeled. *The torn magnetic curtain over Thrae will maintain your health . . . for what little time you have left.* A heartbeat later, a bright flash, and all fell silent.

With a tremendous sigh, Oocaw relaxed her wing and Ian slipped out, dragging his supplies with him. He paused. The dragon had adopted the same color as the ground. Oocaw's chameleon skills served her well.

Thank you for risking your life for me. He stroked the side of the dragon's head. *I am so sorry for your loss,* he channeled.

I am but one.

You are never alone as long as I have breath in my body, Ian responded.

You are your mother's son. The dragon rose and dipped its wing.

Ian climbed up her side, avoiding the injury, and settled in his perch. *We must find her before he does.*

Oocaw lifted her head toward the sky and at the same time raised her wings. A powerful downward thrust and she shot into the air. The dragon pumped her wings like never before, lifting them higher with each thrust, rocketing toward the safety of the cloud.

Ian scanned the ground between flaps, but from what he could tell, his father did not return. A moment later they burst through the cloud, and Oocaw leveled off above.

How did you know father was coming? Ian asked.

His presence disturbs all. Oocaw responded.

Ian pondered what the dragon meant. If Aeros disrupts the energy of Thrae, then perhaps his whereabouts could be tracked on Earth.

The clouds thinned, and then disappeared altogether. Ian welcomed the cool air above, for the land below him stretched like the Mojave Desert.

Were there once many like you? Ian channeled.

At the beginning, we were many, Oocaw responded. *But long ago, Aeros took my kind to Earth for battle. Few returned.*

Dragons weren't native to Earth, but their stories were based in truth.

Oocaw turned and headed for a mountain in the distance. As they drew closer, a dark patch appeared midway in the tallest peak. The dragon coasted, then reared back and her talons gripped the rocky ledge. She ducked her head and entered the cave, her scales turning to the same shade as the surrounding rock walls.

Ian pressed against the dragon's back to avoid getting clocked by the ceiling.

A few yards in and Oocaw rested on her belly, drawing her feet up underneath.

Your home? Ian channeled.

I require rest. We go at nightfall, the dragon announced. She tucked her head under a wing. A few minutes later, rumbling snoring echoed throughout the cavern.

Ian's curiosity about a dragon's lair superseded any need for sleep and he wandered farther into the cave. He expected to find a heaping pile of bones, but the cave was sparse. Perhaps that was only in fiction, he mused. Farther back, he stopped and gazed at crisscrossed scrapes along the cave wall. It looked to Ian like a frenzied assault on the rock. On closer inspection, there appeared to be blood embedded in some of the deeper grooves. The scrapes reached to the ceiling and were several yards in length.

Beyond, small, shallow scrapes close to the ground gave Ian pause. Oocaw had brought Rayne and his mother to her den. Rayne had wandered deeper into the cave like Ian and carved her initials into the rock. He bent down and ran his fingers over her scratches. A fortnight ago, he thought he'd killed her and would never see her again. When Patrick and Jaered told him she was alive, a part of him wasn't sure he believed them, convinced that they had told him the lie to keep him hopeful, cooperative—motivated. Ilyak had told him that the Mother to them all had a young woman with her.

The initials carved by Rayne's own hand brought tears to his eyes. It wouldn't be much longer.

The cave extended for a mile or more while the odor of sulfur grew intense. His eyes stung and he covered his mouth with his shirt, exploring further. At the far end, Ian stopped short of a ledge and watched trails of vapor rise in large columns ahead of him. When he peered over the edge, he discovered it was a lava tube, with a molten pool far below, bubbling and brewing. Upon further study, he saw that the tube had no opening above, which explained the concentrated gas.

He turned back, struggling to breathe while the sulfuric oxide burned his nose and lungs. By the time he reached the mouth of the cave, his coughing had ceased, although his eyes continued to sting.

Oocaw resembled a huge snoring boulder. Ian found a hammock-like curve in the dragon's wing joint and fell into a dreamless sleep.

With a groan, Oocaw rose to her feet, disturbing Ian's bed and his slumber. He landed facedown on the cave floor and the cool rock's impact woke him in an instant. As he got to his feet, the dragon shook and ruffled her wings, nearly decapitating him. He ducked in time and scurried over to the cave wall, out of her reach. Dusk bled into evening beyond the mountain, and Ian drew upon his keen night vision to see where his provisions had been dropped.

I am weak, she channeled. *I must have my fill to reach our destination.* With that, she backed out of the cave and took flight.

Ian was anxious to reach Rayne and his mother, so this wasn't what he had hoped to hear. Given the desolation of the land they had passed, he couldn't imagine how far Oocaw would have to travel to find enough to fill her dragon belly. He stepped to the ledge and waited until Oocaw's journey took her out of sight. Then he opened his pack and found a couple of Sophenna's biscuits and some cured pig that Ilyak had packed for him. Thirsty from the salt and dry biscuits, he grabbed his canteen and went in search of a stream, having drained what he'd brought. There'd been no water on his exploration of the den, so Ian stepped out onto the ledge and leaned over as far as he dared. The ledge gave way to a sheer rock wall below. If he'd had his climbing gear, he might have been able to traverse it, but wasn't about to risk free-climbing. The rocky walls to either side of the cave mouth looked promising. He scanned the mountain above to see if there was a natural stream, or possible snow melt coming from above, but found nothing to suggest a water supply.

A *swoosh* from behind. Huge claws gripped Ian, lifting him into the air. A flutter of chocolate-colored wings, and then a giant bird landed inside the cave and smashed Ian against the rock floor. He glanced over his shoulder just as a chiseled beak poked toward him. He twisted around and with his freed arm, he knocked the beak away with enough force that it stunned the bird. A thunderous *squawk!* Ian was lifted a couple of feet off the ground and shaken like a rattle. Not about to be the gigantic eagle's dinner, he grabbed his pant leg but was flung with too much force to reach the knife. A second later, the bird paused long enough for Ian to whip the knife from its sheath and he cut a deep slash in the bird's leg. With an ear-splitting *squawk*, the bird dropped its meal, folding its injured leg up underneath its breast.

Its injury didn't deter the bird and, hopping on one leg, it fell into a frenzied pecking with Ian as the target. He rolled back and forth to avoid the jabbing beak, but the bird didn't relent, intent on getting its fill.

TWENTY-TWO

an gave a forceful kick at the oncoming beak. It stunned the bird enough that he could roll off to the side, then he bolted to his feet, running with everything he had toward the rear of the cave.

The bird took off after him with its jabbing, snapping beak. Several yards in, Ian stole a glance over his shoulder at the bird. Its injured leg was drenched in blood from the gaping wound and it slipped on the wet surface. The giant bird slid, crashing against the cave wall. Then it shook its head and with an echoing *squawk*, managed to get up and continue the pursuit.

The sulfuric oxide stung Ian's eyes and burned his lungs. He grabbed his shirt and covered his mouth, but kept running. Half-blinded by the fumes, he relied on the increasing heat from the volcano tube to tell him how close he approached.

The bird had caught up, and with a snip of its beak, dug a scrape into Ian's back. "Ahh," he moaned. He lunged forward, sliding on the rock toward the ledge. The bird's momentum was too great and it tumbled over Ian, smashing him, face and all, against the ground. The giant bird rolled into the lava tube. One final *squawk*, and it landed in the molten lava with a bubbly splat.

A coughing fit racked Ian's chest. He curled up and weathered it, gasping for enough oxygen to replenish his spent muscles, but the toxic fumes denied him. His core ignited at the same time a rumble came from deep within the planet. A plume of lava shot into the air behind him. With his thoughts focused on the mouth of the cave, Ian shyfted.

He rolled onto his back and sucked in the fresh air while his pulse took its time to ease. He didn't know how long he lay on the cool rock while professing thanks to the planet for giving him an ounce of his power when he needed it the most.

More parched than ever, Ian's search for water would have to wait. He'd be a meal for the pickings if he stepped outside again. So he lay on his back pondering this strange, desolate planet where dragons, giant piranhas and massive birds of prey roamed. What other creatures ruled this planet?

Oocaw returned a while later and stepped into the cave. The lower half of a long fish hung from her teeth, and with a swoop of her head, the tail plopped inside. She crushed the bony cartilage and swallowed with an extended neck.

This explained why Ian hadn't found a pile of bones. He stood up at another revelation. Oocaw had been to an ocean, or what was left of one. While waiting for the dragon to return, he'd studied his mother's map. From what he could tell, they were somewhere near Peru on his Earth. If there was enough ocean left on the planet, it explained how there were clouds and a valley like Ilyak's.

You are sufficiently refreshed? Ian channeled.

We go now, Oocaw announced.

Ian grabbed his readied supplies and climbed to his perch. *Oocaw,* he channeled. *Will we pass fresh water on the way? I am in dire need.*

The dragon snorted in answer and took off into the night sky. The moon was more than a crescent and shone bright enough that Ian could make out the landscape below. He dragged out the blanket to throw over himself. He lay against the dragon's neck, faint and weak from dehydration. The inside of his mouth was like cardboard and his lips had cracked; he tasted blood whenever he ran his tongue over them.

Ian estimated an hour or more had passed when Oocaw dropped from the sky and swooped in a circular pattern, lowering to the ground. The dragon had brought Ian to a trickling stream in a rocky hill. Oocaw leaned down from her boulder perch, and while Ian dismounted, she lapped at the water, splashing buckets' worth in all directions. He found a location upstream from her drinking spot and fell to his knees, then dipped both canteens into the water at the same time. He drank ravenously from one and filled it up again before twisting the cap tight on both.

Oocaw dipped her wing at his approach and he climbed to her back. *Thank you,* he channeled.

Mother-of-us-all would not want you to die on my watch, she replied.

He chuckled. *That is a very Earthly thing to say.*

The youngling said it. I took it as my own. Oocaw took off for the sky.

With a huge grin, Ian rested his head against her neck and closed his eyes. Oocaw liked Rayne.

The warmth of the day beat down on Ian and he pulled the blanket off and sat up. He had drifted off after getting the water and slept most of the night. He stretched, then drank his fill from one of the canteens.

They were above the parched land that seemed to go on forever. Ian wondered if the polar ice caps had melted and that's why some ocean remained. He pulled out the last biscuit and nibbled on it, then found a sliver of jerky and made the most of his meager breakfast. The wind in his face wasn't helping his chapped lips, and he buried his head against the dragon's neck to give them some respite.

A few minutes later, he flexed his sore back and peered at the horizon. A crimson cloud rose high above the land and billowed taller than Oocaw was flying.

Can you fly around it? Ian channeled.

No, the dragon replied.

Ian scrambled to pull out the protective suit that Sophenna had handed him. He slipped into the pantsuit but struggled with lining up the helmet within the suit's lip. The cloud loomed closer, and Oocaw didn't slow.

He twisted the helmet back and forth, assuming that there was a right way for it to fall into place, but no matter how he twisted it, it wouldn't drop down into the lip. With a jerk, he took it off and perused the edge, saw the two links on opposite sides, then slid his gloved finger along the ring at his neck until he found the other piece of the buckle. He pulled the helmet over his head, keeping everything lined up with his other hand and it fell into place, a heartbeat before Oocaw flew headfirst into the poisonous cloud.

The buckles were latched, yet there was no hissing of air. Without it, he'd suffocate. Ian patted the control panel at his chest and looked down, but it was impossible to see below the lower rim of the helmet. He grabbed the pack and fumbled at opening it with the thick gloves, while cussing at the top of his lungs for not taking time to check out the suit before he needed it. He rummaged through the pack for anything reflective, paused at the thought of Sophenna's knife, then resumed cussing louder than ever. It was strapped to his leg, inside the suit.

Ian spied the canteen hanging at his knee. He pulled it by the strap and positioned it across from him. The scarlet air between him and the canteen wasn't thick, thanks to Oocaw flying through the cloud at such a speed, but the side of the canteen was soiled. Ian swiped at it with the sleeve of his protective suit, unable to use his spit. The side was cleaned enough for him to reflect the panel, although not with much clarity. He pressed a green button on the panel, but crackling sounded at his ears. Coms, right, he thought, and pressed it again to turn it off. A yellow flashing button looked promising and he pressed it, but as far as he could tell, nothing happened. The remaining button was blue, and he pushed it. A hiss of air came from inside the suit— at the same time, Oocaw emerged through the methane cloud, and the bright blue sky loomed overhead.

Ian breathed a sigh of relief and turned off the oxygen, then removed his helmet. In the distance, a shimmering bubble appeared at the horizon. Oocaw fell into her landing pattern, circling the ground until she dropped close enough to land. This landing was the smoothest one yet.

I cannot go closer, she channeled, as her scales turned sandy and dull.

Why? Ian asked.

I must stay under their radar, she responded.

He smiled. *Did the youngling teach you that one?* he channeled.

She taught me many things. Oocaw turned her head and faced Ian. He swore there was a glint in her eye.

He stuffed the helmet back in the pack and slung everything over his shoulders. He climbed down and walked up to Oocaw. *Will I see you again?* he asked.

If Mother Thrae deems it so, she responded. The dragon dipped her head and peered at Ian with one eye. *Keep safe and live long, young Heir.*

Thrive well. May you command the skies for all eternity, he channeled. He stroked the scales behind her ear and she leaned into it, purring. Oocaw rose to her full height and flapped her wings, then took to the heavens, blending into the sky. With a heavy heart, Ian watched her path until she was but a dot. He hoped that someday they would meet again.

He searched the sky for the methane cloud, but it appeared several miles away. There wasn't a breeze to carry it in his direction, so he slipped out of the suit and stuffed it back into the sack. He took inventory of his clothes and battle scars. He'd weathered much to get this far.

Ian set out, walking toward the domed city, apprehensive at how he would be received in the Primary's penal colony. He gave into happier thoughts, enthused at seeing Rayne, and excited, yet restless, to meet a mother he thought dead. Each step across the barren wasteland, taking him closer toward the unknown.

TWENTY-THREE

It had been three days since the trio, along with Saxon, had returned to the auditorium in Greenland. Eve dispatched a few rebels to southern Africa to follow the clue, but had forbidden Patrick from traveling again, holding him to his promise that he would train harder once they found Tara.

No one broached the angst stirring inside them. Ian had not returned from Thrae with Rayne. Eve confirmed that Aeros had also not returned. Whether that was promising or not, was anyone's guess.

Jaered and Tara had fallen into sync, ganging up on Patrick till the bruises resembled a tie-dye shirt, and his muscles begged for the comfort of his bed.

Today, neither one held anything back in his training. By midday Patrick stumbled onto the bleachers for a much needed break and took inventory of his wounds. Saxon jumped up next to him and licked the cut on his face while Tara and Jaered sparred on the gym floor. Tara was everything Patrick wasn't, and while watching the two of them, he understood how competent Jaered was. Hell, competent didn't begin to describe the skills the guy had.

Tara stepped in delivering forceful blows, then used the weight of her body to subdue Jaered on the mat in a choke hold.

"Give," he said, but she took a second longer to relent before slipping off of him. Whatever hatred she had for Jaered, he gave her a chance to bring it to the mat today, and she hadn't held back.

Tara wiped the sweat from her brow and when Jaered offered a hand, she took it and got to her feet.

"That was a first," Patrick said. Saxon snorted.

Jaered pulled his shirt off and swiped at his face, then the back of his neck. "I'm hitting the showers." He exited through the double doors.

"I'm starting dinner," Tara tossed at Patrick. "Afterward, you and I are going for a run."

"Goody," he said, running his tongue over his swollen lip. Since returning, Patrick had lost eight pounds, but from his daily summation, had gained some muscle.

An hour later, Patrick wandered into the kitchen. "It smells great," he said. Tara tore some kale for a salad. Saxon lifted his head at Patrick, then went back to his sprawled-out nap on the floor. Patrick stared at him with envy.

Tara dropped a piece of kale next to Saxon. The wolf sniffed it then returned to his slumber. Patrick wasn't a big fan of the stuff either.

"Don't take this wrong, but I'm surprised at how well you cook," Patrick said.

"I had a great teacher," she said with a faraway look in her eyes.

"I miss the old days, too," Patrick said. "But at least Milo is safe."

"Be helpful, and wash these." She handed him some fresh carrots.

He took them from her and headed to the sink. "You like ordering me around, don't you?"

"Someone has to keep you in line. It's obvious that Jaered couldn't." A smug expression lifted her face as she sliced an end off a cucumber. "What's his story, anyway?"

"I know very little," Patrick said. He set the dripping carrots down next to the cutting board. "He's not big on sharing."

"But you trust him," she said. It wasn't a question.

"My mother trusts him with her life, that much I know. I still have a hard time wrapping my head around all of this. The fact that Ian, Jaered and I are related is so . . . surreal." Patrick rubbed his shirt where his Seal rose on his chest, then grabbed a knife and sliced a carrot.

Tara paused at what she was doing. "Why did you risk everything to find me?" She looked up at him. "Given who you are, a Duach, you were stupid to do that."

"Isn't it obvious?" he said softly.

She shook her head and looked away. "I was raised to be a warrior. Ian's protector. I don't know how to be anything else."

Patrick left the blade stuck halfway through the carrot. "I don't know how to be anything but human. I guess we're both a mess, aren't we?"

A hint of a grin curled the edge of Tara's mouth, and she returned to her chopping. "Then we're each other's mess."

Patrick stared at her, fighting the urge to leap over the island that separated them and sweep her off her feet in a passionate kiss. But Tara was complicated, and he needed to take it slow; at least that's what he told himself in a feeble attempt to wash away his cowardice. Would she have no choice but to reject him if he told her how he felt? She was Ian's guard, and along with Saxon, Ian's Channel. There had never been any room for Patrick. He returned to his chopping with more forceful strokes.

Jaered appeared in the doorway and held up his cell. "Eve's people have eyes on Willoughsby. He's in Johannesburg." He regarded Tara. "What do you want to do?"

She gave Patrick a hopeful stare. "We're going to South Africa," Patrick said.

TWENTY-FOUR

Tara and Patrick elected Jaered to make the call and convince Eve that finding Willoughsby was only the first step. Tara and Bhutto were confident they could persuade the scientist to come out of hiding, and finish his research with the rebels in secret.

Patrick stood in the hall and caught bits and pieces of Jaered's conversation with his mother. He had to admit, he was jealous that his mother trusted Jaered's opinion more than his. Tara had gone for a run along the glacier with Saxon. The two had been pretty much inseparable since Ian left. The wolf was in his element in Greenland, but he didn't know how the animal would fare in South Africa.

Beyond the door, the bedroom grew quiet. Patrick wondered if Jaered was simply listening to his mother when the door flew open.

"What's the verdict?" Patrick said.

Jaered headed down the hall. "It's a go, but with a catch," he said.

"Sounds like Mother." Patrick followed him into the kitchen. Jaered approached the center island. "The mission is to retrieve Willoughsby, but if we can't . . ." Jaered grabbed an apple from the basket on the counter.

Patrick stepped away from the refrigerator. "We're not killing him."

"He's been working on a theory that can stop Aeros from sucking energy from the earth, but if the Primary or Aeros get their hands on him, they can turn his science against us and speed up the damage tenfold. Earth won't have a chance to survive." Jaered didn't take a bite, and instead, spun the apple around in his hand.

The gesture reminded Patrick of Ian practicing with his sleight-of-hand balls. "Then we'll get him to come with us by any means necessary," Patrick said. They'd lose any trust Tara had if they were forced to kill the old scientist. Joule would never forgive them.

"Whatever, just know that it's plan B," Jaered took a huge bite.

"What's plan B?" Tara asked from the doorway. Saxon plodded in and lapped like a rabid dog at his water bowl. She wiped the sweat from her forehead with the back of her arm.

Jaered and Patrick exchanged a glance. "We're going to Johannesburg," Patrick announced.

Tara's face lit up. "Do I have time for a shower?"

"Hell yeah," Jaered said between chews. "I'm not shyfting to the opposite end of the world with stinking passengers."

The second she was out of earshot, Jaered gave Patrick a discerning look.

"It's going to work out," he said, sounding more confident than he felt.

"It better," Jaered dropped the unfinished apple in the trash.

Jaered shyfted them to a back alley where rotting food filled the nearby trash cans, and their odor assaulted Patrick's nose. A horde of flies scattered at their arrival, then buzzed past Patrick's head in a steady stream on their return to the cans. Wooden crates, some intact, others broken, lined the walls of the surrounding buildings. Dusk had set in, and the cool evening did nothing to erase the chill of the journey. Patrick was disappointed that Jaered did the shyfting, but his cousin's corona wasn't visible like Patrick's.

Saxon sniffed around the base of a nearby trash can. At the end of the alley, a man tugged on his earlobe. Jaered met up with him, and they spoke in hushed voices.

"Eve has rebels everywhere," Tara said while keeping one eye on Jaered and his contact.

"It's a big world," Patrick said. He was in awe of what his mother had orchestrated right under his nose, and couldn't imagine how she kept her secrets from his father. For the first time, he wondered if that was why they were living two separate lives.

Bhutto rubbed his hands. "I'm not looking forward to telling him about Joule."

"We'll figure out a way to get her back," Patrick said. "But first, we need to get him to a safer place."

A moment later, Jaered gestured and they joined him at the street. "The team split up yesterday, covering the two liquor stores in the city that sell the brand. Willoughsby was spotted this afternoon, purchasing a bottle in the store around the corner. One of ours tailed him when he left and he saw the scientist go into an apartment upstairs from the laundromat across the street. He thinks he's still in there."

Patrick put his hand on Tara's back. "Are you sure you want to go with Bhutto?"

"I was with Ian when we visited him and Joule in the Congo." She tossed Jaered an evil eye, no doubt reminded how Jaered and Eve had lured them there under false pretenses.

"We'll convince him to come with us," Bhutto said.

"Besides, Saxon is coming, too." She patted the wolf's head.

"If his behavior is odd, or if he has someone with him, get out fast," Jaered said. "If he trusts you, come to the bar across the street. We'll be waiting there and we'll slip out the back. I'll shyft us to the auditorium. Eve will meet us there."

"You can shyft that many people?" Tara looked impressed.

"Just get him to the bar, I'll take care of the rest," Jaered said.

Patrick hated that it had to be her and not him, but Willoughsby had never met Patrick or Jaered, and had no reason to trust anyone but Bhutto and Tara. They stepped into the street and made their way across. Saxon ran ahead and sniffed at the base of the staircase. His ears perked up.

"Something's wrong," Patrick said. He took a step but Jaered held out his arm, stopping him. "Wait. Trust her instincts, not the wolf's."

Patrick's breaths came quick and shallow as the duo continued, walking up the staircase and disappearing into the shadows.

The stairwell reeked of cigarette smoke and urine. Tara held her breath against the stench and made it to the upper landing. There were two doors on either side. Bhutto knocked on the one that opened onto the apartment over the laundromat below.

Voices blared from a television in the apartment behind her. It made it difficult to tell if Dr. Willoughsby was inside or not. Tara knocked again. No one answered. She'd made the decision that Jaered's intel was wrong, when the door flung open. Dr. Willoughsby gave her a dark look, but when he regarded Bhutto, recognition set in and his agitation grew into concern.

"What are you doing here?" He poked his head out of the doorway and glanced beyond them. "You shouldn't be here," he hushed. "How did you find me? Are you alone?"

"It's just us." Tara took a step toward him. "We need to talk to you."

"Joule is in trouble," Bhutto said.

Dr. Willoughsby's eyes softened, but the rest of his features remained tense. "I know," he said.

Tara held he hand up. "Saxon, stay." The wolf sat at the alert at the top of the stairs. She pushed her way into the apartment and Bhutto closed the door. "We're here to take you someplace safe," she said.

Dr. Willoughsby wrung his hands and his back sagged. "You shouldn't have come."

Tara grew rigid, then spun around at a moan. Bhutto slumped to the floor. A man grabbed her from behind. She thrust her elbow into his side and stomped down on the bridge of his foot. He yelped but kept her in a tight grip. She tried to thrust her head back and break his nose, but he pressed his face against the side of her head and left her unable to maneuver.

Growls and scratches came from the other side of the front door. "Scream and I'll kill Dr. Willoughsby," he hissed in her ear. She froze. There was something familiar about the voice. It was Komodo, one of the Primary's Elite guards.

The growls grew fiercer and the clawing rose up the door as Saxon fought to get inside.

"Better yet, we'll kill the wolf." A Pur guard stepped in front of Tara and gave her a pompous grin. It was Falcon, captain of the Primary's Elite guard. She glared at him, then reared up and kicked him with both feet square in his chest. A prick at her neck and a second later, Tara's world swirled into an endless void.

Patrick stared out the window of the bar while holding the beer glass between his hands. He sat up with a start. Saxon rushed down the stairs and paused at the bottom turning his head like radar. Then he rushed up the stairs, and repeated the frantic gesture. "Now do you believe something's wrong?" Patrick said.

Bhutto stumbled down the stairs and Saxon circled him on the sidewalk. Jaered shot to his feet, withdrew his wallet from his back pocket and tossed some American currency on the table. "Time to go."

"We aren't leaving without her!" Patrick shouted. The man and woman at the table next to theirs looked up, then resumed their conversation. Bhutto rushed into the bar with Saxon at his heels.

"Hey, dogs aren't allowed in here," the bartender said.

Saxon planted all four paws and growled up at the man, baring his fangs.

"He isn't staying." Jaered grabbed Patrick's elbow and led him, not too gently, to the back of the bar. Bhutto and Saxon rushed after them. He pushed open the bathroom stall doors, one after another, and with the coast clear, he shyfted everyone to the local safe house.

"What the hell!" Patrick shouted. "We need to go back for her!"

Bhutto rubbed the back of his neck. "They knocked me out. But by the time I woke up, Ms. Tara and Dr. Willoughsby were gone."

"The Pur guard?" Jaered asked.

"The apartment was dark and I didn't get a good look, but I suspect so, yes," Bhutto said.

"This is a nightmare." Patrick slumped down on the arm of the couch. "The Primary has Tara."

"First Joule," Jaered said. "And now Dr. Willoughsby."

"Your rebel contacts set us up!" Patrick shot to his feet with clenched his fists.

"I suspect they got to Dr. Willoughsby long before our contacts found him," Jaered said. "The Pur guard used him to bait us."

"And we stepped right in the shit." Patrick looked around the room. "Where are we?"

"A safe house in Johannesburg," Jaered said, pulling out his cell. "A rebel team will meet us here within the hour."

Patrick peered at him while his core simmered deep in his chest. "You seem prepared."

Jaered faced Patrick. "And that surprises you?"

"They could have shyfted her anywhere," Patrick said. "Where do we even start?"

He held up a black remote. "Prepared, remember?"

"What's that?" Patrick asked.

"I bugged her," Jaered said. He turned a dial and a green screen appeared. "Her tracker will tell us exactly where the Primary is keeping her, and hopefully the Willoughsbys."

Patrick grabbed Jaered's shirt and backed him up against the wall. "You bastard! You used her!" Bhutto pulled on Patrick's arm, but he didn't relent.

"The Primary keeps his special prisoners in a secret location. We've had no idea where. This was the best option we've had in a while," Jaered said. "This isn't about you, or her."

Patrick let him go and stormed away.

"What can I do?" Bhutto said.

"I'm shyfting you and the wolf back to the auditorium," Jaered said. "When we rescue them, we'll meet you there." A moment later a bright flash lit up the room behind Patrick. All was quiet.

His mother and Jaered had planned this. Nausea swelled and snaked up Patrick's throat. He found the bathroom and splashed water on his face, then paused and looked at himself in the mirror. They were willing to do whatever it took to stop the Primary and Aeros, even if it meant the lives of those he loved. If the need arose, could Patrick do the same?

PART TWO

In times of battle, not all your enemies are on the other side.

TWENTY-FIVE

Ian ran out of water by the time he reached the massive dome. Up close, its energy shield shimmered in the bright sun, casting sparks that dissipated a few inches from its surface. The energized structure rose several stories high and was wider than four football fields from one end to the other. He reached toward the energy curtain, but hesitated and dropped his hand, unsure of what effect it might have on his core, or the dome.

He walked around the base, unsure how to gain entrance. From what he could tell, there weren't any security cameras, much less doorbells. The dome disappeared into the ground, and Ian had no idea how deep it reached. There had to be an entrance, somewhere, or was it truly a prison only the Primary could access?

But his mother and Rayne had come here, he argued with himself. If they could get in, so could he.

The intensity of the sun formed droplets of sweat and Ian swiped the back of his neck with his hand, then dried it on his shirt. The desolation of the planet continued to disturb him, and while he followed the curvature of the dome he tried not to imagine Earth suffering the same fate. His core had been all but dead since he'd stepped out of the vortex in the storage room days ago. Was it because Thrae's core was dying? Ian's steps faltered, but he remained on his feet. He gazed upon the barren soil surrounding the dome for as far as he could see. He harbored faith that they could stop Earth from suffering this fate, but was there a way to reverse Thrae's?

More than two-thirds of the way around the base of the dome, Ian stopped at what looked to be an unshielded entrance to a tunnel.

He peered inside but all he could find were carved adobe steps leading down into darkness. He pulled his saddlebag packs higher on his shoulder and descended with caution. The air grew cool the lower he ventured but the dirt walls remained hot to the touch. He stopped at the bottom, facing a wooden door without a handle. He pressed his ear to it, but silence met him on the other side. He rapped on the door in a beat identical to the one Catherine had used to gain access to the cavern at the Northern Colony.

A few minutes passed and then, with a drawn-out *creak,* the door opened.

A brute of a man stared at Ian. He was bare-chested, bald and tattooed over most of his body. He eyed Ian's pack as though judging if there might be something worth stealing. "Where'd you come from?" the man grunted.

"I'm searching for Mother-to-us-all," Ian said.

He pushed past Ian and looked up the stairwell. "How the hell did you get here?"

Ian hadn't anticipated that question. "My transportation is my own. I wish to see Mother. I know she's here," he said in a more commanding tone.

The brute spit at Ian's feet, then walked back inside, but left the door open behind him. "You want to be here, then be here." The second Ian shut the door, the brute leaned down and got in his face and it took everything Ian had not to turn away at his stench. "But not just anyone takes our water and provisions without proving their worth to Stag." He turned and disappeared into the darkness of the tunnel and his voice floated out of the void. "You've gained admittance, but it's up to the Acumen if you stay."

"What's the Acumen?" Ian asked.

"A battle to test your worthiness." The brute's chuckle pricked the back of Ian's neck.

Ian felt his way down the tunnel, doing his best to keep up with the brute who obviously knew how to navigate it in pitch black. Several minutes later, a hatch opened and Ian blinked up at the bright light, magnified that much more by the massive dome overhead. He climbed out into a wide dirt street lined on either side with single-story adobe dwellings. His escort let go of the hatch and it banged shut, kicking puffs of dirt into the air. Ian waved to keep it from snaking up his nostrils.

The brute walked down the dusty street. Grimy men in soiled clothes were scattered about the township. They were of all size and build, many working on roofs, carrying clothes in baskets, or repairing structures. Others rested in the shade or conversed in low voices. A couple were missing an eye, others a hand, some a leg. Everyone paused at their tasks and watched Ian with curiosity or apprehension as he walked by.

"Where are the women?" Ian asked.

"Women are powerless," the brute said. He turned his head and spit in the middle of the street, then wiped his mouth with the back of his hand. "They have no place in Stag."

Ian found most of the population stoic, and to his dismay, emaciated. "How many live here?"

"It's not my job to keep the books," the brute said. "Last I heard, about five hundred."

They had walked for several blocks when, between the buildings, Ian noticed a sizable agricultural field in the distance. Cornstalks and other vegetable plants looked like they needed more than a little tender loving care.

They turned a couple of corners and Ian's guide came to a stop at a pavilion in what appeared to be the center of town.

A broad-shouldered man in his early fifties with salt-and-pepper hair sat behind a wooden table. Unlike others Ian had passed, this man wore a clean, collared shirt. He listened to someone recalling events from across the desk while nodding or yawning as the plaintiff relayed information.

He held his hands up, stopping the plaintiff's recount in mid-sentence. "Look, I get what you're upset about, but unless he has violated colony law, I can't intervene."

"But this isn't the first time he's taken Roxy," the plaintiff said.

The man got up and walked around the desk with an air of authority. He threw his arm around the plaintiff's shoulder and turned him toward the street. "He only does it because he knows it upsets you. Be patient, don't say anything, and I'm sure she'll show up on your doorstep soon."

He left the plaintiff to his mutterings and approached Ian and his escort. He strolled around Ian, as though sizing him up. "I am Horace. Who seeks refuge in Stag?" the man said.

"I do not seek refuge," Ian replied. "I only seek consult with one who resides here."

"He claims he is looking for Mother-to-us-all." The brute scratched a sore on his arm.

"Mother-to-us-all never graces us with her presence." The man peered at Ian with heightened curiosity. "We are only visited by Aeros, when he wishes to hunt, but even he has not sought sport in quite some time."

"I was told that Mother was headed here. She had about a four day's head start, a week at the most," Ian said. Had something happened to her and Rayne? If Oocaw had deposited them in the same vicinity, then it had to have happened on the walk to the tunnel. "I must find her and her companion. It's a matter of life and death."

"You will not find life here, there's only death." Horace signaled to the brute. "Constrain him until the Acumen."

The brute grabbed Ian's arm in a painful vice, but Ian struggled and dug in his heels. "I mean no harm to the colony," he shouted at Horace's retreating back. "I only seek Mother's counsel. If she is truly not here, just let me go so I can find her."

A deep and hearty laugh came from Horace, and he turned around with a wicked smile. "You obviously have transportation. I could use a way out of here."

The brute dragged Ian down the street and opened a door to a building without windows. The only light came from slits in the ceiling between rotting and broken slats. Three long cages lined the back wall. A handful of men were divided up among them. Ian's escort brushed his hands over Ian's torso and upper legs, but never discovered the knife sheathed at his lower calf.

The brute unlocked the cage at the end and pulled Ian inside. An old, feeble man looked up long enough to check out his new cell mate, then dropped his head. The brute pulled Ian's bags off his shoulder, leaving rope burns behind.

"I mean no harm," Ian yelled. "I only seek counsel."

"No one cares what you want, only what we need." The brute locked the cell and walked to the opposite end of the building. He sat on a rickety, short stool and rummaged through Ian's things.

Ian licked his lips. "Can I get some water, please?"

"Here, you can have some of ours." A man in the cell next to Ian's dipped a battered tin cup in a water pan and then handed it to him through the bars.

"Thank you," Ian said. He drained the mug and returned it to the man. He grabbed the bars and stuck his face through the slat while the brute checked each piece of his gear. When he removed the protective suit, he dropped it along with the helmet on the floor as though he'd seen one before. This surprised Ian. From what he could tell, the township didn't appear to have much in the way of technology.

The brute pulled out a piece of jerky that Ian had missed. He smelled it, then licked it. A grin spread wide and he stuck it in his mouth like a lollipop, sucking on it. He caught Ian watching him and pulled it out of his mouth, then held it up. "You got more of this?" he asked.

"That was my last one," Ian said.

The brute grunted and stuck it back in his mouth. When he had finished pilfering Ian's possessions, he stood and tossed everything in a crate, then carried it outside.

Ian leaned his forehead against the bar with racing thoughts. Where the hell were Gwynn and Rayne? Had they changed their destination since Oocaw had brought them here? If so, what kind of transportation did they find? Where would they have gone? Ian turned around and leaned against the bars. The old man in the corner kept his head down but had stretched out his legs. His feet were filthy and his hair disheveled. Blood and drool wet the front of his shirt. Both earlobes were missing.

Who had done such atrocities to the poor souls here? If it was the Primary, he truly was Aeros's brother. Ian slid down the bars and sat with his knees pulled up.

"Where'd you come from?" A man in the adjoining cell scooted over. "I've never seen you before."

"I came from a northern colony," Ian said.

He gave Ian a puzzled look. "You meant to come here? Are you missing some marbles?"

"I'm looking for someone. I thought they were here." Ian reached between the bars. "I'm . . ." He hesitated. "I'm Galen." It felt disconcerting to use his old mentor's name. Galen's loss to a Duach psychopath a few months earlier still stung. There were so many loved ones who'd succumbed in the battle to protect Earth. Tara's twin sister, Mara, brought the greatest ache whenever his thoughts fell to her.

"Proctor." The man shook hands. He pointed over his shoulder. "Nguyen is in here with me. Tweedle Dee and Tweedle Dumb are next door to us." Nguyen jerked his chin in Ian's direction. The two teenagers in the farthest cell turned their faces in unison. They were identical twins.

"Deek," one of them said, and raised his hand.

"Twiddle," the other one said.

Deek shoved his brother. "That's not your name."

"That's what he called me," the boy said, rubbing his shoulder.

"He made a joke about us, that's all." Deek grabbed his brother around the neck and pointed at him. "This is Dunn."

Ian held his hand up. "Galen." He turned toward the slumped man in the corner. "What's your name?" The man didn't respond.

"Don't know if he can answer," Proctor said. "I don't think he can hear. And his tongue's been cut out, so I suppose he'll make the ideal cell mate."

Ian stared at the tortured man. "Who did that?" he asked.

"The Primary. He's judge, jury, and executioner on both planets." Proctor turned a keen eye on Ian. "Which are you?"

"What do you mean?" Ian said.

"Duach or Pur?" Proctor said. "What else would I mean?"

Ian scooted next to the bars. "Everyone here is a Weir Sar?" It would explain why women weren't part of the colony.

"Mostly," Proctor said. "And all are from Earth. Me . . ." He touched his chest, "I was born and raised in the heart of America. I was a banker and worked to keep farmers above water."

"Why are you here?" Ian asked.

"Because I was ratted out to be a Duach." His jaw bulged and he spoke between clenched teeth. "I couldn't help how I was born. I lived my entire life by the Weir code, and just because my corona was the wrong color, I was taken from everyone I loved and stuck in this hellhole."

The man's words cut Ian to his core. The Primary had raised him to view all Duach as his enemy, the Pur's enemy. It was the worst kind of bigotry, and he was ashamed that it took him coming to Stag for him to recognize it.

"I'm so sorry for all that you've lost," Ian said, as the weight of the Pur's transgressions fell upon his shoulders and bent his back. He'd been born the Pur Heir and had been the figurehead for all the Primary's transgressions. Was that why the Primary had secluded him from Pur and Duach alike? Not for his protection, but to be a faceless scapegoat. "How can Duach and Pur be this close together without triggering the Curse?" Ian said.

Proctor lowered his voice. "Thrae's energy is so weak, that no one's core functions here."

It explained Ian's lack of powers once he stepped out of the vortex in the storage room. Could he shyft in Oocaw's den because he had been next to the lava tube, a direct link to the planet's core? "If that's the case, how can the Primary and Aeros come and go?"

He shrugged. "Beats me. But they can shyft in and out with no problem. That's how we got here."

From over Proctor's shoulder, Nguyen stared at Ian with interest. "Pur," he said. He leaned forward. "Something about you is familiar."

"I'm a Pur," was all Ian offered. "Maybe our paths crossed somewhere."

"Maybe," Nguyen said and leaned back again the wall. "I know I've seen you somewhere before. I'll figure it out."

Ian turned his back to them and stared at the old man in the corner while the throb in his neck took its time to subside. He'd walked into a snake pit.

TWENTY-SIX

The clatter of metal against metal woke Ian from a restless sleep and he sat up with a start. He peered over his shoulder at the cause of the commotion. The brute was back, running an aluminum mug along the bars of their cells.

How long had he been out? The sunlight streamed through the slit in the roof. Ian brushed himself off and stood. "I need to talk to Horace."

"Horace has better things to do than listen to your yappin'," the brute said.

"Keep quiet and keep your head down," Proctor hushed from next door. "It's the Acumen."

The brute opened the closest cell first. The second he swung back the gate, one of the twins took off out the door at high speed. "No!" his brother yelled. A *thud* came from outside the building as though the twin had been knocked down the second he emerged from the building "Idiot!" his brother said and waited next to the cell with his arms crossed over his chest.

"That was Tweedle Dumb," Proctor muttered under his breath. He and Nguyen were let out, then Ian.

The brute eyed the old man in the corner. "Hey, you, get out."

"I think he's deaf," Ian said.

He entered the cell and nudged the old man's shoulder. The guy slid onto his side and lay motionless. The brute checked the man's pulse with a finger to his neck. "He's more than deaf, he's dead." He exited the cell and motioned for the others to start walking.

Ian took a final glance at the old man, and swore he'd make the Primary pay.

They were led outside with two other men at the ready to guard them. The twin rubbed the back of his neck and was helped up by his brother. Everyone was led to the pavilion where a crowd had gathered, standing around in a circle.

He'd seen enough movies to figure out that this was some kind of test, and from the size of the circle, in all likelihood, combat was involved. He scanned the faces of the crowd, searching for anyone familiar, but scrutiny and sneers stared back.

Horace stepped into the middle of the circle and cleared his throat. "I give you our newest arrivals," he shouted. "The Acumen will decide if they're worthy of sharing our food, drinking our water, and if they can pull their weight for the good of the colony."

Ian studied the others from the corner of his eye. The twins were solid of build, but he was concerned if the slower one could hold his own against an experienced adversary. Nguyen looked like he could outmaneuver someone with his slight build, but landing blows against a solid jaw might break a few of Nguyen's bones. Proctor came across as meek, but if he had grown up on a farm, he might be able to overcome an opponent.

Horace grabbed a basket off his desk and walked back to the center of the circle. He held it up in both hands, turning around to face everyone. Cheers, shouts, and whistles rose to a thunderous level. "We choose without prejudice, who determines their worth," he shouted.

The brute that had pilfered Ian's things, approached Horace, and reached into the basket. He pulled out a stone and looked at it, then held it up. "Richter!" he yelled.

A man of medium height and build slipped out of the crowd while removing his shirt. He tossed it to the crowd and stepped up, taking his stone from the brute. The crowd went wild.

"Richter has accepted the challenge!" Horace announced.

Richter had a patch over one eye and a diagonal scar across his chest. His bronze skin glistened in the sunlight. Ian guessed he'd been in the colony for a while. He regarded the basket, wondering whose names were on the stones, and figured "without prejudice" was loosely interpreted around here.

Horace strolled past the newly arrived as they stood shoulder to shoulder at the edge of the circle, and stopped at Proctor. "Do you accept Richter's challenge?"

Proctor wrung his hands. "What choice do I have?"

"There is always a choice," Horace said. "If you choose not to prove your worth, then you can take your chances in the barrens."

"Is that where the losers go?" Ian asked.

Horace regarded Ian. "It's where we all go, eventually."

"So one way or another, it's a fight to the death," Ian said. Many of the men within earshot chuckled.

"Let's get this over with." Proctor followed Horace to the center of the circle. He reached toward Richter, but instead of shaking his hand, the man grabbed Proctor's arm and swung him around, then flung him to the side.

"It looks like we are underway!" Horace said with a sly grin. He took his place at the edge of the crowd and stood with his arms crossed.

Proctor stumbled and landed facedown in the dirt, then looked up at Richter, who circled him like he was lunch. Proctor spit dirt out of his mouth and bolted to his feet. He held his fists up and shuffled his feet like a trained boxer. Ian gave in to a sigh of relief. He might hold his own after all.

Richter pulled his fists up and danced from foot to foot as if ready for a match. He brushed his nose with his fist and thrust one fist out, and then the other, back and forth. Ian couldn't tell if he was mocking the man or boasting that he'd had training as well.

Proctor made the next move and feigned with his left, then came in with his right and caught a piece of Richter's jaw. The glancing blow didn't stun his opponent, and Richter came in with an uppercut that landed square with Proctor's lower jaw. It sent him staggering back.

Richter bent down and rammed Proctor's abdomen with his head. Proctor fell onto his back and Richter landed on top of him. The back of Proctor's head bounced against the ground and he lay staring up at the sky, gasping for air.

His opponent pinned Proctor's arms and punched him with his bare knuckles, cutting open the bridge of his nose and splitting a gash over one eye. Blood splattered with every one of Richter's blows.

"Oh shit," Nguyen said, standing next to Ian. "I thought he had a chance."

Ian's stomach knotted. He rushed into the center of the ring and held his hands up. "Stop!"

Richter paused and leaned back. Horace gave Ian a backhanded wave. "This is our way."

"Why?" Ian said. "Because you see anyone new as a threat? Is this how you beat them into submission, so they'll follow you blindly?"

Horace threw him a hateful glare. Had no one questioned Horace before? "Stay out of this, or take his place," he snarled.

"What if I take all of their places, Proctor included," Ian said and gestured toward the vagabond group. "I fight anyone of your choosing, and if I win, we all become one with Stag."

Cheers rose from the crowd while others laughed.

A spark of amusement flitted across Horace's face. "And if you lose?"

"What the hell are you doing?" Nguyen hissed. "You'll get us all killed!"

"I'll take a chance on him," Deek said with a nervous glance around the crowd, "rather than go into there with one of their choosing." Dunn nodded.

"But what if he loses?" Nguyen said, staring at Ian like he was measuring his worth.

"Would you rather get beaten up first?" the twins said in unison.

Nguyen stared at Proctor for several seconds, then stepped back into line with the twins.

"This one has already proven he's not worthy," Horace said and nudged Proctor's leg with the toe of his boot. Bloody gurgles spouted from his mouth.

"He's from farmland in the heart of North America," Ian said. "He might not be a worthy fighter, but he could help with growing your food." Proctor opened a swollen eye and lifted his head enough to regard Ian. His look spoke volumes.

Ian went to remove his shirt, but hesitated. If this group saw the Heir's Seal on his chest, it might be the end of him. He lifted both hands. "Who will challenge our worth?"

The brute stepped up with a sneer. "I'll take him." He pulled his shirt off and dropped it at his feet. His tattoos were distorted by scars of every size and configuration.

Horace regarded Ian with a raised brow. "You prove your worth against Stellan, and I'll accept your pathetic group. But if you lose, the barrens will not be kind."

"I get it," Ian said. "Let's be done with this. He paced back and forth, sizing up Stellan's weak points. He couldn't find any.

Stellan walked into the center and punched his hand with his fist. His biceps and triceps flexed and bulged. He'd been here a while, Ian surmised, working his way up to be Horace's right-hand man. Ian dug in the heels of his boots and took a stance. He brought up his hand and motioned Stellan to come and get him. The man dropped his head and charged.

TWENTY-SEVEN

Stellan had more brawn than brains, and Ian skirted off to the side using the brute's own shoulder to glance the blow. But the man reared up and spun around, screaming at Ian.

He walked away, turning his back to the brute as a taunt. Stellan rushed at Ian, but at the sound of his approach, Ian sideswiped him and grabbed the brute's outstretched arm. With a flip, Ian landed on the guy's back. Gasps came from the crowd.

Ian wrapped his arms around Stellan's neck and squeezed a balled fist against his carotid artery, pushing his forehead against the back of the brute's neck for leverage.

Enraged, Stellan twisted every which way, trying to loosen Ian while clawing at his arms wrapped around his throat. Stellan changed his tactic and managed to land blows with a fist that split open Ian's cheek, but he held on as tight as ever. Stellan reached high enough with his other hand that he got a solid grip on Ian's shoulder while staggering from loss of blood flow.

Ian hung on, but Stellan dug his fingers into Ian's shoulder blade and pulled him off his back, tossing him away. Ian moaned when he landed hard against the ground. The brute dropped to one knee, choking.

Ian slowly got to his feet. The guy had dislocated his shoulder, and his arm hung limp at his side. He sucked air into his lungs and fought to erase the pain from his face.

Nguyen glanced between Ian and his limp arm and from the look on his face, the guy knew what'd happened.

He faced the recovering Stellan and stuck the hand of his injured arm into his belt to stabilize his arm. Then he rushed Stellan. He sprinted off the ball of his foot, went airborne, and wrapped his legs around Stellan's neck before the brute could stand. A twist of his body, and Ian brought the guy to the ground, face first. He sat on Stellan's shoulder blades and brought his elbow down on the back of Stellan's head like a hammer.

Dust mixed with spittle burst across the ground and Stellan went limp. Ian cradled his injured arm, and with one last check that Stellan was down for good, he slipped off and collapsed onto the ground.

Stunned, the crowd stood with gaping mouths. His fellow prisoners threw their arms up and yelled, running toward Ian. Nguyen supported Ian's injured shoulder while one of the twins grabbed him from under the other arm. Together they helped him to his feet.

Deek raised Ian's good arm and shouted in triumph. "Winner!" He slapped Ian's back and grabbed him behind his neck, shaking him. "I knew you were a good bet!"

Horace approached and looked at the prisoners, then rested his gaze on Ian. From his expression, Ian wasn't sure the man would uphold the deal. After an eternity of scrutiny, Horace patted the backs of those closest. "You are all one with Stag," he said, then turned and addressed the crowd. "They are now of us!"

Cheers and whistles rose from the crowd. Ian caught more than a few jeers. He looked around. "Where's Proctor?"

"A couple of men grabbed him when you started the fight." Nguyen bent Ian's arm up and pressed it against his chest. "Hold it here until I can repair it for you."

Ian chuckled. "Should I call you Doc?"

"I've been many things," Nguyen said under his breath.

"You can take him to the infirmary." Horace signaled to a man with one arm. "Show them where."

"Is Stellan okay?" Ian asked.

Horace laughed. "He'll be fine. But you made sure of it, didn't you?"

"I don't know what you mean," Ian said as they half walked, half dragged him to the infirmary.

Nguyen pulled a wooden chair next to a support beam and indicated for Ian to sit. "Grab the beam with your other arm and hang on. This is going to hurt."

Ian did as he was told. One of the twins leaned against Ian's arm wrapped around the pole and placed a gentle hand on Ian's good shoulder. "I fell out of a tree once. Our town doc had to do this to me, too," Dunn said.

"Yeah, but he cried like a baby," Deek said.

Dunn stuck out his lip. "Momma said it was okay, that everybody cries when it hurts a lot."

Nguyen pressed the tips of his fingers around Ian's injured shoulder, then he cupped Ian's limp arm in both hands.

"It takes a second, but you'll be sore for a while." Deek gave Ian a thumbs-up.

Nguyen planted his foot against the leg of the chair and counted. "One, two." He pulled hard on Ian's arm.

Thousands of searing needles ripped through Ian's shoulder and down his forearm, ending in blazing fireworks at his fingertips. His skin turned clammy, and he became lightheaded to the point of passing out. He leaned his forehead against the pole, and focused on his heartbeat to ease the shock. "What happened to three?" he mumbled.

"I never was good at math." Nguyen grinned. He bent Ian's arm at his elbow and slipped it into the torn opening in the front of his shirt. It held Ian's arm like a sling. Dunn helped Ian to a nearby cot. Nguyen wrapped Ian's shoulder using strips of torn cloth from a nearby basket.

Proctor lay on the cot next to Ian's. A man threaded a needle through the gash on Proctor's face and from his expression, he hadn't been given anything to numb the area. "Thanks for saving our butts," Proctor mumbled, unable to open his swollen eyes. His face was already turning into a kaleidoscope of bruises.

"No sweat," Ian said and laid his head on the cot. "We've got to stick together."

"From what I can tell, it's every man for himself around here," Proctor said. "But thanks for adopting our measly crew."

Ian lay there, mulling over what Proctor said. There were rules in Stag, and a sense of community. The order of things appeared to be based on survival. It might be harsh, but so, too, were their conditions. Ian closed his eyes and welcomed the rest. He drifted off with the hope that his mother and Rayne were safe wherever they were.

Ian's skin prickled at the back of his neck and he opened his eyes. A thin film of moonlight found its way through the window at Ian's head and lit up the foot of his bed. Apart from that, the infirmary was pitched in darkness. The room was filled with snoring, with a few groans and moans mixed in.

A dark shadow moved to Ian's left. At first he thought that Proctor had sat up in his bed, but the figure leaned over

Ian. The odor of cigars stirred Ian's senses. He sat up and gripped his injured arm to keep it against his chest. "What are you doing here?"

Marcus grunted and leaned back in the chair beside his cot. "I've been waiting for you to open your peepers to ask you the same thing." The old Pur general gave Ian a wide smile.

The man who'd protected Ian since he was ten years old was a welcomed sight. The last time Ian had seen the old Pur general, the Primary's Elite guards were arresting him for helping Ian uncover the truth about the Primary.

Ian returned an even wider smile. "I thought I'd never see you again!"

"It took a world away, and half a continent, but it's good to see you, my boy." Marcus patted Ian's hand. "You feel up to answering a volcano-full of questions?"

Marcus had so easily fallen back into his Texas drawl. "No one knows who I am," he said for the old general's ears. "I told them my name was Galen."

He nodded. "Good, but from the way you fought Stellan, some will suspect that you've had training, Horace among them." Marcus grinned. "Yeah, I watched from the back of the crowd. Damn proud of ya boy. Made all that training worthwhile, didn't it?"

Ian swung his legs around and faced Marcus. "How long have you been here?"

"Time fuses into sweltering day after day around here, but it's got to have been a week or more."

"You fought your way in, too." In spite of the scant light, Ian's keen night vision had caught a scab along the general's cheek and a split lip that looked like it wasn't healing.

"I can still hold my own against them young'uns," Marcus said. "But like you, I fought for more than myself."

"Who did you defend?" Ian asked.

"Vael," the old general said on choked words. "They would have sent him out to the barrens for sure. No way could he defend himself."

When Ian had seen Vael last, the Elite guard had followed Ian and Marcus as they tracked down the rebels, Vael among them. The Elite guard had opened fire on the bridge of their ship and Vael lay dying in a bloody pool.

He grabbed Marcus's arm. "Vael survived? No one would tell us anything."

"Dr. Mac stitched him up." Hatred clouded Marcus's features. "What the Primary did to him afterward, that I will never forgive."

Ian's shoulders sagged. The reason for the missing body parts became so clear. "He maimed Vael," Ian said.

"I'll take you to him," Marcus said. "But he's not the boy you knew. Not any longer." Marcus dropped his face into his hands and his shoulders shook, unleashing the horrors the only way he could.

TWENTY-EIGHT

Once Marcus composed himself, he wrapped an arm around Ian's back and led him to the opposite end of the infirmary. The gesture felt paternal, not like before, when Ian had been under the general's protection for more than a decade.

Vael lay asleep on a cot, covered to mid-chest with a blanket. The boy's hands had been cut off. Ian stared at him in shock.

"His power was in his hands," Marcus said. "The Primary let him live, but on one condition."

Vael's eyelids fluttered. "Dad?"

Marcus sat on the edge of the cot and stroked his son's hair. "I'm here, Vael. Ian is with us."

He opened his eyes. "Is Jaered here?"

"He's still on Earth," Ian said, unable to keep the emotion out of his voice. "I'm here to help."

Vael lifted his arms. "You're too late." He rolled onto his side. "No one can help me now."

"We can make the bastard pay," Marcus said in a voice edged in steel.

"You can't kill someone who's immortal," Vael said.

"We're going to try," Ian put a reassuring hand on Vael's leg. "The three Heirs."

Marcus got to his feet. "What are you talking about?"

"I've learned a lot since the Pur guard arrested you," Ian said. "Let's find a place where we can talk."

"No," Vael said and rolled back to stare up at Ian. "Don't shut me out, not now."

Ian and Marcus hunched over Vael. He started at the beginning, when the Weir were first created on Thrae . . .

It took most of the night for Ian to fill them in on what he knew and to answer their barrage of questions. The longer he spoke, the more strength returned to Vael's eyes and at one point, he sat up to absorb the rest. Being told the truth about the Pur, Duach and the brothers that commanded two planets, was enlightening enough. To find out there were three Heirs born of the Ancients brought life back into the father and son.

"So what's become of Rayne?" Marcus said in the dim light of dawn.

"You haven't seen her?" Ian asked. "They would have arrived soon after you did."

"I was occupied with Vael and trying to prove my worth to Stag." He rubbed his face.

"If two women had arrived, we would have heard about it," Vael said. "No way could they have quenched that rumor."

"I need to find them before Aeros does." Footsteps came from behind. Ian glanced over his shoulder. Nguyen leaned over Proctor, as if examining him. "No one can know who I am," Ian hushed. "Refer to me as Galen." Vael and Marcus nodded.

Ian approached Nguyen. "Glad to see you up," Nguyen said.

"I'm surprised you're here so early," Ian regarded Proctor. The swelling in his face had lessened, but the bruises were uglier than ever.

"At least the wounded get a cot." Nguyen straightened up and flexed his shoulder. "The twins and I were given a dirt floor for the night." He jerked his chin at Ian's shoulder. "Let me take a look."

Ian sat on his cot and Nguyen poked his fingers around his shoulder through the bandages. "Good, it didn't slip back out. Don't do any lifting with that arm for at least a week."

The boost back at Ian's estate would have helped to heal him much faster. But that wasn't an option, even if he had been on Earth. The Pur guard would be watching the mansion, ready to arrest anyone setting foot, or shyfting, onto the property.

He had never felt more human, or appreciated their struggles more, than since arriving on Thrae.

"Is he going to be okay?" Ian asked, jerking his chin at Proctor.

"I'm guessing he has an occipital bone fracture, but without the benefit of an X-ray machine, I can't be sure. In time, he'll be up and about." Nguyen put a hand on Ian's good shoulder. "If you feel up to it, let's go for a walk."

They stepped outside. The first rays of sunlight found nooks and crannies between buildings, and already brought with them the morning heat. They walked to the end of the row of houses and Nguyen turned down another street that led to a path behind the shoddy buildings. He stopped at a garden that stretched from the back of the town to the base of the dome. The cornstalks that Ian had seen when first arriving rose high above the other plants but were wilted, and many had leaves the color of butter. He wandered between the rows of squash, broccoli, and melons that were meager at best.

"I know who you are," Nguyen said.

Ian turned. The man didn't appear hostile, but he'd led Ian to a remote plot, away from the awakening township. There were no breezes where air did not circulate by the forces of nature. From across the field came the distinct, muted buzz of bees.

Nguyen crouched and removed dead undergrowth from a zucchini plant. "I was a scientist at QualSton," he said. "I saw you with Dr. Orr there a few months ago. He and I both worked in the genetics lab. I was there when the Pur guard attacked us."

During Ian's visit to the research facility, he had discovered Duach working there, Rayne's father among them. "Yesterday, you claimed you were a Pur," Ian said.

"I am. I tried to prevent them from taking my lab assistant. The Pur guard shined some kind of light into her eyes, then arrested her. They said she was a Duach. All those years I worked with her, I never knew of her heritage." He sighed. "I didn't care. She was an asset to the lab, excellent at her job. A lovely woman."

"And you ended up here just because you defended her?" Ian couldn't imagine such an atrocity.

"I was spared, at first. Then a couple of months later, the guard came to my house. They arrested me and dragged me out, right in front of my wife and children. I was tried as a conspirator, fighting with the rebels." Nguyen stood, but held onto his collection of dead leaves so tight, a few crumbled beneath his fist. He glanced about. "They weren't mistaken. I did collude with the rebels," he confessed. "Ever since they took my assistant."

"Why are you telling me this?" Ian asked. "You could have just kept it to yourself."

"That was General Marcus of the North American Pur forces that you were talking with in the infirmary, wasn't it? He had made a few visits to QualSton over the years." Nguyen leaned close and lowered his voice. "If the two of you find a way to help these people, and those back on Earth, I want to be a part of it."

Ian met his stare. "What makes you think I can make a difference?"

Nguyen lifted the edge of Ian's torn shirt with the tip of his finger, revealing the Heir's Seal on his chest. "I noticed this when I helped carry you to the infirmary." He held out his hand. "It's an honor to meet you, Pur Heir."

TWENTY-NINE

Patrick's pacing grated on Jaered's nerves and fueled his temper. The rap on the door came at the same moment Jaered had made up his mind to tie him to a chair. Patrick stopped in his tracks and Jaered peeked out the front window, then opened the door.

Wyatt, Eve's second in command of the rebel forces, stood on the stoop, dressed in battle gear. His towering presence cast Jaered in shadow. The men flanking him, carried the kind of illegal weapons found in a drug cartel. Wyatt greeted Jaered with a reverent nod.

Jaered admitted them and closed the door. Patrick hung back, and to Jaered's relief, didn't resume his pacing. "Thanks for volunteering," Jaered said.

"If we can infiltrate that hideout, it'll be a coup for us." Wyatt regarded Patrick with a discerning glance. "Who's the squint?"

"The Duach Heir," Jaered said.

Wyatt's lips parted and he dropped to one knee, bowing his head. The group of men followed suit. "We are at your service, your Majesties."

Patrick looked at Jaered with utter confusion.

"Wyatt, get up," Jaered said. "We don't have time for tributes."

He and the men stood. The creases in Wyatt's face hardened. "What's the plan?"

Jaered held up the tracker. "It looks like we're going to Belgium."

Wyatt raised an eyebrow. "That makes sense."

"What does?" Patrick said.

"The Primary is CEO of a bank there," Jaered said. "The same address where they took Tara."

"Was that the bank job you and Vael pulled last year?" Patrick said.

"How'd you know about that?" When Patrick postured to answer, Jaered held up his hand. "Forget it." He grabbed his handguns and stuck them in the holsters at his side. Then he donned a dark leather jacket he'd found in the safe house closet, concealing the weapons underneath. "Ready to take us?" he asked Patrick.

"I can't shyft this many," he said under his breath.

"The safe house is directly over a vortex," Wyatt said. The men grabbed each other's shoulders, and Wyatt placed his gloved hand on Jaered's back.

Jaered grabbed Patrick's arm and tilted the tracker to him. "This is the address."

"We'll be seen," Patrick said.

"It's the middle of the night," Jaered said. "Hold the address in memory and at the same time, imagine a rooftop."

"Both?" Patrick said. "I can barely master one."

"Concentrate!" Jaered cautioned himself not to lose his temper. "First commit the address, then imagine the rooftop." Patrick closed his eyes and inhaled deep, then held his breath with his chest puffed out. Jaered had no idea if it was to brace himself against the effects of shyfting, or from nervous tension. A full second later, Jaered felt the power surging upward from the vortex below their feet. "More," he urged. Patrick's increased power leaked into Jaered's core and together, they shyfted everyone.

They appeared standing on a rooftop. Patrick looked around at the same time his mouth fell open, but Jaered clamped his hand over it. The last thing they needed was a victorious holler.

"Keep your head! Remember why we're here," Jaered hissed. Patrick nodded and he let go.

"Orders?" Wyatt said.

Jaered pulled out the tracker and studied it. "It looks like they're five stories below us."

One of the rebels leaned over the parapet, then held up three fingers. The secret holding cells were two floors underground.

"I can shyft us inside," Jaered said. "We'll figure out how and where to go from there." Everyone pushed their backs against each other, facing outward. Jaered shyfted them to the lobby, drawing more electromagnetic energy than necessary to disable any cameras or security systems.

A guard enjoying a sandwich at the center counter looked up in alarm. He reached for the gun at his hip. One of the rebels shot him in the neck with a tranquilizer dart, and the man dropped to the marble floor. Another rebel dragged him around, then deposited him behind a desk. One of them packed up his lunch, including the half-eaten sandwich, and tossed it in a trash can.

"How long ago were you here?" Patrick whispered.

"A little over a year ago." Jaered signaled for Wyatt and Patrick to go to the elevators. He indicated for the other four to split up, two-by-two and head to the staircases. They disappeared down opposite hallways. Wyatt and Patrick followed Jaered to the elevator, but he held his fist up when he noticed the brass hand above the elevator moving toward the number one. *Ding.* Everyone scrambled and ducked down, out of sight.

The doors opened and a sixty-something woman, dressed in a tailored suit stepped out. She was accompanied by a man wearing a business suit. Jaered froze. It was the Primary.

"Thank you for working late, Annabeth," the Primary said. "But you will fill me with guilt if you work any later. He paused and glanced around the lobby as if noticing something out of place.

Jaered and Wyatt exchanged glances. They hadn't considered anyone other than guards at the bank this late.

"My pleasure," she gushed. "You know you can ask whenever it's needed."

He put a hand on her back. "Let me escort you to your car. It's late."

"It's really not necessary," Annabeth said.

"I insist," he said. They exited through the front doors. The Primary turned and locked them behind him.

Jaered released his breath in a steady stream, then signaled for them to continue.

Wyatt pressed the button while Jaered kept lookout. The doors swished open and they entered. Jared pressed the close-door button with the side of his fist. They stared at the console. According to the buttons, there wasn't a lower floor.

"It takes a key," Patrick said and ran his finger over the keyhole. "I bet that's the way down."

Wyatt pulled out a small case and opened it. He removed a couple of picks and knelt in front of it. He inserted them and began twitching them around. Jaered pressed an ear to the slit between the closed elevator doors, listening for anything amiss.

A couple of minutes passed. "Can you do it or not," Jaered hissed.

"You haven't gained any more patience since the last time we worked together," Wyatt muttered.

Patrick leaned his ear against the elevator door. "If he returns, we're all dead."

"Aren't you a bundle of optimism," Wyatt said. A loud *click*, and the elevator jolted, then descended. He returned his tools to his pocket with a grin.

"About time." Jaered pushed away from the doors. The elevator creaked and shimmied, but kept moving. "I doubt the others will find a way here," he said.

With a grunt, Wyatt swung his gun around and held it at the ready. Jaered removed one of his from inside his jacket and took up position to one side of the doors. Patrick eyed the gun. Jaered paused, then removed the other one and handed it to him.

"You know how to use it?" he asked.

Patrick nodded. "Ian taught me."

"Don't pull the trigger unless you're sure of what you're shooting," Wyatt said.

"Got it." Patrick looked the gun over. When he flipped off the safety, Jaered wasn't sure if that was a positive sign, or not.

"Get back," Jaered said and Patrick pressed his back against the console.

The grinding creaks came to a halt and the elevator stopped with a jolt. Silence. The doors swished open, revealing a dirt hallway beyond. A dim overhead lamp hung from the ceiling midway. There appeared to be wooden slatted doors on one side of the tunnel, every few feet apart.

Wyatt stepped out and swung the tip of his gun back and forth. Jaered slipped out and took a few steps ahead, then motioned for them to follow. The energy in his core fizzled and he pressed a fist against his chest. The Primary used a jam to stifle Sar's core energy. There'd be no shyfting out of here.

"No tunnels, no exits," Wyatt whispered as he wandered down the hall. The elevator appeared to be the only way in, or out.

The fact there wasn't a guard down here gave Jaered pause. Did the Primary keep his special prisoners to himself?

A desk sat off to one side, across the hall from what appeared to be cell doors. Jaered froze and lifted his fist. Wyatt stopped Patrick from taking another step.

The tracking device that Jaered had slipped into Tara's pocket sat on the desk.

Hands grabbed the bars in the second cell's door. "Who's there?" It was Tara.

Patrick rushed down the hallway and stuck his face in the cell window. "We're here to get you and the others."

"Patrick, it's a trap! Get out while you can!" Tara yelled.

"Go!" Dr. Willoughsby shouted from next door. "Save yourselves!"

"We're not deserting you." Patrick stared at Jaered like a dare.

"We can't help them if we're prisoners, too," Wyatt muttered.

The elevator doors closed and with a whining grind and a *creak*, the elevator ascended.

Jaered rushed over to the closest cell and peered inside. Joule Willoughsby lay on the stone floor, unmoving. Jaered used the butt of his gun like a hammer and struck the rusted iron padlock until the door swung open. He hurried over and when she didn't arouse, he checked her pulse. It was weak, but steady.

When he emerged from Joule's cell, he gestured and Wyatt pushed Patrick to the side and struck the padlock at Tara's cell. Patrick ran over to Dr. Willoughsby's lock but after a few whacks had no luck getting it to open. He stepped back and pointed the gun at it.

"Wait!" Jaered shouted. Patrick lowered the gun. Wyatt took over and with a tremendous *smack*, the lock broke open.

"There's someone else." Tara pointed to the farthest cell, beyond Dr. Willoughsby's. "I heard moans.

Wyatt broke open the last cell door and disappeared inside. Jaered waved at the others. "In here." They filed into Joule's cell, one after another. Wyatt set the unconscious prisoner down on the ground next to Joule.

"Oh my god, Dr. Mac!" Tara gasped. She pressed her hands to either side of his face. "Dr. Mac, can you hear me?"

He groaned and his eyes fluttered open. "Tara?" he rasped.

"We should be dropped by the Curse," Patrick said. "Why aren't we?"

"Whatever jam the Primary is using, it's powerful," Wyatt said.

"Go to the back wall and get down." By the time Jaered returned to the hallway, Wyatt had tilted the desk over and crouched down behind it.

Tara snatched the gun out of Patrick's hand. When he went to protest, she put a finger to his lips. "I'm the better shot," she said, then gave him a peck on his lips and closed the door. "Keep them safe," she said between the bars.

"How am I supposed to learn anything if you keep me out of it!" Patrick shouted from the rear of the cell.

"Love you, too!" she shouted.

Creaking and grinding gears. The elevator descended. Jaered pushed his shoulder against the wall across from the desk and planted his feet. He held his gun at the ready while counting off the seconds they had left before the doors would open. Tara crouched down beside Wyatt.

The noises came to a grinding halt and a heartbeat later, the elevator doors swished open.

THIRTY

Jaered gazed past the opening doors and his stomach lurched. Bile rose in his throat. The rest of their team's bodies lay in a heap on the floor of the elevator. When nothing stirred from inside, he signaled for Wyatt and Tara to stay put and crept toward the elevator with his gun thrust ahead of him. *Ding*. The doors moved to close. Jared stuck his foot out and stopped them. They retracted.

Other than their murdered comrades, the elevator was empty. He reached around and hit the button to keep the doors open.

"Goddamn it!" Wyatt stepped up next to him. "They were good soldiers, every one of them."

"Don't move." Jaered had caught a muted, soft *click*. "Take cover!" He dove behind the desk next to Tara and Wyatt landed on top of them.

With a deafening roar, the desk was uprooted and everyone was thrown against the wall. At the same time, searing heat burned Jaered's face as a fireball blasted its way down the hall. Body parts scattered, sticking to walls and the upturned desk.

Smoke bled into the hallway and then lifted toward the ceiling. Wyatt rolled off and Jaered turned onto his back, coughing. Wyatt pressed his hand against his side. Blood leaked between his fingers. Tara grabbed the back of her neck. When she lifted her face, a sizeable wooden sliver stuck out of her cheek. She caught Jaered staring at it and she patted her face, touched it, then pulled it out. Frantic, she scrambled over Jaered and ran into the cell.

The ringing in Jaered's head made it difficult to decipher what was being said, but he thought he heard her yelling, "Is everyone okay?"

He scooted over to Wyatt. "Let me see," came out muffled and barely coherent.

Wyatt groped for his bag. Jaered grabbed it and tore it open to find a med kit inside. He ripped Wyatt's shirt to get a better look, then found the aerosol. "Ready?" he thought he said, but unable to hear himself, he wasn't sure. Wyatt nodded. Jaered stuck the tip inside the gash and pressed the nozzle.

"Ahhh, that crap sucks!" he screamed loud enough to be heard on the streets above.

The wound filled with the aerosol gum and it soon stopped seeping. Jaered looked over his shoulder. "Are they okay?" he shouted loud enough to hear himself.

Tara held up two thumbs.

Wyatt grabbed Jaered's shirt and got in his face. "You're bleeding from your ears!" he yelled.

Jaered touched the side of his head and his fingers came back bloody. He squeezed the bridge of his nose and pressed his hands against his ears. Everything sounded like he was underwater. The blast had torn both eardrums.

Tara appeared in the doorway but stopped short when Jaered motioned for her to stay put. He got to his feet and surveyed the damage to the elevator. It was toast. Nothing but a mangled steel box. What was left of the bodies had been smashed against the walls of the elevator like bloody tissue paper and at the center, a charred blast site. He grabbed the dangling end of a steel beam and leaned in, peering up the elevator shaft, but only darkness stared back. The elevator cables had snapped.

He backed up in a daze at how to get them out. Tara touched his elbow and he startled. "What do you think?" she yelled.

Jaered shrugged. "It doesn't look promising." He found Dr. Mac examining Joule while Dr. Willoughsby cradled her in his arms. "Did the Primary interrogate you?"

"No," Dr. Willoughsby said too softly to be heard, but Jaered could read his lips.

Tara turned Jaered around and spoke, enunciating carefully. "When they shyfted us here, they found my bug right away, then stuck us in cells and left. They were waiting for you to come."

"They couldn't have shyfted you here," Patrick said. He pointed to the floor. "You mean upstairs, then brought you down."

"No." She shook her head. "We reappeared right here, in the hallway."

"One of the guards got a text and walked down there." Dr. Mac pointed toward the shadows at the end of the hall. "I was too short to look out the cell opening and could only hear what was happening. But moments later, they all shyfted here," he shouted. "There's got to be a jam switch of some kind."

Jaered's pulse quickened. "Look for some kind of control box!"

Tara, Jaered, and Patrick split up and combed the hallway, checking out every crack and indent in the surface of the wall for a lever or spring. When the hallway didn't yield anything promising, they searched the cells, but after nearly an hour, the group came up empty-handed.

Dr. Mac finished stitching Wyatt and wound gauze around his abdomen. He tied it off, then removed his bloody gloves and tossed them to the side. Dr. Willoughsby packed the unused supplies back in the satchel.

"Is there something for a headache in there? Dr. Mac pulled out his penlight and flashed it in Jaered's eyes.

"You probably have a concussion," Dr. Mac announced loud enough to be heard.

"I just need goddamn aspirin," Jaered snapped.

The old doctor rummaged through the satchel and handed Jaered some small white pills. He popped them in his mouth and swallowed them dry in spite of the lingering charred taste from the smoke. "How is Joule?" he asked.

Dr. Mac faced Jaered. "I think they drugged her, but I can't know for sure unless I run some tests, or she wakes up, whichever comes first."

"Maybe they controlled the jam from above," Patrick said, then peered up the elevator shaft.

Dr. Mac said something, but his back was to Jaered and it came out muffled. He turned the doctor around. "What did you say?"

"I know it's there somewhere," Dr. Mac said, pointing at the far end of the hall.

"Patrick and Tara, let's check again. The rest of you, be ready to shyft at a second's notice," Jaered said. "If we can turn off the jam, we might be able to escape, but they—"

"Can shyft in to grab us before we can all get away," Tara said.

"Shouldn't I stay at this end and help shyft them?" Patrick asked.

Dr. Mac growled. "I'm a Pur Sar! You aren't getting anywhere near me, lad!"

Patrick gave Dr. Mac a soulful look. Once the jam was off, they couldn't be near each other without suffering the Curse. Jaered saw Patrick weather yet another loss of someone close to him. No wonder he clung to Tara.

"Keep a hand on each other," Jaered told them. "If we find something, I'll get to you and take you to a safe place." Dr. Willoughsby gathered his daughter in his arms and they huddled together.

Jaered, Tara, and Patrick left the others and returned to the end of the hall, but the dim light didn't extend far enough and it was cast in deep shadow. He went high, Tara dropped to her knee and Patrick took the adjacent wall. They worked every inch of the wall with their fingers, feeling for anything out of the ordinary.

A small square felt softer than the rest of the wall. "I've got something," Jaered announced. He scraped at it and peeled back an edge of camouflaged cloth, exposing a button the size of a quarter. He went to press it, but hesitated. "Get ready!" he shouted loud enough for the others near the elevator, then pressed. His core surged, absorbing the tremendous energy. The bank was built on a powerful vortex. The others felt it, too. Jaered heard their hollers from the other end of the hall.

Patrick stumbled back and pressed a fist to his chest.

"Patrick, shyft Tara to the auditorium," Jaered said just as an emerald glow came from midway down the hall. "Go!" Jaered turned down the hall at a full dash, but a group of Pur guards were about to solidify. At the exact moment he would have collided with them, he shyfted the rest of the way, stretched out his arms, gathered the others and shyfted.

THIRTY-ONE

Stellan approached Ian the second he and Nguyen reached the main street. A wide strip of tape stretched across the brute's nose and a swollen bulge came from the side of his jaw. He glared at Ian. "Horace wants a word."

"No shock there," Nguyen said. "You got noticed." The scientist waved to Deek and Dunn across the street and wandered toward them.

Ian followed Stellan to the pavilion. Horace sat behind his desk, tapping a pencil against his tall cup. From the look of it, he was drinking iced tea. Ian wondered what other perks the mayor of Stag enjoyed.

"That was some show you put on yesterday," Horace said at Ian's approach. "You've had training."

"I was in the Pur army for a while." Ian sat on a stool under the open tent and marveled at how the air cooled ten degrees or more once he was out of the sun.

"That's how you know the debunked general," Horace said. He scrutinized Ian. "I was wondering what you and he had to talk about all night."

The man's spies were vast, Ian thought. "I was under his command for a while. I'd met his son just once."

"Yeah, that punishment was pretty harsh. Makes you wonder who the Primary was more furious with, the son, or the general." Horace dropped the pencil and rested his elbows on his legs, then smiled, revealing well-tended teeth. "What's your story?" Ian asked.

"Me? I'm an entrepreneur," Horace said. "I sold minutiae to the wrong side and ended up here." He spread his arms wide. "I need someone like you. You're not like the usual batch. They arrive maimed or broken. You, you're young, brash, and got skills."

"And not missing body parts." Ian regarded Stellan. "At least, not yet." The brute gave him a sly grin.

Horace leaned back in his desk chair and swiveled. "I can make life pretty comfy for those with higher rank."

Ian jerked his chin at Stellan. "He doesn't look so comfy."

The man's chuckle was drowned out by Stellan's growl. "He doesn't have your skills, or your brains." Stellan frowned at Horace.

"I'm sensing a *but* in here somewhere," Ian said.

"See, you do have brains." Horace grabbed Ian's knee in a vice grip. "To gain my utmost trust, I would need access to your transportation."

"You wouldn't believe me if I told you," he said.

Horace's amused expression turned sour. "Try me." His grip tightened.

"I flew here," Ian said.

Horace threw back, laughing. "You're a find, I have to admit."

"No lie," Ian said. "I climbed a mountain looking for a fresh water source, and some gigantic bird grabbed me."

Stellan stepped closer. "A giant eagle got you?" He looked impressed.

"We've lost a few to those buggers." Horace peered at him. "It would have ripped you to shreds. How the hell did you get away?"

Ian withdrew the knife from his leg sheath and held it up.

Horace's shock was fleeting. "You didn't frisk him, did you Stellan?" Silence hovered thick in the air. The brute knew when to stay quiet.

"I could have used this on him in the fight, but I didn't," Ian said. He turned it around and rammed the tip into the desktop deep enough that it remained upright. "Check it, if you want. It probably has traces of the bird's blood on it." He crossed his arms. "The bird dropped me, not too gently, I might add. But I could see the dome on the horizon and headed for it."

"You claimed you were here for Mother," Horace said.

"I am searching for her," Ian replied. "I started my quest at the Northern Colony."

Horace stiffened, but his lips parted. "You know where there are others?"

They were all from Earth, Ian realized. The Primary had brought them directly here. All they knew were the barrens as far as they could see. The prison was much more effective when the prisoners were fed ignorance. "I followed Mother's map," Ian said. "It was in my pack."

Horace closed his eyes and clenched his jaw. "Stellan." Muscles ebbed in the man's neck. "You found a map and didn't bring it to me?"

Stellan looked between Ian and Horace like he was caught with his hand in the till. "I . . . I . . ." he stammered.

"Get it!" he roared. Stellan rushed off.

Horace turned a keen eye to Ian and didn't speak for several minutes as though stewing in his own thoughts. Stellan returned with the folded map in his hand. Horace snatched it and unfolded it, then peered at Ian over the top edge. "You took a river?"

"It was underground," Ian said. "And had some gnarly piranhas with a nasty bite." Ian showed Horace the blemishes on his hand, then lowered the edge of the map so he, too, could see and pointed to the valley. "I healed up here, then made it the rest of the way, with a lot of help from the eagle."

Horace stared at the map. "How many days?"

"Thanks to my run-in with the piranha, I was unconscious for part of the boat ride, but it had to be close to five or six," Ian said. "Granted, some of that was by air."

Horace stood and peered across the pavilion while his fingers twitched at his side. What Ian would have given for

Tara and Saxon to be there, so he could channel and be privy to the man's thoughts.

The plaintiff from a couple of days ago strolled by while stroking the yarn hair on a rag doll. Roxy had returned, Ian mused. One of its button eyes was gone. Everywhere Ian looked, the faces were all the same. Distant—vacant—lost. "If the Acumen weeds out the strongest and most capable of men," Ian said. "Why are there so many of the maimed and broken in Stag?"

Horace gave Ian a sideways glance. "We survive whatever way we can here," he said. "I'm not proud of how."

"What happens to them?" Ian stood. "Eventually."

"The Primary brings us here, for a reason," Horace said. "For his brother."

Ian's pulse quickened. "What does Aeros have to do with the colony of Stag?"

"The sick bastard enjoys the hunt," Horace said.

Ian's chest rose and fell with rapid breaths. "How often?" He grabbed the man's shoulder. "Horace, when does he come?"

"Every few weeks." He pulled away from Ian's grip and leaned against the edge of his desk. "Why does it matter?"

"Aeros is on Thrae," Ian said. "I hid from him, on my way here."

A deep sigh came from Horace. "Then he will be here, soon enough."

Would Aeros's wrath extend to the engineers of Stag like in the Northern Colony? "I need to see your control room," Ian said.

Alarm brought Horace to within an inch of Ian's face, and he gave a subtle shake of his head.

"What's he talking about?" Stellan said.

"He's confused," Horace snapped.

The brute crossed his arms and stood his ground. "I don't think so. He's the one with brains, right?"

Horace grabbed Ian's arm and led him out of earshot. "How the hell do you know about the control room," he hissed.

"I saw them in the Northern Colony. I know they power and control the domes."

"Why should I reveal them to you?" Horace said. "No one but me and the technicians know about them."

"Does Aeros?" Ian asked.

Horace didn't respond, but his expression gave Ian his answer. "You need to warn them that Aeros is coming."

Horace bit his lower lip enough to draw blood. "Stellan, stay here," Horace said. "Make sure we're not followed." He took Ian by the elbow and led him across the pavilion, then entered the building facing his desk. It was a simple dwelling, but unlike the cots in the infirmary, Horace's had padding and a plump pillow. A cast iron kettle sat on a hearth on a corner fireplace. He closed the door once Ian stepped inside, then shut the thick curtains, casting the room in deep shadows. "Aeros never attacks the technicians," Horace said. "They are off-limits and never threatened."

"The Northern Colony thought they were safe, too," Ian said.

He stood stock-still. "No one can know what I'm about to show you," he said. Ian nodded. Horace approached the far wall and stuck his hands behind a tall, wooden cabinet holding books and dishes. With a jerk, the cabinet swung wide, revealing a landing beyond. He ushered Ian inside and pulled a tether, swinging the cabinet back into place.

"Why are you trusting me?" Ian asked.

"If Aeros is after you, he must have reason to fear you. That's a plus in my book," Horace said. "And if your claims of evading him are true, then I want you on our side."

Horace flipped a switch. Small lights lit the edge of the spiraling stairs, lighting their way and the two men followed a narrow, wrought iron staircase. It ended at a lower level with white wooden walls and aluminum fixtures. Horace approached a door and pulled out a set of keys, searched through them until he found the one he needed, and unlocked the door.

They stepped into a modern, antiseptic room. Three rows of consoles, two men seated at each one, filled the center of the room. The engineers faced a far wall that held a large monitor where lights blinked on and off a map of the town and its domed borders. To one side, five monitors depicted a shot of Stellan standing in the pavilion, the entrance to the dome, the infirmary, a well with men pulling buckets of water up, and the garden.

"Red's coming," one of the engineers announced.

A crimson patch hovered at the north edge of the main screen and creeped closer toward the map of the town.

"How long?" Horace said.

"Fifteen, maybe twenty minutes," the engineer said. "But systems are good."

"The methane cloud?" Ian said. Horace nodded. Ian marveled at Stag's control room and its contrast to the living conditions above ground. The engineers looked healthy and well nourished. There wasn't a speck of dust from what he could tell.

"This is the heartbeat of our existence," Horace said.

Catherine had referred to the Northern Colony's control room in the same way. "They get first rations," Ian said.

Horace stuck his keys in his pants pocket. "If they go, we won't be far behind. Everyone in Stag is my responsibility," he said, then his voice took on a sharp edge. "What aren't you telling me?"

"What do you mean?" Ian asked.

"You didn't get here like the rest of us." Horace turned on Ian. "No one travels the barrens, we don't dare, yet you know more than most beyond our dome. Why are you really here?"

"I'm trying to find Mother, and her traveling companion," Ian said. "Her name is Rayne and Mother is protecting her from Aeros. She ended up on Thrae by accident and I need to get her back to Earth before he finds us."

Horace leaned his hands against the railing that separated the entrance area from the main floor and consoles a few steps below. "If they got this far, they didn't seek refuge." He regarded the monitor. "We'd have seen them."

Ian studied the screens. Could they have gained entrance without anyone knowing?

A bright flash obscured one of the screens. When it faded, Aeros stood staring into the camera. His face drew into a wicked grin, then he stepped out of view.

"Sir," one of the engineers said.

"Keep your positions and stay alert." Horace made to leave, but hesitated and turned back to the room. "Arm yourselves," he said.

"But," one of the engineers said.

"Just do it!" Horace shouted. "Barricade the door once we leave. Don't open it for anyone but me."

Ian left with Horace close behind. The second he shut the door, he glared at Ian. "It looks like he found you."

"Where was Aeros when he shyfted here?" Ian said.

Horace regarded him. "Near the garden, why?"

"If Aeros and the Primary can shyft here, there must be a vortex," Ian said, remembering the storage room at the Northern Colony.

"There isn't," Horace said. "Trust me, I would have found it by now."

"Where's the energy source for your dome?" Ian asked.

"No one knows," Horace said. "The instruments and dome were in place long before any of us arrived here."

"There's got to be a vortex, and a powerful energy source for the dome. But both would have to be located far enough from the controls not to interfere with them."

"You think the vortex and the energy source are one in the same?" Horace said.

"That much energy could easily mask the existence of a vortex."

"There was a cave-in a while back, but all we found was a sinkhole," Horace said. "A few of us started digging, but eventually gave up when we didn't find anything."

"Where was this?" Ian asked.

Horace's expression lifted. "On the opposite side of the garden."

THIRTY-TWO

They returned to Horace's quarters and Ian pushed the cabinet back against the wall. Activity created flickers of light through the crack between the curtains. Horace opened the door to his quarters, but when he stepped out, the townsfolk were fleeing toward buildings. Slamming doors and windows came from all directions. Aeros stepped into the heart of the pavilion and strolled up to Horace's desk.

Horace gestured for Ian to stay inside his quarters, then shut the door behind him. Ian stood at the window and peered out the slit between the thick curtains, turning a keen ear to the voices beyond in the pavilion.

Horace addressed Aeros next to his desk. "What brings you here?"

Stellan looked beyond Horace toward the door. When Ian didn't emerge, he gave Horace a disgruntled glance, but remained mute.

"That's what I love about you. You always get right to the point." Aeros turned around, as though studying the surroundings. His gaze settled on the window where Ian stood, and he stilled. A heartbeat later, Aeros turned back to Horace. "You are the consummate businessman."

"Hunting people down and murdering them isn't business," Horace said. Ian wondered if the town's mayor was as calm as he appeared.

"You aren't so different from me," Aeros said. "Your former profession killed thousands, perhaps millions. At least I look my prey in the eye instead of letting others pull the trigger."

"I may be punished for my former profession," he said. "But making a living isn't the same thing as sadism."

Aeros flicked his hand. Horace's head tilted back and he was lifted a couple of feet into the air. He groped at his neck, choking and kicking. "Don't believe for one minute that you are immune." Aeros dropped his hand and Horace slumped to the ground. "No one is immune!" he shouted and looked about.

Stellan stepped in and helped Horace to his feet, but kept an eye on Aeros.

Aeros picked up Horace's pencil and pressed his finger to the sharpened tip. "I am searching for someone."

"Check with the Primary, he knows who he's brought here." Horace rubbed his throat.

"He's not a guest of my brother's."

"We are far from guests," Horace said.

Aeros gripped the pencil in his fist. "He would have gained entrance from the barrens."

Horace chuckled and spread his arms. His voice rose. "You expect me to believe that someone can travel across the barrens . . . and survive?"

Ian grew apprehensive at Horace's aplomb.

"Listen to you." Aeros took a step toward Horace, holding the pencil. "Your attitude seems to have changed since I was here last."

"Nothing ever changes," Horace said, staring him down. "Especially my attitude."

Aeros wagged his finger at Horace, then turned around, scanning the surroundings. "Boldness is fueled by only one thing. Hope." Aeros said it so softly that Ian wasn't sure he'd heard him right. A moment passed, then Aeros spun around and whipped his wrist.

Stellan stiffened with wide eyes, and then reached up, pulling the pencil from his neck. Blood squirted everywhere and flowed over his neck and across his shoulder. The brute took a step toward Horace, trying to speak, but chokes and gags were all that came out. He collapsed across Horace's desk with blood gushing from his wound. Horace pressed his hands around Stellan's neck, but a few seconds later, the brute's thrashing came to a halt and he went limp.

Horace placed a bloody hand on Stellan's back. "The only hope we have around here, is for a quick death like his."

His shoulders quivered and he turned on Aeros. "I'm the one who egged you on, why him?"

"Because not everyone deserves a quick death." Aeros regarded Stellan's body with an expression that boiled Ian's blood. The man enjoyed his handiwork. "Now, let's get down to business," Aeros announced.

"No one has asked for refuge," Horace spat. "You've wasted your time coming here."

Aeros ran the tip of his finger around in the blood next to Stellan's body. "I would question a few before taking you at your word."

Horace snorted. "I would know before most."

"Perhaps," Aeros said. He raised his bloody finger and smelled it, then wiped it off on Stellan's shirt. "Then again, the ones who would truly know would be the engineers, am I right?"

Ian's pulse revved. He glanced about Horace's quarters. The sole exit was the door leading to the pavilion.

"They would have reported it to me immediately," Horace said.

"We shall see." Aeros headed for the door to Horace's quarters.

Ian rushed across the room and slipped behind the cabinet. He took the stairs down, two at a time and didn't steal a breath until he'd made it to the floor below. If the engineers had followed orders, the door would be barricaded. He glanced about the small space and found an air vent behind the staircase, near the floor.

An intense tingling in his core made him pause. Ian felt along the wall's surface and stopped at a subtle pulse against the adjoining wall. Voices overhead. He pulled off the vent screen and entered feet first, then pulled the vent into place at the same moment steps came from the upper staircase. With a deep inhale, Ian backed up a few more inches into the vent, far enough not to be noticed, then drew upon his training to still his heartbeat.

The view between the screen vents allowed Ian to see their legs. The men stopped at the control room door. Knuckles rapped on the metal.

"What's wrong with your key?" Aeros said.

"A rumor spread that there was a surplus of food hidden inside the dome. I didn't want the curious to happen upon the control room."

A terrified voice called out. "Who's there?"

"It's Horace," he said, then hesitated. "Open up."

Scrapes and voices came from the other side. A deadbolt clicked, and the door opened. Aeros pushed in and disappeared into the room.

Horace didn't follow, but backed up a few steps toward Ian's hiding spot. "Get out and find the vortex," he whispered. "I'll buy you as much time as I can." He entered the control room, then locked the door with a metallic click of the deadbolt.

By the time Ian slipped out of the vent and shut it, shouts came from the other side of the door. An urge to help them gave him pause, but Ian realized he could do little good without his powers. His rush up the stairs was followed by terrifying screams coming from the control room. With a heavy heart, he shut the cabinet, drowning out the horror below.

THIRTY-THREE

Ian left Horace's residence, unable to shake the torture below his feet.

The rest of the township was out of sight, no doubt cowering behind closed doors, yet Ian kept his head down. If they were questioned by Aeros, the less they saw of him, the better.

He wanted Marcus's help to find the vortex, but when he reached the infirmary, it was empty except for Proctor propped against the wall with Nguyen spoon-feeding him from a bowl.

Ian changed his mind. The old general's effort should be focused on protecting his son and maybe others. He headed for the garden.

Abandoned farm tools were scattered on the ground between vegetable plants. Ian kept his head down, grabbed a shovel and gloves from a basket sitting on the ground, then bent over and lifted a few of the dismal leaves on the plant, examining the vine. If Aeros checked the monitors, Ian would appear as an oblivious worker tending the garden. From the corner of his eye, Dunn strolled down a far row carrying a basket filled with melons. The twin glanced in Ian's direction but didn't approach or call out. A moment later, Ian slipped into the corn rows and made his way down the narrow path, peering between stalks for any sign of a sinkhole.

A camera was attached to a post at the opposite end of the garden. The lens swiveled toward the workers slipping into the garden to collect their gathered food baskets. He crouched down behind the thickest leaves of the stalks and studied the camera to determine if it was on a programmed sweep, or activated by movement. If this was where Aeros had appeared, the sinkhole had to be nearby.

Beyond the post, a slightly raised edge of dirt gave Ian a surge of hope.

The camera swung toward Ian's hiding spot at the same moment shuffling footsteps approached from behind. The camera had reacted to Dunn's appearance.

"What're ya doin'?" Dunn asked. Ian motioned for him to get down. The twin sat on the ground cross-legged, then leaned over Ian's shoulder. "That a camera?"

"See that red dot under the lens?" Ian said.

Dunn squinted and pointed. "That itty-bitty one?"

Ian pulled his arm down, but the camera had swung back in their direction. "It reacts to any movement that we make," Ian said. "I don't want it to know we're here."

"I wanna play hide-and-go-seek with the camera, too," Dunn said.

Dunn's remark gave Ian an idea. "Is Deek here?"

"Yeah, you want him to play?" Dunn's excitement drooped. "He's better than me. I always get caught."

"Then you'll win, because that's the way we're going to play," Ian said. "Stand up, go back the way you came and get him, but when you bring him back here, both of you stay low. I don't want the camera to find you, or Deek. Okay?"

He gave Ian an enthusiastic nod, then started to crab-walk away.

"Dunn, stand up," Ian said. "You only have to hide when you come back."

He gave Ian a thumbs-up from over his shoulder and stood tall strolling down the path.

As Ian predicted, the camera followed his movement. If Aeros watched from the control room, the flutter of leaves and other activity at the end of the corn row was caused by Dunn coming and going. When the twin reached midway down the path, the camera swung back toward men carrying baskets of picked vegetables.

Dunn returned with Deek. They both crouched down and moved slow between the rows of cornstalks.

"What's up, fearless leader?" Deek said.

"His name is Galen," Dunn whispered.

"I'm looking for something, but I don't want the camera to pick up where I am, or where I go." Ian pointed toward it.

"Distraction," Deek said, and gave Ian a two-finger salute. "No problemo."

"Take it over to where the tomato pickers are," Ian said. "And make sure everyone's attention is on the two of you."

Deek turned to his brother. "Remember what we were fighting about when Momma spanked us and grounded us to our rooms for a week?"

Dunn scrunched his face in contemplation. "No."

"Then you won't look like you're acting." He grabbed Dunn's shirt and dragged him away, but kept his hand pressed against his brother's back to keep him low and out of sight.

Deek didn't make Ian wait long. Shouts came from the direction of the tomatoes.

"You broke the heads off my G.I. Joes!" Dunn screamed.

"Yeah, well, they were stupid!" Deek yelled. "You shouldn't have thrown my Superman down the well!"

When the camera fixed on the twins, Ian rushed out in a wide, sweeping pattern and reached the pole without the lens turning toward him. He paused and pressed up against the pole. The boys were running and ducking behind the bushes, tossing tomatoes at each other. One struck a worker in the face and he wiped the lumpy scarlet off with a scowl. The other workers yelled for them to stop wasting the food.

Ian backed up and made sure the camera didn't swivel in his direction. His heel caught on a rock and he fell backward down a steep grade. The loose dirt offered no traction, and Ian clawed, trying to slow down. But he couldn't and fell head first into the sinkhole.

His shoulder took the brunt of the impact and he rolled over onto his back, thankful he hadn't landed on his injured shoulder. The overhead sun lit up the hole in a rectangular strip of light. Once he caught his breath, Ian got to his feet and took in his surroundings. The walls were perpendicular, yet jagged and about ten feet tall. When he turned, a carved-out opening at one end led farther underground in a sloping grade. Ian followed the branching tunnel that appeared to lead under the garden, but soon came to a dead end.

Ian stood with his ear pressed to the dirt wall. A subtle tickle rose in his core and he pressed his palms against it. A suppressed electromagnetic pulse answered back with an identical beat to what he felt in the Northern Colony's cave.

The energy column had to be just on the other side, but how thick was the dirt? Ian looked around the ground and found a sharp-edged rock. He scraped away dirt, but it was slow going.

A stutter in the energy's pulse stopped him cold. Aeros's voice drifted toward him. Ian retraced his steps, but hung back in the opening at the sinkhole.

"You two will be fun," Aeros said. His voice came from above.

"Do you want to play our game?" Dunn asked.

"Who the hell are you?" Deek said, but his tone morphed into apprehension. "Is that blood on you?"

Ian slumped against the dirt wall.

THIRTY-FOUR

eros's laugh ignited Ian's core. "I suggest that you run."

A single set of running footsteps—not two. Ian leaned out, cautious not to make a sound, and saw the top of Deek's hair from below.

"Who the hell are you?" Deek said. "What's going on here?"

"Apparently, your brother is the smart one." A flash of brilliant light was accompanied by a horrendous scream, and then a groan.

"That is a sample of what I'll do if you don't run." Aeros's voice was so low and guttural, Ian had to strain to make out his words.

Scrambling. Weak steps that picked up speed as they grew distant. Silence. Was the megalomaniac counting off their head start? One minute, two. Or had he sensed Ian at the bottom of the sinkhole?

Several minutes later, with a grunt, footsteps faded in the direction of the town.

Ian rushed down the adjoining tunnel and back to the wall. He ignored the sharp rock he'd been using and opened his palm as his core regained its strength the longer he was in proximity to the energy column. A core blast sputtered to gradual life and grew in volume. He stepped back and flung it at the shallow hole he'd created.

A blast of dirt burst into the tunnel and coated Ian from head to toe. It hadn't punched through, but Ian repeated the attempts and on the third blast, a hole the size of a watermelon confirmed Ian's suspicion. He stared at the shimmery column of pulsing energy and reached in, then focused on absorbing the raw electromagnetic energy, bringing his core to full strength.

The blessed tingling sparked every nerve in his body. He closed his eyes, and shyfted.

Ian reappeared in Horace's quarters.

"Ian!" Marcus and Horace sat on the edge of the cot. Marcus's hand was pressed to Horace's side while Stag's mayor grimaced.

"He took a core blast trying to save the engineers," Marcus said. "But the heat cauterized the wound."

"Like hell took a bite out of me." In spite of his injury, Horace's excitement couldn't be contained. "You found the vortex!"

"It's camouflaged by the energy source, just as I suspected." Ian looked in the direction of the cabinet. It hung open. "The engineers . . ."

"The twin's escapades stopped their torture," Horace said.

Marcus grimaced. "They're alive."

"Aeros went after the boys. At least from what I could see on the monitor. I don't know where he is," Horace said.

Ian peered out the drawn curtains. "How many shyfters are in Stag, do you know?"

"Enough to get most back to Earth," Marcus said. "But it'll take some time to replenish our cores for that kind of energy draw."

"I punched a hole in the wall, but the tunnel off of the garden is too narrow to get them out quickly." He regarded Horace. "Do you have an ax?"

There's one in the storage room on the other side of the pavilion," Horace said. He pulled keys out of his pocket and tossed them at Ian. "The longest one is the one you need."

"I'll be back in a second." Ian opened the door a crack and checked that the coast was clear. Then he rushed out and approached the building behind Horace's desk. He unlocked the door and went inside.

Shelves lined the room, piled with odds and ends of personal belongings. Six environmental suits hung on hooks along the far wall. An ax lay on the floor beneath them.

Ian grabbed it and returned to Horace's quarters, then ran down the stairs to where he'd felt the energy pulse earlier. Ian swung the ax at the wall. Marcus came down just as Ian broke through to the other side. It led to a dirt tunnel, similar to the ones at the Northern Colony.

"What's that?" Marcus said.

"If I'm right, a way home." Ian handed him the ax. "Open this up enough for people to get inside. I'm betting it'll lead to the underground energy column. When you get there, you won't be able to feel the vortex like we can on Earth. The energy from the column masks it. Tell the shyfters to stick their hands in the column; that will trigger the shyft." Ian headed for the stairs.

Marcus yelled. "Where the hell are you going?"

"I put a target on the boys' backs. I've got to try and stop him."

"You can't take on Aeros alone!" Marcus shouted. "The best thing you can do, is get away. I'll let everyone know about the vortex."

One of the engineers appeared in the doorway. "What's going on? Has Aeros returned?"

The consoles and blinking lights beyond the doorway gave Ian an idea. "No, but I could use your help." He backed the engineer into the room, and shut the door while Marcus's ax chopped at the wall from the other side.

"I need you to bring the dome roof down on us," Ian said.

"Are you insane?" the engineer said.

"That would kill all of us," the other one shouted. He was hunched over a console cradling his arm.

"I have a plan," Ian said.

"Your plan's too risky," Marcus growled. "Let us save as many of the others as we can while he's occupied."

"A true hero wouldn't turn his back on the boys," Ian said. Or was he trying to make up for turning his back on the control room technician's? He held his hand up when Marcus postured to protest.

"You need to leave us. For the greater good," Horace said.

At Horace's words, Ian paused. Stag's mayor confided that he was an arms dealer who had chosen to sell to the wrong side. "You're in league with Eve."

The old general's eyes flew open and Marcus took a step back, placing himself between Horace and Ian. A decade of protecting Ian returned in an instant.

The gesture wasn't lost on Horace. He chuckled. "I can't believe I didn't see it till now. I am in your service, Pur Heir." He winced as he straightened and got to his feet. Horace brought a fist to his chest and gave a slight bow, albeit with a groan. "The rebels will fight by your side until we no longer walk the universe."

Marcus's shoulders relaxed when Horace dropped back to the cot. Ian grabbed a piece of charcoal from Horace's fireplace and scraped it across the hearth, writing down the coordinates. "Shyft everyone here. They'll be safe. I'll meet you there as soon as I find Rayne."

Marcus stepped next to Ian, and a moment later, he erased the coordinates with his hand. "I'll tell the others."

"Use my distraction to get the others downstairs. Once Aeros leaves, we can use both the garden tunnel and the control room tunnel to evacuate everyone."

Ian shut the door on the old general's growls, crossed the pavilion, and snatched the map that had fallen under the desk. He entered the storage room, grabbed one of the environmental suits off a hook, and slipped into it. He folded the map and stuck it next to his chest, then zipped up. After grabbing a helmet, Ian stood in the doorway, turning a keen ear to the air. A door banged open one street over. Screams, but they did not ring of death.

Ian had counted on Aeros searching one residence after another. If the megalomaniac was anything like his former protégé, Ning, he enjoyed the pursuit. The pyro had claimed there wasn't anything sweeter than the smell of fear.

He made his way to the infirmary. All was silent. Ian glanced in the window. Several cots were uprooted from their neat rows. Blankets were strewn everywhere. A few rolls of bandages had landed against the wall, having left a trail halfway across the room.

Proctor got to his feet with Nguyen's help as Ian stepped inside. "What's going on?" Nguyen said in a subdued voice. "Who the hell is that?"

"Aeros, and he's hunting the twins." Ian caught the subtle tilt of Proctor's head toward a pile of blankets that had been swept up into the corner. A couple of cots were overturned on top. Ian glanced out the doorway and listened, but Aeros didn't appear to be nearby.

When Ian stepped closer, the corner of a blanket fluttered. He mouthed, *Dunn?*

Nguyen gave a slight nod. "He ran in seconds after the guy left."

Ian dropped to one knee. "I'm going to find Deek," he whispered. "Then take you both to a safe place." A whimper came from the mound. Ian placed a gentle hand on it. "Stay still and be quiet. Close your eyes and feel the sun's warmth on your face, seeping in through every pore." Ian didn't know how else to soothe him other than to share his own training. "Put your hand on your chest and count the beats of your heart, but make them come slow, not fast."

"I don't wanna play anymore. I want my brother. I wanna go home." The mound quivered.

Dunn's childish voice struck a nerve and Ian clenched his teeth to control the flood of emotions that threatened to overtake him. "If the bad man returns, stay as quiet as a mouse. No matter what you hear."

The top of the mound moved as Dunn nodded. Ian gave him a pat for following directions.

"I'm not going anywhere," Proctor said.

"Me neither," Nguyen said. "But hurry. That guy terrifies me, too."

Ian left them and hunched down between buildings, making his way toward the garden.

THIRTY-FIVE

The frightened engineers didn't have faith in Ian's plan until he showed them the tunnel.

An eerie silence hovered over the garden when Ian arrived. A handful of minutes later, a sizzle like a short in an electrical cord came from overhead. Ian raised his eyes. Thousands of sparks rained down upon the town. Some landed on a thatched roof several blocks over. The thatch smoldered at first, then flames shot into the air.

It took only seconds for the entire roof to be engulfed, and as other roofs burst into flame, smoke filled the inner circle of the town. Then it spread in all directions, snaking its way throughout the intersecting streets. From his vantage point, additional roofs caught fire and added to the swelling haze.

Ian scanned the area as smoke rose to the pinnacle of the dome overhead. As hoped, it grew thick and dense, and then lowered enough to make visibility difficult.

"Uh," came from the smoky haze on the opposite side of the street. "Let me go. Can't you see we're about to be toast!" Deek broke into a coughing fit.

The protesting teen sparked the little energy left in Ian's core. A gust of wind took him by surprise and he ducked below the zucchini plants. The air cleared enough for him to see two bodies. Aeros used his power to summon wind and disperse the smoke, but the nearby flames and dried timber were too great. The smoke swirled back unto itself seconds after Aeros cleared the air in front of him.

"What is this!" Aeros roared. He let go of Deek and the teen stumbled toward the garden. He slumped to the ground next to Ian. Ian pressed his hand over the teen's mouth.

Deek blinked, from surprise or the smoke, Ian couldn't tell. The teen nodded and bent over, doing his best to stifle his coughs.

"Ahhh!" Aeros's shout penetrated the haze. "Are you so desperate to stop your incarceration, that you would destroy yourselves along with your chains!"

Deek moved his lips as if about to speak. Ian pressed a hand over his mouth. The teen's head stuttered beneath Ian's gag as he settled into a coughing fit.

"I leave you to your funeral pyre!" Aeros walked down the path one row over, and a few minutes later, his footsteps came to a halt. It sounded like he'd walked to the security camera pole. A brilliant white flash lit up the haze for a second before the smoke snuffed it out.

The teen fell onto his back, unable to stifle his coughing fit. "My brother," he rasped.

"Safe, with the others." Ian helped him up. "Come on, there isn't much time before this place comes down on our heads.

Ian blew the smoke away, clearing as much of a path ahead of them as he could. He didn't have Aeros's wind power, but what he could do was enough. With Deek in tow, the two of them made it to Horace's quarters. From what Ian could tell, the prisoners had gathered in two groups, separated by the pavilion.

Vael approached with a coughing man at his side. He indicated for the guy to rest at the back of the line. "Stay here. It'll be your turn soon enough."

"Are there more?" Ian asked.

Vael coughed and nodded. "A few, but I got it."

"Why are they separated?" Ian asked.

"Whatever is shorting out the dome, shorted out the jam. People were dropping from the Curse and we had to separate everyone into groups of Pur and Duach." He leaned in and stifled a cough. "Let my dad know I'm okay." Vael turned back to the town and disappeared down a side street.

Ian found Nguyen at the doorway. The scientist waved his arms, directing groups of four and five men each. He smiled at Ian through the haze and threw his arm around his shoulders when he approached. "You made it!"

"Where's my brother?" Deek asked.

"He's downstairs at the entrance to the tunnel," Nguyen said. "He's waiting for you." The scientist held his hand up to stop the next person in line, then motioned for Deek to go in next.

"Don't be a martyr," Ian said to Nguyen. "Make sure you get back. This rebellion needs more men like you."

Nguyen pursed his lips. "Perhaps, but our universe needs you."

Ian followed Deek down the winding stairs. Dunn stood in the corner, clutching a rag doll with a missing button for an eye. The doll's owner had an arm around Dunn.

"Dunn!" Deek shouted before he reached the bottom.

His brother looked up and when their eyes met, Dunn turned to the plaintiff and handed him the doll. "Thank you. I don't need it anymore. That's my brother." They threw their arms around each other, and Deek buried his face in his brother's neck.

Dunn patted his back. "We go home now," he said and took his brother's hand. Deek swiped at his cheeks, and didn't let go.

An emerald burst came from inside the control room. A shyftor ran out and hurried through the tunnel opening, knocking Marcus to the side with an obligatory, "Sorry, coming through."

Marcus gave Ian a grunt. "Is that bastard gone?"

"For now," Ian said. He remembered Jaered's warning about Aeros knowing that Ian parashyfted to Thrae. "Thrae's electromagnetic energy might be too compromised, but if Aeros can feel the changes in the fields of the planet—"

"He'll notice our parashyfts," Marcus said. He waved those in line to hurry through, then stuck his head in the tunnel and shouted. "Get your butts moving! We don't have much time!"

Ian threw his arms around the boys' shoulders and pulled them close. "You can't go home, not right away," he said.

Dunn made to protest, but Deek put a hand on his brother's chest. "He's right. They'll come and take us again." Dunn's eyes flew open and he shook his head.

"Once they stop looking for you, you'll see your mom again," Ian said. "I promise."

"Thank you," the twins said in unison. They burst out laughing. "Jinx!" they shouted.

Ian grinned. He knew the perfect safe house for them. He and Marcus helped the boys climb through the tunnel opening, then he rushed into the control room and snatched a pen off the console. He returned and wrote an address on the general's hand. "Take them here. It's where your geeks are hiding out from the Primary." He rested the helmet against his hip. "I saw Vael above. He's helping to get the last of the people here."

Marcus motioned for the next group to go inside the tunnel. "Find Rayne and get your butts back to Earth. How am I going to find you?"

"I'll find you," Ian said. Fighting his way up the stairs was made all the more challenging by the bulk of his suit. When he exited Horace's quarters, he told Nguyen to speed things up, then ran back to the garden.

The smoke made visibility impossible, and Ian's eyes and throat stung. He found the camera pole and dropped to the ground, breathing as much undisturbed air as he could. He removed the map, studied it and decided where to go next. Then he folded it and stuck it back in his suit. Ian rose to his knees, and zipped the suit to his chin.

His elation at the successful evacuation was short-lived. A couple of minutes later, a shimmering light appeared. Ian stuck his helmet on and secured it. He had to buy some time.

Ian felt at his breastplate and found the oxygen button. The second that Aeros's image solidified, he pressed it, then headed for the sinkhole. The camera whined and came alive at his movement.

Aeros roared at the top of his lungs.

With a twist, Ian slid feetfirst into the sinkhole, and landed in a crouch. He sprang for the outlying tunnel and slipped into the opening. A rumble, and then clumps of dirt fell behind him. Aeros had jumped down into the sinkhole.

A flash of light lit up the inner tunnel. Ian pressed against the dirt wall as a core blast missed hitting him by a couple of inches.

"Who are you?" Aeros snarled.

Ian froze. His father couldn't tell who was in the suit. "I hear you're looking for me!" he shouted.

A silent pause. "Ian?" Aeros hissed.

Ian took off for the energy column as fast as the suit allowed. A core blast landed at the ground behind his feet, searing the back of his legs. Ian didn't look back.

The end of the tunnel loomed closer and Ian picked up speed, then reached out. His gloved fingertips connected with the column and his hand, then arm, punched into the energy. A fraction of a second before he would have crashed into the tunnel wall—Ian shyfted.

He reappeared in the center of the square. To his dismay, there were several groups left to enter the building, and he waved his arms. "Run! Hide!" he shouted, but the waiting prisoners stared at Ian and didn't budge. He removed his helmet. "Aeros is coming back, save yourselves!"

Instead of taking cover in the outlying buildings, the mob made a mad dash for Horace's door. But the mix of Pur and Duach triggered the Curse, and it dropped many of them to the ground, Nguyen included. He writhed on the ground while trying to keep them from trampling everyone.

A few of the inmates weren't Sars, and one ran up but kicked Nguyen in the head trying to jump over him. The scientist collapsed back, motionless. A fight broke out at the doorway. Ian ran up but was shoved by a falling body, and the two of them ended up on the ground. His helmet rolled away. "Stop!" he shouted, but his plea fell on deaf ears as the Primary's prisoners fought to get off the hellhole of a rock.

A bright flash came from behind. Aeros's laughter bellowed above the chaos. Ian scrambled to his feet and faced his father. "Leave them. I'm the one you want," he said.

"What can I do to them that they aren't already doing to themselves," Aeros said with his face painted in amusement. He closed his eyes and spread his hands wide as a nearby raging blaze lit up his face in fiery blood red. "Let me help them along." He brought his fists together with a *smack!*

Ian was tossed backward and landed hard against the crumbling building. It knocked the wind out of him. Terrifying screams came from inside the remains of Horace's quarters, which had collapsed on top of those stuffed inside. A core blast formed in the palm of Aeros's hand.

"No!" Ian's hand shot up. "Don't!"

"Stop!" Vael rushed over.

A smirk spread on Aeros's face and with the flick of his hand, the core blast shot at the building.

Vael jumped in its path, then stiffened. He'd taken a direct hit, and with a wobble, he dropped to the ground. Ian cradled him in his arms. Marcus's son gazed up at Ian. His eyes glassed over.

Tears clouded Ian's sight and he set Vael down gently. When he moved to get up, Nguyen's bloody head was visible between the blocks of adobe. The scientist's eyes were fixed in a deathly stare.

A core blast slammed into the remains of the building, and then another. The thatch ignited and Ian backed up as their means of escape turned into a funeral pyre. How many had perished? What of those already downstairs? When he turned, his father was admiring his handiwork. What Ian would have given to tear that smug expression off his face. But instead, he walked over and grabbed his helmet while his father relished in their deaths.

Ian took off down a side street, headed for the sinkhole, but the smoke made it difficult to know which direction to turn. Once Ian came upon the vegetable plot, he followed the rows to the camera pole, then leaped into the sinkhole at the exact moment Aeros shyfted behind him. Ian landed in the bottom and stifled a groan when his ankle took the impact of his fall. He limped as fast as he could toward the energy column.

"I will find you, Ian!" Aeros shouted from behind, gaining on him. "There's no place on this planet that you can hide from me!"

Ian fell against the far wall and stuck his arm into the vortex. At the moment of his shyft, he heard an enraged scream.

THIRTY-SIX

Jaered let go of the punching bag and stepped away. "Take over," he said to Tara, then headed for his cell phone. It had buzzed twice, then fell silent. He checked the code on the screen, and called Eve back. "Have you heard something?"

"In a way," Eve said.

"What's that supposed to mean?" Jaered wiped his face with his shirt. He caught voices in the background. It sounded like Eve was in a public place. "Where are you?"

"The alarm triggered at the safe house. A couple of us came to retrieve Ian and Rayne . . . but it wasn't them," she said. "The rest, you've got to see for yourself." An emerald glow formed in the center of the gym floor. Wyatt's image solidified. He nodded at Jaered. "He's there to babysit the others until you get back," Eve said.

"What is it?" Tara said and loosened her gloves. She and Patrick abandoned the punching bag and hurried over.

"Did Ian return?" Patrick asked. "And Rayne?"

"No, not yet," Wyatt said. "But Jaered is needed elsewhere for a couple of hours."

"I'll let you two know something when I do," Jaered said. He shyfted to the safe house and appeared in the farmhouse's living room. Stunned, he absorbed the scene in front of him. The house was filled with prisoners from Stag.

A man pulled Jaered out of the vortex. "Sorry, but we don't know if more are coming."

There was a taped-off section at the center of the living room, and the others were making sure men were steering clear of it.

Eve motioned for Jaered to follow her. They walked down the narrow hallway of the farmhouse and ascended the back staircase. "Pur and Duach shyftors have been parashyfting their fellow prisoners here at an alarming rate," she said.

Jaered stopped in his tracks from a mixture of shock and elation. He had tried to help the prisoners of Stag while living on Thrae, but couldn't figure out how the Primary and his father shyfted in and out without a vortex field.

She opened one of the bedroom doors. Marcus sat on the bed with a drooped head. The old Pur general wore a Stag uniform.

"What's going on?" Jaered asked.

"Since you're from Thrae, I guess you'd know all about Stag," Marcus said.

Jaered glanced at Eve, but she nodded. They were beyond keeping secrets from the old general. "How did you know?" he said.

"Ian told me as much," Marcus's gaze rested on Eve. "He told me everything. He found a hidden vortex and made it possible for all of us to escape." Grief quivered his bottom lip. "Not all . . ."

It was what Marcus didn't say that caused Jaered's core to cool. "Was Rayne with him?"

"The boy hadn't found her yet," Marcus said. "As far as I know, he's still looking for her."

"Vael didn't make it," Eve said softly.

Jaered punched the wall. His knuckles throbbed as the impact vibrated up his arm and through his shoulder.

"He stayed behind to help with the waiting groups," Marcus said. "But the building collapsed, and then there was a fire. Bodies fell down the stairs and the entrance was blocked. Everyone rushed into the tunnels. I don't know what happened to those left above."

"They just stopped coming," Eve said.

"Vael told me about you," Marcus said. "He never came out and said it, but he thought of you like a brother."

"How many?" Jaered swallowed his grief.

"At last count, about four hundred," Eve said. "We've had to separate them. The Pur are in the corn field and the Duach are in the backyard. Some of those have spilled over into the barn.

Marcus took a deep breath and let it out in a gradual stream. His years on the battlefield kicked in and his features hardened. "Those men can't go home. There were mutterings while they waited for their turns to shyft to Earth," he said. "If you'll have them, you'll gain some recruits with pretty strong motivation."

"We'll put them to good use," Eve said. "And do what we can for the maimed."

"Don't hesitate to use me in any capacity. I've still got some fight left in me." Marcus left them alone in the bedroom.

"I know what you told me about the Primary's punishment, but these men." Eve said. "Now that I've seen it firsthand . . ."

"We'll get him," Jaered said with more conviction than he'd felt in a while. "We'll get them both."

"I've called for help," Eve said. "But the Primary will dispatch the Pur guard to check out the fluctuation in the field soon, if he hasn't already."

The safe house was compromised. Jaered ran his fingers through his hair. "There's no way to let Ian know not to shyft here when he finds Rayne."

"In all likelihood, they'll be stepping right into a trap," she said.

"We need to get these men out of here." Jaered headed down the hall. "I can take about twenty at a time. But first I'll get Patrick. He can help."

"Do you think that's wise?" she asked.

"We're past protecting him, Eve." Jaered stared out the back window at the gathered Duach making their way toward the barn. "Patrick needs to see what he's fighting for."

A maternal smile crept across Eve's face, and she left him.

Jaered shyfted to the auditorium. Patrick didn't let up on the punching bag, landing one solid blow after another.

Tara met Jaered's stare with apprehension. "What's happened?" she asked. Patrick connected one last blow to the bag, but Tara had let go, and it swung back at him. He caught it before it knocked him on his butt. Jaered inwardly grinned. Patrick had also increased his coordination and awareness of his surroundings.

"About four hundred prisoners on Thrae were shyfted to the safe house coordinates here on Earth." Jaered motioned for Wyatt to take off. "Get back, they need you." The rebel shyfted in a shamrock cloud.

"Prisoners," Patrick said.

"Were they Duach?" Tara asked.

"Political prisoners of the Primary," Jaered said. "They were both Pur and Duach. Not all were Sars."

"What of Ian?" Patrick said.

"He was the one who found a way for them to shyft back to Earth," Jaered said.

"That sounds like him," Tara said with a grin.

By the scowl on his face, Patrick didn't share her elation. "But Ian and Rayne didn't come back with them."

"He's still searching for her." Jaered hoped he sounded more convincing than he felt. Where could Gwynn have taken her?

"The longer he's there . . ." Tara's words trailed off.

"The better chance Aeros has to find them both," Patrick voiced what she couldn't.

"There is one silver lining to everything." Jaered returned to the punching bag. "Many of the prisoners want to join the rebel forces. Your General Marcus is among them."

Tara brightened up. "He's alive? And Vael, too?" Jaered's hesitation gave her the answer. "Oh, god." She turned away.

Patrick dropped his face. "Poor Marcus."

"Ian might not have found Rayne yet, but he managed to stack our deck against Aeros, and the Primary," Jaered said. "First, we have to get them to safety." He gripped Patrick's shoulder. "You're coming with me. We need your help relocating them."

Patrick tossed off his boxing gloves. Jaered shyfted them to the farmhouse. A gunshot whizzed by Jaered's face and he knocked Patrick to the floor. The odor of metal filled the room. They'd shyfted into the middle of a gun battle.

"The Pur guard?" Jaered shouted to one of Eve's men.

"Worse, his Elite guard," the guy said. He twisted upward and fired out the cracked window.

"Stay here, and keep your head down," Jaered told Patrick. He trench-crawled to the cabinet across the living room, and pressed the release at the base. The cabinet's sides fell open, exposing half a dozen rifles.

He grabbed one, whistled, and tossed another to the man at the window. Then he brought a third to Patrick.

"Remember how to use it?" he shouted over the gunshots. Patrick chambered a round like a pro. "Where's Eve?" Jaered yelled to no one in particular.

"She and Wyatt left to prepare some new locations. Some of the shyftors took a bunch of the men with them," the man at the dining room window said. He cowered at a volley of shots that took out the window above him, and showered him in shards of glass.

"What about the Stag prisoners?" Jaered said. "Where are they?"

"The Pur are keeping their heads down in the corn field. All of the Duach are held up in the barn." The man swiped at a cut across his cheek. "The Elite guard approached from the front of the house," the rebel said. "Everyone scrambled pretty fast."

Patrick trench-crawled to the taped-off section of the room. "Don't do anything stupid till I get back."

"Where the hell are you going?" Jaered yelled, but when he glanced over his shoulder, Patrick was gone.

At the first lull in the bullet exchange, Patrick appeared in the middle of the room with Tara. They'd retrieved another dozen rifles, along with Jaered's favorite, from the auditorium gun safe. Jaered reached toward him and Patrick tossed him the rifle.

A voice called out from the front lawn. "I'm going to assume that you don't have any shyftors left, or you'd be long gone," he said. "Give up and come quietly so no one has to get hurt."

"That's Falcon," Tara said. "He's their squad leader."

"Then Komodo is definitely with them," Patrick said. "Those two are inseparable."

"They're the ones who kidnapped us in Johannesburg," Tara said.

Jaered kept low and settled under the window. "Just leave us alone. Whoever you're after, they're long gone. Leave us in peace," he shouted.

"Nice try, but the magnetic field disruption was too great. "We came for answers."

"Who's been in the barn before?" Patrick whispered.

"I have," Jaered said, lifting high enough to peer out the lower edge of the window.

Patrick held up a couple of the rifles. "Let's give them something they didn't count on."

"They already know we have firepower," the man next to Jaered said.

Tara grinned. "But they don't know we have the numbers."

Jaered grabbed the rest of the rifles from the cabinet. "I'll be back in a minute." He stuffed a couple of boxes of ammo in his jacket and zipped it up, and then slipped the straps of the rifles Patrick had retrieved over his shoulder.

Bullets ripped through the front door. The Elite guard had short attention spans. Jaered shyfted to the barn.

It was packed with the Duach prisoners, hunched down and eerily calm and quiet. It occurred to Jaered they'd had ample practice hiding from Aeros during his hunts in Stag. He lifted one of the rifles into the air. "Who's a good shot among you?" Several hands rose above the sea of heads. He passed out the rifles and instructed them to divide up the ammo. "Get to the hayloft upstairs and find as many vantage points as you can. Pick them off only when you can do so with confidence. Don't waste ammo." He turned to the rest of them. "Everyone else, barricade yourselves in here the best you can and find safe places if they open up on the barn."

One of the prisoners grabbed a sickle hanging from a hook. "I ain't going back," he said. The crowd voiced similar conviction, and most of them searched for any kind of weapon they could find.

"Who among you are shyftors?" Jaered asked. To his dismay, no one raised a hand.

"They took several men to the new location," one of the prisoners said. "They haven't returned yet."

"Who's a Sar?" Jaered asked. From the show of hands, about a third. "Get to the loft with the others, he said. If I need you, I'll be able to grab you quickly."

"Why?" one of them asked.

"Because they're Pur Sar soldiers," Jaered said. "And at the cost of you dropping from the Curse, so will they." He shyfted back to the upstairs bedroom inside the farmhouse, then peered out between the drawn curtains and counted five soldiers hiding behind various vehicles and tree trunks. By the look of it, they were focused on the house and hadn't crossed the dirt road behind them.

Jaered rushed to each window in the upstairs rooms and in all, counted twelve Elite guards. He heard voices downstairs at another lull in the gunplay and he shyfted into the middle of the taped zone.

Patrick had left to give the rebel at the back of the house a fresh rifle, but was dropped to his knees before he entered the kitchen. A moan at the back door bellowed out of the doorway.

Tara pulled Patrick back into the living room and he recovered. "You okay?" Patrick called out.

"Yeah, but steer clear from now on," the rebel said from the kitchen. "No more surprises."

"Got it!" Patrick said.

"Get upstairs and stay there," Jaered said. "You'll have a better vantage point."

"Come on," Tara said. The two of them headed for the back hall.

"Coming through," Patrick called out as they approached the kitchen doorway.

But they both groaned until Tara got Patrick clear of the narrow hall junction.

A moment later, footsteps came from overhead. Jaered grabbed the rest of the rifles and shyfted to the corn field where he'd spotted the Pur prisoners. He passed out the rifles and then gestured directions, unwilling for the wind to carry their voices. The prisoners nodded in understanding, and he left them when gunshots rang out.

Jaered crouched down a few feet from the end of the corn row and studied the Elite guard from behind, but stiffened when his attention fell to the guard behind the massive oak tree. The man held up a grenade—and pulled the pin.

THIRTY-SEVEN

I f he shot the man, the Pur prisoners would lose their advantage of a rear attack and be vulnerable to weak protection. Jaered scanned the area and hesitated when he spotted the overhead power lines. He raised his hand and sent an energy burst at the transformer. It exploded in brilliant fireworks as metal and wires rained down breaking the power lines loose. They hit the ground, whipping about like snakes. Jaered flicked his wrist and one of the sparking lines connected with the soldier before he could fling the grenade.

The Elite guard screamed and writhed where he stood as the grenade slipped out of his hand, then rolled down the lawn toward the old pickup truck parked in the driveway. A couple of Elite guards scrambled from their hiding spot as the grenade exploded from under the vehicle. Mangled car parts and ignited gasoline flew in all directions. One of the Elite caught fire and stumbled down the driveway screaming.

An Elite guard walked out to the road, raised his handgun and fired. The flaming man fell to the ground, motionless. The smell of burning flesh blew in Jaered's direction.

The Elite guard turned around with his chest heaving and murder dripping from his eyes. "I don't believe in coincidences! Show yourself or I'll tell my men to open fire on the field!"

It was Falcon. Jaered raised the rifle and took aim. Out of the corner of his eye, a fireball hurdled toward him. He fell back as it struck the cornstalks overhead. Those closest to him were engulfed in flames. Jaered rushed back toward the other Pur prisoners, ducking from the onslaught of automatic weapons.

The Pur prisoners returned fire in spite of Jaered waving his arms and motioning for them to wait. It gave their position away.

Jaered hunched down at the men in front. "I can shyft about twenty of you," he said.

"Ask the others," the first Pur prisoner said. "I can hold my own with a rifle." The armed men behind him nodded. Two more said to take others before them.

He worked his way to the back of the row and handed his rifle to the last unarmed man. He motioned for the remainder to grab the shoulders of those closest, so he could shyft them.

An explosion came from the direction of the house, but Jaered couldn't see through the rising smoke and flames.

Jaered hesitated, unsure what was happening. If the house was compromised, he had to get back to Patrick and Tara. A horde of Stag prisoners rushed into the corn field between the rows. The man at the front of their line groaned and grabbed his chest.

"Wait!" Jaered yelled. The running men stopped cold.

"We overtook them!" a voice shouted from several feet away. "They shyfted their sorry asses out of here."

Jaered worked his way up to the front of the line. "You okay?" he asked the bent-over man.

"Yeah," he said. "They retreated."

Their Duach rescuers gave Jaered a broad smile upon his approach. "When it became obvious they were focused on all of you in the field, we decided to take your advice. We snuck up on them and they started dropping like flies," he said. "They saw our numbers and hauled out of here."

"But not all of you were Sars," Jaered said.

"They didn't know that." The Duach prisoner grinned.

Jaered chuckled. "You realize that the Duach just saved a bunch of Pur."

"Bet it won't be the last time," the Duach prisoner said with a smirk.

Playful hoots and hollers rose from the field as word spread fast who'd saved their butts. The band of Duach prisoners raised their rifles and returned hoots of their own.

Jaered stepped out of the corn field. The front of the farmhouse was gone. Jaered made his way through the rubble and stood at the base of the steps leading up to what used to be a porch. He could see into the living room, the dining room, and the two bedrooms that faced the front of the house. Rubble lay in a pile across the porch, and sparks from exposed outlet wiring hung and sizzled from the edges of the gaping hole.

Patrick grabbed an edge of the remaining upstairs outer wall and leaned out. He gave Jaered a curt wave. "Glad you made it."

"What the hell happened?" Jaered said. "A grenade wouldn't have done this."

"It wasn't a grenade," the rebel at the front door said.

"It was as if the front was just torn off, from the inside out," another rebel said.

Jaered entered the house. Their medic attended to a rebel's arm.

When the medic caught Jaered's hesitation, he held up a thumb. "Took a through-and-through. He'll be fine."

"Any other injuries?" Jaered asked.

"A few bullet grazes and a couple of large splinter extractions are in my future, but so far that's all," the medic said without looking up. "Lucky sons of bitches."

Jaered made his way up the back staircase and walked down the upper hallway. A strong gust of wind whipped up and a few pictures swung, and then one dropped to the floor with a shattering of glass. He stepped over it and met up with Patrick in the bedroom. The furniture was surprisingly tidy.

"What happened?" Jaered said.

Tara and Patrick exchanged nervous glances. "It was me," Patrick said with his hands pressed under his armpits.

Jaered gave him a discerning eye. "What do you mean, you did it? How?"

"We could see that you and the others were in trouble," Tara said. "Komodo set the field on fire while Falcon gathered the others and opened fire."

"Tara and I each took one out with the rifles, but then one of them turned his on us," Patrick said.

"It was an automatic," Tara said.

Jaered walked over to the outside edge and peered down. At the structure's creaks and moans, he stepped back with care.

"Patrick went ballistic," Tara said. "He fell on his butt and scrambled away, propped against the bed."

"I threw my hands up and screamed," Patrick said. "That's when it happened."

"The front of the house . . . flew away." Tara gave Patrick an uneasy look.

"I don't know what I did," Patrick said.

Jaered surveyed the damage. He'd never been able to conjure this much power at once. He thought back to Greece and The Rising that Eve had put Patrick through in order to bring his new powers to the surface. Jaered hadn't been present when it happened, but Eve had told him about it.

"Are you going to tell my mother?" Patrick said like a twelve-year-old caught breaking a window.

"You don't get it, do you?" Jaered wandered into the adjoining room to measure how far his power reached. "This is exactly what your mother and I have waited for."

THIRTY-EIGHT

A bright emerald cloud formed in the middle of the auditorium. Wyatt appeared with Marcus. The old general took a couple of steps and turned around, taking in his surroundings with a bulging pack on his back. He planned to stay a while.

Saxon ran circles about him and sniffed at his boots and pant legs.

"I thought I'd never see you again." Tara flung her arms around Marcus's neck. "I'm so, so sorry about Vael."

"We're going to get those bastards." Marcus regarded Jaered with sad eyes from over her shoulder. He swiped at his nose with the back of his hand and pulled away. "This looks like an Olympic training facility."

"Eve has deep pockets," Jaered said. "It costs a lot to save the world."

"Don't get me started," Marcus said. "I was in the United States Army." He dropped his pack to the gym floor. "Where's Patrick?"

"Up here." Patrick sat in the top row of the auditorium.

Marcus stared up at him with his fists resting on his hips. "I hear you're some kind of hero in the making. They must be pretty desperate to put faith in your wimpy ass."

"I don't have the luxury of time like Ian's had, or Jaered." Patrick stood and crossed his arms. "But I'll get there."

Marcus grunted. Jaered caught an amused spark in his eye. "Well, get your butt down here and let's figure out how far apart we need to be, so I can whip you into shape."

"Just what we need around here, another drill sergeant." Patrick took one cautious step after another down the stairs.

"Who're you calling a sergeant, grunt! You'll address me as General!" Marcus yelled. He sized up the others from over his shoulder. "This bunch are pussies compared to what I'm going to put you through."

Patrick's holler could be heard from inside the auditorium. Saxon jumped at the picture window at the end of the gym, then took off through the double doors and ran out. Jaered and Tara hurried after the wolf and ended up outside, not bothering to grab jackets on the way.

"What happened?" Tara stammered between chattering teeth.

"The boy formed a core blast!" Marcus couldn't hide the pride in his voice. "Show them." Marcus stood at the base of the snowy hill and gestured.

Patrick raised his palm and stared at it, and stared, and then stared some more.

"Well?" Marcus said. "Don't make me stand here with egg on my face!"

"If you did it once, you can do it again," Tara coaxed.

They stood dancing in place and rubbing their arms from the cold, waiting. Jaered wondered if it was too cold for the fire to form, but the auditorium had been built over one of the most powerful vortexes on the planet. "Focus on drawing energy, not on the core blast," Jaered called out.

When nothing happened for another handful of minutes, Marcus stuck his fists on his hips. "Get it back or you'll feel some pain, boy!"

Patrick shuddered, but then a stuttering ball of crimson energy formed in his hand. Everyone came alive. "Yes, you can do it!" Tara shouted.

The ball grew in volume, filling up his hand and painting Patrick's face in scarlet. He turned halfway around and pulled his arm back. With a flick of his wrist, he flung the core blast. It struck a few feet from the base of the nearby glacier.

A gigantic crack formed at the impact site, then spread in all directions, growing wider and deeper with each yard.

Chunks of ice fell from the edge of the overhead cliff and Jaered rushed at Patrick, tackling him to the ground a second before a large chunk would have flattened him. Marcus scooped up Tara and they shyfted. Patrick opened his arms, and Saxon leapt into them. They shyfted.

Jaered took off for the equipment bag at the base of the hill. A snowy chunk of ice hit his back and sprayed cold needles across the back of his head and shoulders. He snatched one of the handles at a full run and shyfted inside the auditorium.

"Ugh!" Patrick and Marcus had drawn into fetal positions, pressing their fists to their chests. Jaered grabbed Marcus and dragged him away, while Tara did the same to Patrick, headed in the opposite direction. Several feet later, they both lay still on the auditorium floor, catching their breath.

"I'm too old for this," Marcus said, panting.

Jaered stood at the large picture window, watching the calving glacier in the distance. A few minutes later, the rumbling and vibration ceased. Chunks of blueish ice, most bigger than a tractor, sat in a massive pile.

Patrick joined Jaered at the window. "Damn. I did that?"

"A lesson not to be forgotten," Marcus said from across the gym floor.

"What lesson?" Tara said.

"That undeveloped power can be a dangerous thing," Jaered said. He slapped Patrick on the back of his head.

"Ow!" Patrick rubbed it. "It's not like I did it on purpose."

One last glance at the icy mound, and Jaered headed for the kitchen. "I need a beer," he announced. Eve wouldn't appreciate that her multimillion-dollar training facility was almost crushed by a glacial avalanche.

"How many more powers do you suspect he has?" Marcus joined him in the kitchen and snatched the opened beer from Jaered. He took a swig.

"I don't know. No one does. Same goes for Ian."

Marcus's squint pushed his eyebrows together like one long caterpillar. "What do you mean, like Ian?"

"When he was revived in the modified boost, we restarted his core. It was supposed to open him up to all of his powers."

"You mean to tell me that Ian's inability to master his full complement of powers was engineered?" He set his bottle on the counter with such force, beer sloshed out. "Who did it, the Primary?"

"Why would you think the Primary?" Jaered said.

Marcus wiped the splash away with the side of his hand. "Because he fiddles with anything that threatens him."

"Ian's mother was behind it," Jaered said.

"I've got questions coming out of my ears," Marcus growled. "You going to answer them?"

"If you tell me what happened to Vael." Jaered stared at Marcus like a dare.

Marcus looked down at his feet and his nostrils flared. "The Primary condemned Vael to Stag with me."

"And?" Jaered said. He had to know the truth.

"The bastard cut his hands off," Marcus snarled between his clenched jaw.

Jaered's breaths came quick and he retrieved another beer from the refrigerator. Before he could close the door, Tara snagged that one and reached inside for another bottle.

"If we're celebrating, we can't leave Patrick out." She left them in the kitchen.

Jaered grabbed one for himself, but grasped it so tight, he could have shattered it. "I'm sorry for getting him involved."

"You're fighting a good fight," Marcus said. "He hadn't had something to believe in for a long time. He died saving others." The old general's lip quivered. "No father could be more proud."

Jaered blinked away the threatening tears, then wandered into the gym with Marcus at his heels. He raised his bottle. "To Patrick, for not leaving us homeless."

Patrick and Tara clinked bottles, and then took swigs from the opposite end of the gym.

"Here, here," Marcus said and downed half his bottle in a drawn-out gulp.

"And to the fallen who have gotten us this far." Jaered and Marcus locked eyes. "To Vael."

The old general nodded. "To my son and his ultimate sacrifice."

Patrick and Tara sobered, and lifted their bottles. "To Vael," they said in unison.

A shimmering emerald cloud formed in the center of the auditorium and grew in width. Patrick and Tara scurried into the upper rows.

Wyatt and five other rebel troops' images solidified. The rebel lowered his gun when he caught sight of Jaered holding a beer. "What the hell?" he said. "There was a disturbance in the instruments for this location."

Jaered tilted his beer in Patrick's direction. "Ask him."

"Look outside," Patrick said.

The rebels walked over and stood at the picture window. "Eve's going to blow a gasket." Wyatt tossed a grin at Jaered from over his shoulder. "But in a good way."

Eve sipped her tea and looked out the window of her plane. Jaered drummed his fingers on the table that separated them. It wasn't like her to avoid a topic. Whatever this was about, he wasn't going to like it.

"You should be proud of him," Jaered said. "He still needs to keep his cool under pressure, though, but that will come with more experience."

"He's progressing faster than I'd predicted," she said.

"Not fast enough as far as I'm concerned." Jaered straightened up in his seat. "What's this meeting really about?"

"What do you mean?" She didn't pull her attention away from the window.

"I could have caught you up on his progress from the auditorium. Patrick would have loved to give you a demonstration."

"There will be time for that later." She ran her finger down the side of her iced tea glass. "The Primary is increasing his efforts to weed out the rebels, and now he's added Stag's escapees to the hit list."

"So, what does that have to do with me?" Jaered stared at her, confused. This news wasn't anything they hadn't anticipated.

"The longer Ian and Rayne are on Thrae, the scales tip in Aeros's favor. I don't have to tell you what a catastrophe it would be if he should find either one, or both," she said. "And with the farmhouse compromised, we need to get word to Ian before he returns."

The pulse in Jaered's neck throbbed. He knew where this was headed, and more than anything, he didn't want to hear the next words come out of her mouth.

"You have to go to Thrae," she said.

"You know what you're asking." He met her intense gaze. "I'll be putting everyone in the Northern Colony at risk."

"What makes you think they haven't been dealt a severe blow already?" Eve leaned back in her seat. "Think, Jaered. Your father's been unable to get his hands on Ian. And now his playground has been taken away from him. We both know how he can be when he's out of control."

"Just shyfting there will condemn anyone left alive." He pushed out of the airplane seat and paced in the narrow aisle. "I wouldn't know where to begin to look for them," he hissed.

"We need Ian and Rayne back here in one piece," Eve said. "You may be the only one who can make a difference at this point. I know my sister and how she thinks, but you know Thrae as well as she does. We must put our heads together and figure out where she could be protecting Rayne."

Jaered paused with his hand on the seatback in its upright position. "You want me to scour that planet based on hunches."

"That's more than what Ian started with." Eve leaned back in her seat. "Find them. Bring them back before Aeros destroys that entire planet."

THIRTY-NINE

Ian had shyfted to the one place on his mother's map that made no sense. The one crossed out, in what would have been Australia on Earth. He'd made his way out of the vortex building and had searched about a third of the abandoned dome when he was forced to take a break.

He plopped down on a large chunk of cement while his stomach growled in anticipation of a lunch break that wouldn't be coming. As hard as he tried, he couldn't recall the last time he'd eaten.

The city lay in ruins. From the looks of it, the inhabitants had been much more progressive than what he saw in the bleak existence of Stag, and more on the same level as the Northern Colony.

A sizable rat emerged from a crack in the nearby rubble. The rodent weaved around the crumbled asphalt and approached. It sniffed at Ian's boots, then lifted its head, pressing its front paws together as though begging for what Ian couldn't give.

The battle in his stomach raged on and he licked his lips wondering how raw rat meat tasted. He decided he wasn't that starved. Not yet.

What Ian needed was water. The search for a well, or any working faucet, had come up dry. He chuckled at the unintended pun.

There was a huge gap in the dome's ceiling as though it'd taken a direct hit from an outside force that had exposed the city to the elements overhead. Its hanging beams were twisted and broken in a torn spider web. If he stared at the opening long enough, it appeared that connecting wires were still intact, but it was impossible to tell for sure from the ground.

What had Sophenna told him that day she handed him the map? A catastrophe had decimated the colony. From the number of skeletons strewn about the city, whatever had taken out the dome must have been sudden and unexpected.

Memories of those left behind in Stag triggered Ian's grief and he bent over, resting his elbows on his legs. He hoped that shyftors had returned to save the rest, but Ian feared that Aeros had gotten to them first.

A massive crimson shadow lit up the rubble ahead of him and headed toward his resting spot. He stood and retrieved his helmet that had rolled off the slab and onto the ground. A gigantic methane storm descended on the dome while Ian twisted and secured the helmet in place. He pressed the button, turning on the oxygen flow.

The third button flashed on and off. The oxygen flowed, so what was the apparent warning about?

Red mist seeped in through the gap in the dome. Ian continued his search for a trapdoor in the ground, anything similar to what he'd seen in the middle of Stag. Thus far, he hadn't found an intact structure where his mother and Rayne might have found refuge. Unsure how much time he had before the oxygen ran out, he picked up his speed. His peripheral vision was obliterated by the helmet, but Ian didn't waste precious oxygen and kept his cussing to himself.

The poisonous methane filled the ruins and turned the air blood red. Lightheaded, Ian's steps faltered and he stumbled, landing on all fours, gasping for air. The hissing taunt at his ears didn't let up. Why was it so difficult to breathe? He crawled, disoriented.

The hissing was drowned out by shouts and running footsteps. Ian fought to raise the helmet to see where the sounds came from. A pair of environmental suit boots kicked up dirt a few yards ahead. Ian rolled onto his back, mesmerized by the abstract light show while a heavy curtain shut on his eyes.

Whispers drew Ian out of his dreamless sleep, but in his groggy state, he couldn't make out what they were saying. It sounded like an argument. He went to take a deep breath, but it triggered a coughing fit and he rolled onto his side with his lungs burning. The voices fell silent.

He was in a small room and he'd been laid out on a cot, similar to the ones in Stag. For a few seconds, he thought he'd been brought back to the prison colony, but the walls were wood paneled, not made from adobe, and he dismissed the panic attack as nothing more than a nightmare.

"Ian," came from the doorway.

He looked up at the sound of her voice, at the woman he thought was lost to him forever. Rayne knelt down next to him with damp cheeks glistening beneath her crystal blue eyes. The cruel fate that they could never touch filled him with angst. He was desperate to throw his arms around her and hold her tight. From the torture creasing her face, she felt the same.

"What are you doing here," she asked when she found her voice.

"I'm here to take you home." He sat up on the cot.

"You shouldn't have come," she said. "Aeros is after me."

"I know." Ian coughed. "We need to get out of here before he figures out where I shyfted to."

Alarm widened her eyes. "You've seen him?"

"He caught up with me at the prison colony." Ian stood on shaky legs, but they soon gave out and he collapsed back onto the cot.

"You're lucky to be alive," Rayne said. She withdrew his environmental suit they'd stuffed under the cot, and she stuck her arm deep into it. Two of her fingers wiggled out a hole at the back leg.

"It must have ripped when Aeros attacked me."

"Then you're extra lucky to be alive," she said with a weak grin that melted Ian's heart. She pursed her lips. "Are Patrick and Tara okay? Where are they? Did anyone else come with you?"

"They're back on Earth." Ian drew a deep breath and released it in a slow stream. He rose to his feet and this time, stayed erect.

The small room shook and dust rained on them. "Our instruments indicated a meteor shower was on the way," Rayne said. "Looks like it's here." She rushed out of the room and Ian followed her down a hallway that led to an open area. Two bodies clad in environmental suits had stepped out of their quarters and were closing the door behind them.

"Damn it," Rayne reached for a suit hanging on a hook. "I told them not to go without me." She kicked off her shoes and slipped into the suit.

"What's going on?" Ian said.

"They went to check the dome." She zipped the suit up to her neck. "It's not in great shape and they're afraid the power grid will crash from the storm."

"I'll go." Ian grabbed the helmet from her.

Rayne snatched it back. "Don't be a hero, Ian. You can barely stand." She stuck the helmet on and secured the buckles like she'd done it multiple times. "We'll be back. There's crackers and water in the cupboard behind you," she shouted through the faceplate.

"I've come too far to lose you again." Ian pressed his hands to the sides of her helmet. "Be careful."

"You know me so well." She let herself out and Ian stood in the doorway taking in every nuance, every step until she disappeared around a corner in the hallway.

Ian closed the door. Beeps came from down the hall and he went to investigate. A single control panel, similar to the ones in the other colonies, sat in the middle of the small room. A monitor displayed a grid in the shape of the dome. A red patch to one side of the apex blinked, and Ian assumed it was the damaged section. He sat in the chair and watched as dozens of dots approached the grid from the north. The meteors were about to strike.

Two blue dots emerged outside the dome and then stopped. He followed the third blue dot as Rayne turned one corner and then another until she paused at the edge of the dome. Her dot emerged beyond its boundary and joined the others. *Their coms are working*, Ian realized, and that small bit of news gave him comfort. Rayne wasn't alone.

The blue dots worked their way around the edge of the dome. Ian shot to his feet. To his horror, they were headed for the meteor shower side. An alarm sounded and the room filled with strobing scarlet at the same moment the first dots impacted the dome. A dead panel came alive with a dozen blinking lights.

Unable to figure out the panel controls, Ian ran back to the cot room and grabbed his suit, then opened every closet and cupboard he could find in the sparse five-room quarters. In the last drawer, he found a roll of duct tape and inspected every inch of his suit, ripping off tape with his teeth and repairing it as fast as he could.

When Ian checked his tank, he discovered that he'd used two-thirds of it evading Aeros and searching the dome. He hadn't come across extra tanks or a nozzle to fill it, so he returned to the monitor and checked their progress. They were walking into the heart of the meteor shower.

A video feed switched to a view of the suited bodies walking along the dome's perimeter. Chunks of rocks and dust were kicked up all around them. Ian donned the suit and secured the helmet, then rushed out the front door.

FORTY

Rayne stumbled, but the solid pull on the tether in either direction helped to keep her on her feet. The dust clouds swallowed Liem and Gwynn in front and behind her. The pressure of the cord around her waist was a beacon of comfort.

They'd come out to inspect the dome a week earlier, soon after arriving, but the air was clean then and they didn't need to wear their suits. Everything looked so different this time, and she was disoriented.

Between the confining suit and the dust cloud, her claustrophobia seeped in and her breaths grew shallow and rapid. Sweat formed across the back of her neck and her skin turned clammy. Moisture clouded the inside of her faceplate.

"How are you doing?" Gwynn's voice sounded in Rayne's ear.

"I'm okay," she said, but it came out raspy.

"You're lighting up the dust around you," Gwynn said from behind. "That indicator on your chest tells me that you're not breathing right."

"Take deep breaths, Rayne. Focus on the dome, not the storm," Liem said.

Gwynn had warned Rayne not to touch the dome itself for fear she'd corrupt the delicate system, but the shower of meteors made it a challenge. Many were the size of a large suitcase. Rayne couldn't help but stoop whenever they came crashing toward her but they bounced over their heads and landed a few feet away, kicking up clouds of dust. Gwynn had promised they would, thanks to the curvature and force field emitted from the dome.

"I'm getting more activity ahead." The edge in Liem's voice put Rayne on the alert.

"We'll turn around," Gwynn said. "There's no need to take any more chances. The power grid is holding up on this side."

The ground beneath Rayne's feet shook with a tremendous shudder and stopped her mid-step. The small rocks at her feet bounced across the ground like marbles. She peered through the dust cloud at the sound of sizzling scrapes from above. A boulder the size of a small car, had struck the dome and it slid down the slope. They were directly in its path.

"Run!" Gwynn shrieked.

The tether tightened and Rayne stumbled. Liem and Gwynn had taken off in opposite directions. Rayne's arms flapped like she wanted to take flight. Too terrified to speak, she fell to the side and crashed headfirst against the dome.

The tether loosened as the sizzling grew deafening and she crouched, ducking her head the best she could, in spite of the helmet.

Gwynn covered Rayne, pressing her against her chest. Liem crouched nearby, unable to come in contact with Rayne.

The boulder bounced over them, but it snagged a piece of Gwynn's helmet and she was thrown off to the side, jarring Rayne out of her embrace.

"Gwynn!" Liem shouted, but she didn't answer.

Rayne scooted over to her and discovered that her helmet was cracked down the middle and she bled from her nose and mouth. Rayne shook her, but she remained limp. "She's not responsive!"

"I'll get her," Ian said. "Get back inside the dome."

"Ian! What are you doing here!" Rayne said, lifting her face to find him approaching.

He dragged Gwynn away. Rayne disconnected the tether when Ian slung Gwynn over his shoulder.

"Come on, we need to get out of this storm," Liem said.

They followed the base of the dome back to the door and Liem punched the large, round button. The doors swished open. Liem offered to carry Gwynn once they were safe inside, but Ian waved him off and followed them back to the apartment.

Once inside, Ian laid her on the cot, then dropped to one knee, coughing and sputtering. Rayne removed his helmet.

His tank read empty. It was then that she noticed the blinking light on his chest plate.

"I need the first aid kit." Liem pushed in and removed her helmet. Everyone paused at the bloody trail down the side of her head. Rayne grabbed the kit from the other bedroom and opened it.

Liem removed a pen light, then checked Gwynn's pupils. "Go, I'll take care of her," he said, removing bandages and iodine from the case.

"I want to stay," Ian said.

"There's nothing you can do to help," Liem said. "She'll be all right, but I need space to tend to her."

"Come on Ian, I'll make you something to eat." Rayne went to grab his arm, but retracted her hand at the last second. Their eyes met, both of them filled with pain at the familiar occurrence. He followed her out and closed the door, but not before steeling one more glance at his mother. Rayne's heart leapt out to him. This wasn't the reunion she'd hoped for, for either one of them.

She slipped out of her suit and hung it up. Ian did the same in silence, then grabbed his shoulder and turned away, but not before Rayne caught his grimace. "Are you okay?" she asked.

"I dislocated my shoulder in a fight. I wasn't supposed to lift anything for a few days." He held his arm against his chest.

Rayne inhaled deep as the ache swept over her. "I would throw my arms around you if I could," she said softly.

"Back at ya," Ian said, and gazed at her with such sorrow. "I forgot how much this hurts." She gave him a weak nod.

He sat in the chair at the kitchen table and leaned back, rubbing his face. "How did you get here?"

"Liem shyfted directly here with the supplies we were going to need. Gwynn and I traveled by boat and then," she smiled wide, "by dragon." She moved about the kitchen, preparing to heat some canned soup. "When we were dropped off just outside of Stag, Liem met us there and we hiked a few miles to a cave vortex that he knew about, and then he shyfted us here." Rayne found the old-fashioned can opener and used it. The second she pierced the lid, the smell of chicken noodle soup wafted up toward her. "The vortex was weak. Liem struggled to pull enough energy to shyft us here."

"I shyfted into a basement vortex room at the other side of the dome. Is that the only one?" Ian asked.

"I don't know, but it sounds like the same one we came through." Rayne grabbed the crackers and opened the box, then set it on the table in front of him. How long had it been since they'd been together? Close to a month, maybe more. She found it unnerving that she struggled to remember the estate, his mansion, their walks around the lake. What had happened since she became stranded on Thrae? Rayne blinked, aware that Ian had said something. "What?"

"How long have you been here?" he said.

"I'm not sure," she said. "Time is strange here. The days and nights seem much longer."

"I was told that the planet's rotation has been disturbed." Ian grabbed a few crackers from the box. "It would affect all sense of time. Days, months, even their year would be longer than Earth's . . ." Ian slipped into a lecture on the physics of the planet while he nibbled on the crackers. The longer he spoke, Rayne's heartache diminished and warmth spread throughout her limbs like a soothing bath. The familiar had returned, and with it, the comfort she felt whenever he was near. She paused at stirring the pot of soup and stared at its swirling contents.

He fell silent. "I love you," he said with such emotion that it took her breath away.

She turned on her heel and the spoon slipped from her hand. For once it had come from his heart, not his head. Unbridled emotion flowed from his eyes and pierced her heart, opening a wound and bleeding it dry. She fell into the chair across from him, unwilling to keep dammed what she'd kept bottled up inside. She stretched her clasped hands toward him. He reached out and rested his on either side a hair's breadth away.

"It took chasing you across two dimensions, and an entire planet . . . but there it is," Ian whispered.

"I killed you." Her lower lip quivered.

"I begged you to do it," he said.

Rayne sniffed and wiped her nose with the back of her hand. "You tried to burn me up," she said playfully.

"I tried to burn Jaered. You got in the way." Concern crept into his expression and for the first time, his eyes scanned every exposed inch of her. "You're all right, I didn't hurt you?"

She shook her head as the memories from that night churned. "Aeros took Jaered, he was seriously burned. Is he?"

"Fully recovered. Beat me up for doing it to him. I returned the favor. I guess we both had it coming." Ian's tone had changed, like it always did whenever their conversation touched upon Jaered.

Rayne got up and cleaned the spoon in the sink. She stirred the soup in silence. The familiar had its downside.

"I know why he's so obsessed with you. Why you can't seem to let him go," Ian said in such a gentle way that Rayne paused and faced him. "I spent some time with Sophenna. She showed me the pictures," he said.

"Kyre was five months pregnant when Aeros killed her," Rayne said. "What Aeros has done to his home world . . . I understand his rage . . . his drive."

"His conviction," Ian said and looked up at her. "It's contagious, his need to fight back. Until I stepped onto Thrae, I had no idea who, or what, I've been fighting for. I do now."

"Jaered's not your enemy, Ian," Rayne said.

"No . . . he's my brother." He leaned back in the chair. "As is Patrick."

"You're wrong," Rayne said. "Gwynn is your mother, Sophenna is Jaered's, and Eve is Patrick's. They're sisters, that makes you cousins."

"We share the same father," Ian said.

She stared at Ian as it sank in. Why hadn't Gwynn and Sophenna told her the rest? The pot spurted and bubbled behind her. Rayne turned off the stove and ladled two bowls of soup, then joined him at the table and set one in front of him. "Dig in. Gwynn and Liem told me about Stag. I can't imagine you had much to eat."

"I want to hear about your travels," he said.

"Wasn't Oocaw amazing!" Rayne blurted.

"I know!" Ian brightened, then leaned over his bowl. "It smells good." He waited for her to begin, then picked up the spoon, staring at it. "I can't take you back, not until I can talk with my mother."

She smiled. "I can't wait for you to meet her."

FORTY-ONE

an stood still, staring at the bedroom door. Liem and Rayne had left to scout out water, but he knew the real reason. It was to give him and his mother time alone. He lifted his fist, hesitated, then knocked.

Shuffles came from the other side, then scuffling steps. The door opened a crack, then wider and his mother gazed at him with eyes brimming in tears.

"They told me you were here." She threw her arms around him.

The warmth . . . the love that he felt in her embrace, filled him in a way he'd never felt before, and he yearned for her to never let go. He buried his face in the crook of her neck and his chest heaved. "They told me you were dead," he whimpered.

"A day hasn't risen and set that I haven't thought of you," she said.

Her voice and touch were so gentle, yet strength poured from her and seeped into Ian's core. It ignited at the sound of her voice and churned in his chest. She lifted her head and kissed his forehead, then pushed away. He lingered in the doorway. "Your wound, are you all right?"

"I just need some tea." She led him to the kitchen and he leaned against the counter while she prepared it, unwilling to separate them by even the kitchen table.

He absorbed everything about her. Her ebony hair had a thick streak of lightning where she was graying, and it was wavy and long. Her eyes were as deep as twilight and her skin an olive tone, so similar to his. He thought back to Sophenna's fair skin and how blond her hair was, almost white. Eve was shorter and more petite than her two sisters, with strawberry-blond hair. Patrick joked that his mother dyed it the same color all his life. Given Patrick's coloring, Ian wasn't so sure.

Gwynn paused long enough to hold up an extra mug, Ian gave her a tight-lipped smile and shook his head. She filled the tea strainer with fresh tea leaves from an assortment of different bags. The one she chose reminded Ian of Milo's fall baking with its apples-and-cinnamon perfume.

"Are you the tallest of your brothers?" She asked like they were at a family reunion.

"Yes, he said. "Have you ever seen Patrick?"

She lifted her face and bit her lower lip. "The last time I saw him, he was three, maybe four. I last saw Jaered when he brought Rayne here. He's the one I've watched growing up."

Ian clenched his teeth. His mother had more of a relationship with Jaered, than her own son. "The Primary kept us apart," he said.

"To punish my arrogance, he banned me to Thrae." Gwynn blew across the surface of her mug, then took a sip.

"Wanting a child doesn't make you arrogant," Ian said.

"It wasn't conceiving that angered him," she said. "It was how."

Ian leaned against the counter. "Genetics."

"Sophenna bore Jaered nine years earlier. Aeros had raped her, like he'd done thousands of times before. Patrick was born three years after when Eve got her way with him. I had to bear the third Heir. But Aeros was too savvy, and our feud had lasted for centuries. He would never have trusted my wiles. Another means was necessary."

"One of your sisters got his sperm and you used it to conceive." Ian ran his fingers through his hair.

"We may have created the enemies of our enemy," she said with raised shoulders and a thrust-out jaw. "But don't believe for a second that you weren't cherished, and loved deeply."

"Yet, you created soldiers more than children," Ian said.

His mother got to her feet and met his gaze. "I've born thousands of children and watched them, and their children, and their children's children die. Lived more lives than you can imagine. I stopped counting how many husbands I've lost over the centuries." She leaned in and Ian smelled apples on her breath. "If you and your brothers succeed and stop the tyrant that is Aeros, you will not only be cherished above all others, but by the Weir race and humans alike, for all eternity. You may not have had the life you wanted, Ian, but will you have the victory that we all deserve?"

Unable to respond, he dropped his gaze to the floor as her words sank in, stilling his heart and quenching his anger.

"Perhaps you shouldn't have come," she said, replenishing the steamy water in her mug.

"Jaered claimed he couldn't come back," Ian said. "But he wouldn't tell me why."

She returned to the table. "Jaered spent most of his life defying his father. When it became obvious that he couldn't reverse his father's destruction of Thrae, he took the fight to Earth."

"He connected with Eve," Ian said.

"And slowly, methodically, brought many of Thrae's Sars to Earth. Liem is one of the few left in the Northern Colony."

"Come back with me," Ian said. "We'll return and take Sophenna, too. I can't protect you here, but Eve can keep you safe on Earth."

"Sophenna and I can't leave Thrae," Gwynn said. "Aeros has sucked too much of its core energy."

"What does that have to do with you?" Ian asked. "You and your sisters aren't Sars."

"But we are Ancients," she said. "We have a direct connection to the planet, just like Aeros and the Primary."

"Is that why Aeros can shyft freely around Thrae, but I need a vortex?"

She gave him a guarded stare. "You're powerless on Thrae?" He shook his head. She stood and abandoned her cup, gripping the back of chair. "You had to have shyfted here," she said.

"I had to come in contact with the vortex column in Stag to do it. The same for the other shyfters there," he said. "The only other time I was able to shyft without a vortex, was when I was in the lava tube in Oocaw's den." Her breaths came shallow and rapid. "Why, what does that mean?" he asked.

His mother didn't respond at first. "Thrae's core could be so compromised, that it's only fueling the columns left to run the domes." She paced the floor with her finger to her lips and didn't acknowledge him for a handful of minutes. She had transformed from his mother to the scientist that she was, in mere seconds.

"What does that mean?" Ian said.

"The planet is in more trouble than I thought. If Aeros becomes aware of it, he could bring destruction to every other living soul or creature left on Thrae," she said.

"With a chain reaction," Ian added.

The door creaked open and Rayne stuck her head in. A wide smile and glistening eyes peered at Ian through her faceplate. At his sober demeanor, her expression drooped and she pushed into the room with Liem carrying in a spare environmental suit.

Rayne twisted her helmet, but hadn't turned her oxygen off and a tremendous hiss burst out as she lifted it over her head. Liem reached around her and pressed the button. A tense silence hung in the room.

"What is it?" Rayne asked, glancing between Ian and his mother. "What's wrong?"

"Thrae's core is weaker than I thought," his mother said. "We need to take some measurements, Liem."

"Now?" He paused with his gloved fingers on his zipper.

"Be a dear and retrieve my pack from the control room, Rayne." She took off and Ian's mother grabbed one of the environmental suits off the hook. "Take Rayne to Earth."

"I can help gather the data," Ian said.

"Aeros is still out there." She stepped into the suit and pulled it up to her shoulders, then slipped into the sleeves. "Your priority above everything else, is to protect Rayne." She zipped up the suit and Liem handed her the helmet from the spare suit.

Rayne passed her the bag but didn't let go right away. "Will I see you again?"

Ian's mother hesitated and she gave Rayne a gentle smile. "From the moment you arrived on Thrae, we've always been on borrowed time," Gwynn said. She placed a gloved hand on Rayne's cheek. "You are so much like Kyre, yet, refreshingly your own person. I'm glad we've had this chance." Rayne threw her arms around Ian's mother. Gwynn leaned in and whispered something in her ear. Rayne nodded and pulled away, swiping at her cheeks.

"Let me help you," Ian said, unwilling to abandon her after such a short time together. He still had so many questions, things to share.

"My priority is keeping Thrae alive until you can defeat Aeros," Gwynn said. "Perhaps, one day, we will revive this planet together." He hugged her like he never wanted to let go. It took his mother to separate them. She brushed his bangs out of his face and leaned her forehead against his. "I love you," she whispered. "More than the universe itself."

"I will make you proud," he said for her ears only.

"Oh, Ian." She cupped his chin. "You already have." They left with a shish of the door.

"What do you need to pack?" Ian said.

"Not much," Rayne said.

"Grab it." Ian opened the cupboard. When searching for the duct tape, he remembered seeing a water bottle. It was in the second cabinet he opened, and he topped it off with water Rayne had brought back.

"You're your mother's son," Rayne called out from down the hall.

Ian paused. He'd seen the resemblance right away, but his mother was methodical, worked from her head more than her heart. If Ian was honest, he did, too.

Rayne set a small backpack down near the suits, then went about opening all of the kitchen cupboards.

"What are you doing?" he asked.

"Taking inventory of the supplies they have left. Looks like there's enough for a couple more days." She shut the cabinet doors. "But they'll have to ration the water."

"Jaered gave me coordinates for a safe house. We'll go there first," Ian said.

"The red cloud is hanging around outside." She checked the oxygen tank on her suit. "I'm almost empty."

"Mine reads empty," Ian said.

"The tanks to refill ours are in a nearby building. I think it used to be a hospital." She donned the suit. "Liem showed me where he found them."

"Why didn't you bring any here?" Ian asked.

"They were too big, and heavy," Rayne said.

They helped each other with their helmets, then Ian grabbed Rayne's pack and they left to find the hospital.

In his search for the others, Ian hadn't gone into all of the buildings. He didn't need to. Most were nothing but crumbled walls and empty structures, having lost their interiors long ago. The apartment they'd brought him to was part of a research facility with hermetically sealed doors. For the first time, it occurred to Ian that the bedrooms had once been offices and the kitchen, a break room.

They stepped outside and were met with a blood-red sky. "This way," Rayne said over their coms and led him down one of the streets. They made a couple of turns and she paused at the far corner. "There." She pointed at a large structure. Most of its windows were busted out, but a few remained. Tall letters spelled out the hospital's name over the entry. Most had fallen off, but a few pieces remained with rebar poles sticking out like loose hair. There wasn't enough for Ian to guess what it had been called.

Ian's core burped deep in his chest. He didn't know any other way to describe the odd sensation. He stopped with a fist pressed to his chest while Rayne crossed the street, headed for the entrance. It took a few seconds to realize he wasn't with her, and she turned around. "What's wrong?"

"I don't know," he said. "Something happened to disturb the energy field."

She looked up and turned around. "The dome looks okay to me."

"It wasn't the energy around us," he said. "I think it came from Thrae itself."

"Come on," she yelled. "Let's fill up and get out of here."

He hesitated before following. His mother was right. Thrae was weaker than everyone realized. If the core disintegrated, the domes would fail. Without a way for shyfters to evacuate those remaining on the planet.

The nozzle attached to the hospital oxygen tanks didn't fit the opening to Ian's valve, and they searched the rubble for something to act as a go-between. Rayne found a baby bottle nipple in what used to be a nursery, but the pressure was too great and it popped right off when she turned the handle. She scrambled to shut off the flow.

"Shit! There's got to be something we can use," she said and disappeared down the hall.

Ian grasped the doorjamb to keep upright. His oxygen had run out and he tried to conserve what was left inside his suit. He wouldn't make it out of the hospital doors, much less to the vortex.

He stumbled back into the hospital room and collapsed against the wall, trying to focus on something, anything to dispel the blurred vision. A gulp of air cleared his sight. From his lower position, Ian noticed a valve extending from the wall behind the bed's headboard.

He crawled over and with the last of his strength, pushed the bed from the wall. The nozzle appeared smaller than the other ones they'd found. He grabbed the shoulder strap to his tank and pulled it toward him, then pressed his shoulder against the wall and slid upward to a standing position. The tank was light enough that he could hoist it up onto his hip and he dropped the top against the wall, nozzle to nozzle. It took three tries, but he finally got them to connect, only for his legs to turn to mush and he collapsed to the floor before he could secure the connection.

"Ian!" Rayne rushed in and peered at him through her faceplate.

He lifted his finger and pointed upward when his voice failed him. She looked up, then grabbed his tank and pushed the nozzles together.

"I'll get it, Ian, hang on!" she said, but then screamed in frustration. "Damn these gloves, I can't turn the bolt hard enough for a tight fit. She stepped back and tugged on the Velcro strips that kept her gloves snug.

Ian batted at her legs for her to not expose herself to the poisonous gas, but to his horror, she removed one, tightening the Velcro back around her bare wrist. She brought the nozzles together and tried the bolt again.

His lids grew too heavy to keep open, and as they shut on him, hissing leapt into the room at the same moment he slid the rest of the way to the floor.

FORTY-TWO

Jaered stepped out of the vortex a fraction of a second before the field fluctuated. He reached out and felt the waning energy, fully aware of what it meant. He had to find them, and fast, or they'd all be stranded on the dying planet.

The desolate city hadn't changed much since he'd been here last. From the sizzle of the dome overhead, the column of energy had continued to flow, protecting nothing but ruins and the natural elements that clung to life when those higher on the food chain had succumbed long ago. He feared that his beloved home world couldn't cling to life much longer, and that even the ruins of a once vibrant world would soon turn to dust. In spite of the urgency, he took a second to imagine Earth with the same fate. It expedited his steps.

A crimson cloud of death hovered over the city. Jaered had come prepared, aware that the dome was exposed when a meteor had penetrated the structure about a decade ago. Additional tiles had fallen off since he'd last been there, and a gaping hole stared like an all-knowing eye from overhead. The exposure wasn't a good omen.

Jaered lifted his wrist and checked his oxygen gauge. A full tank would give him enough time to search the ruins, but he had no intention of it taking any longer than necessary. The fluctuation in energy might have masked his arrival on Thrae, but if his father still searched for Ian, the slightest disturbance might gain his attention.

Every step kicked up dirt and the methane cloud limited his visibility. He made his way down the main street, sweeping the tracker out in front of him. Warm-blooded images appeared on the screen at his sleeve, but to his dismay, they were too small to be human.

He'd no sooner reached midtown when a tall image appeared to his right, about a hundred yards away. He froze where he stood as the shimmering red and gold heat signature walked at a fast pace in and out between the thick slabs of concrete. It moved in the same direction as the vortex, but too fast for it to be a person searching the area. If it was his father, he was on his way out, but if it was Ian . . .

Jaered hurried, following a parallel course, one block over, and slightly behind the image. At this rate, the person would reach the vortex a handful of minutes ahead of Jaered, and would be gone by the time he reached it. At each step, Jaered fought to pull energy from Thrae to shyft ahead, but whatever tingling he felt, dissipated.

The person stopped and Jaered caught up, aligning himself with a city block's width between them. To his shock, the image turned and retraced its steps. Jaered made his way to the same city block as the image, then pressed against the upright building wall, and peered around the corner.

Whoever was in the environmental suit had bent over something in the middle of the street with their back to Jaered. He crept closer, keeping himself near the building, and studied the figure. The person's build was tall and lanky enough to be his father, but everything about their movements told Jaered it wasn't.

Jaered stepped away from the building. "Ian!" he shouted, but realized that his helmet had muffled most of it and with cautious steps, he approached the figure from behind and touched their shoulder.

The person spun around. A startled Gwynn stumbled back, knocking her equipment, tripod and all, to the ground. It took a couple of seconds for her to recognize Jaered through their masks, and his aunt relaxed. She caught her breath with one hand resting against Jaered's shoulder. "Oh my god, where did you come from!"

"Are you alone?" Jaered said and looked around. "Is Rayne with you?"

"Liem's setting up some instruments in the building down the block. Rayne was with us, but Ian came and they left about half an hour ago."

Jaered's pulse raced through his veins. "They left? Where was he taking them?"

"I don't know; we weren't there when they left." Gwynn shrugged from beneath her suit. "He'll keep her safe, Jaered. You can trust that."

"They're far from safe," he said. He turned to go, when his core released a plume of heated energy and he bent over, groaning as blistering heat burned his throat and seared the inside of his mouth. Rumbling. Rocks in the street bounced about like spilt marbles. Deafening creaks came from the surrounding buildings, and they swayed as the earthquake grew in force. Jaered grabbed Gwynn's sleeve. "Run!" he yelled. They took off down the street as chunks of concrete cracked off the building façades and showered around them. Jaered dodged the bigger ones and jumped over the smaller pieces, but Gwynn broke out of his grasp when she tripped over exposed rebar.

He helped her up and they kept going. A shadow raced toward them, and Jaered glanced up. A building at the end of the street was falling directly in their path. He pulled Gwynn toward the sidewalk and dove through a window display, rolling to a stop inside a store. Gwynn skidded to a stop beside him. He jumped to his feet, grabbed her, and pushed them both up against a thick center beam in the open room. The falling building in the street slammed against the side of the store and it tore away, mixing with the crumbing multi-storied office building beyond.

Gwynn screamed. It took a second for Jaered to recognize that she was screaming Liem's name.

The quake had decimated most of the remaining high-rises in the heart of the downtown area, and it had taken a while for Jaered and Gwynn to climb out. He raised his arm to shield his eyes from the bright sun streaming in through the dome. "Maybe he shyfted in time?" Jaered said while lowering the protective shield on his helmet. At her silence, he discovered that she had removed her helmet, and hadn't heard his question over the com. "Liem was a shyftor, he could have escaped," Jaered said gently.

"He knew where I was." Gwynn turned her back to him. "If he shyfted, he would have come to me."

Jaered removed his helmet and shut off the oxygen. "I have to get to Ian and Rayne. Could they have shyfted to the Northern Colony before returning to Earth?"

She regarded the remains of the building that had completely collapsed, and released a heartfelt sigh. "Ian mentioned going back for your mother," Gwynn said. "I told him she couldn't leave, but . . ."

"He's stubborn enough, he might have tried. Jaered grabbed Gwynn's sleeve. "Come on, we've got to shyft back now if I have any hope to still intercept them."

They raced for the vortex, hampered all the more by the dust and towering mounds of crumbled buildings.

"This was massive," Gwynn said from behind.

"I know," he said. "Thrae won't last much longer."

She stopped him. "She is already pulling energy from the electromagnetic dome columns to brace herself against the meteor showers. If they don't decimate her, the earthquakes will."

Her words fueled his steps and he broke ahead of her, reaching the vortex building a few moments before his aunt.

The building had cracked in half but they still had access to the staircase and descended to the lower level. They soon discovered that part of the ceiling had collapsed, blocking the short walk to the vortex room. Jaered pushed his shoulder against a beam, but it was wedged across their path and wouldn't budge.

Gwynn grabbed Jaered's shoulder. "Why are you so scared? What aren't you telling me?"

"The place where Ian is parashyfting Rayne was compromised. They're walking into a trap."

The news energized Gwynn. She tugged on the beam while Jaered pushed, but it wasn't any use.

He pressed his palms against it and dropped his head, focusing on drawing energy into his core, and when it sputtered to life, he captured that much more from the nearby field. A second later, the beam disappeared.

Together they pushed debris to the side and opened the door wide enough for the two of them to slip through, but they were forced to leave their helmets behind. Gwynn grabbed Jaered's hand and at a full run they jumped into the column of energy—and shyfted.

FORTY-THREE

Ian and Rayne stumbled through the remains of the city, fighting to make their way to the vortex building. When he had arrived, Ian committed the location to memory and believed he could retrace his steps, but the side visit to the hospital and the ensuing quake had changed the landscape.

Liem had shyfted them there in the dead of night, and Rayne wasn't much help in navigating what was left of the city.

Neither of them gave voice to their dread as they weaved in and out and over piles of rubble for what had to be a handful of miles of devastation. It took them stopping for a drink of water for Rayne to broach the painful truth. "Your mother," she said. "Maybe they were beyond the dome."

"She survived," he shot back, then gave her a pained grimace at how severe his tone had been. "She's an Ancient, she can't die." He stared across the remains of the city with a heaving chest. Rayne offered him water but he waved it off. "I don't know where we are," he admitted.

She looked around, studying their surroundings. "We came from that end of the dome," she said, pointing. "You and I both recall walking almost straight across from the vortex."

"But there's no more straight anything," Ian said. "We could be way off course."

Rayne screwed the top back onto the water bottle and tucked it under her arm. "Then we follow the curvature until you recognize something, because I'll drag you to hell with me before I die in this fishbowl."

She stared at him with such conviction, that it brought Ian to his feet. He reached toward her. "I'll carry the water," he said.

"I've got this." She gave him a backhanded wave to get moving. "Get us the hell out of here, preferably while we're still standing."

It took another hour or more for them to reach the last street before the edge of the dome. Ian stood with his back to it, looking in one direction, and then the other. A steeple had fallen off a building and lay crooked against the ground. The clock in its tower was familiar and Ian headed for it. Rayne followed in silence. Her steps had grown slower and she was no longer keeping up with him, so he matched his steps to hers as the sun set.

He stole glances in every direction, praying for a glimpse of his mother and Liem making their way toward the same location, but they were out of sight, if they were alive at all.

The footsteps behind him came to a halt. "We can't leave, not yet," Rayne said.

He turned at her tearful plea. "The last thing she told me was to keep you safe."

"And she told me to take care of you." Rayne walked up to him. "But part of that includes her now, doesn't it?" She brushed her nose with the sleeve on her shirt. "Neither one of us can leave Thrae without knowing she's safe."

Ian mulled over his options. "I'll shyft you to the Northern Colony. If my mother and Liem aren't there, I'll return with others to search for them," he said. "Sophenna can hide you until I return."

Rayne stared off in the distance while chewing on her lower lip. "Agreed." She marched by him, but not before tossing the empty water bottle in his direction.

He caught it with one hand, then followed her, hoping he wasn't making a grave error.

It could be the same building, but Ian wasn't positive. The quake had parted it down the middle like a torn roll opened to welcome a pat of butter. He led the way downstairs, but paused on the lowest step. Someone had cleared a path in the short hallway and the door was ajar. Ian remembered he'd closed it behind him. It was then that he noticed the two discarded helmets.

"They made it out," he shouted, and ran over, clearing more debris out of the way. Then he tugged on the door to open it further, but it didn't give. They slipped out of their helmets and into the vortex room that doubled as the energy source for the dome. The second he stepped inside, his core sputtered to life and he pressed his palms to the column, absorbing as much power as he could until his chest swelled with searing heat.

Ian pulled away from the column. "Ready," he said.

"How are we going to do this?" Rayne asked. "I don't want to drain you."

"Jaered taught me how to control my core during a shyft." He lifted his face to the energy column that disappeared into the ceiling of the room. "I've replenished my core, but there's no guarantee this will work until we try."

"You've really got to work on your pep talks." She stepped close. "This is going to hurt you, isn't it?"

"We'll be there before you know it," he said. Ian grabbed her hand. In an instant, thousands of needles raced through his body and threatened to tear his core apart. He fought to keep his pain from her intense gaze, and shyfted.

They appeared in the Northern Colony's storage room and let go of each other's hands. Rayne's entire body shivered from head to toe but she gave him a sly smile at the same time. "You know what this means," she said.

A noise from the other side of the metal door caught Ian's attention and he turned away. "You'll be tagging along on my field trips from now on."

"Yep," she said.

Ian pressed an ear to the door and focused on the sounds beyond. At a muted scream, he drew back. "Something's wrong. Stay here."

"Like hell," she said.

"Rayne, be reasonable," he hissed.

"You must have me confused with someone else." She pressed against the door. "Have we really been apart that long?"

He knew better than to argue with her, and he looked down at the crack below the door. The amber light wasn't strobing like the last time he'd shyfted into the room. Every red flag in his head waved with vigor, but they'd come too far to desert the others.

The door was bolted from the other side. Ian peered along the miniscule gap between the door and the frame. "Stay back," he told her. Rayne settled against the stacked crates. He pressed his palm against the door where the bar was latched and with his other hand, reached toward the vortex in the middle of the room. Energy leapt out from the vortex like a lightning bolt and passed through his arm, into his core, and out his opposite hand. Ian slid his palm along the door and with a metal scrape from the other side, he kept sliding his hand as though lifting the bar out of the brackets.

He let go and from the loud scrape, it was too soon. The bar slid back into place.

He focused on drawing power again, and this time, kept a keen ear to the other side as the bar swung far enough that when he let go, it slipped out of the brackets and fell to the floor with a clatter.

Rayne rushed toward the door but Ian stopped her with a raised hand. "You can come, but you have to promise me that you'll do what I say."

She gave him a subtle nod. He stepped out into the hall. The motion detectors caught his movement and turned the nearest light on, but left the rest of the long hallway in darkness.

The screams had ceased and Ian motioned for Rayne to follow. Ian led them down the hallway with their journey lit by the motion detectors overhead. A sound of running footsteps caused Ian to stop, and he held out his arm for Rayne to do the same.

The runners approached from a perpendicular hallway, but soon slowed their steps. "Who's there?" a frightened voice said. "Stay behind me," the woman added at a child's whimper. "The light is triggered. I know someone's there."

Ian peeked around the corner. The woman held back a small child around the age of three or four. When Ian stepped out into the hall with Rayne, the woman gasped and fell to one knee. "Your Highness, you've returned."

Rayne took her elbow and helped her up. The child grabbed her mother's skirt with one hand and didn't let go of her filthy stuffed toy with the other.

"I heard screams," Ian said.

"What's going on?" Rayne looked beyond the woman but the dark hallway offered nothing but deep shadows.

"Aeros is here. He found an entrance to one of the tunnels." She pressed the child against her. "He came upon the cave and went mad with rage. He's ripped many to shreds. The rest of us fled, but there's nowhere we can go he won't find us now." She grabbed Ian's sleeve in both hands and buried her face against it, sobbing.

He grasped her shoulders. "Was Sophenna there, have you seen Gwynn?"

"Or Liem?" Rayne said.

The woman stilled. "Sophenna escaped with many others, but they headed down a different tunnel."

Rayne's face contorted with fury. "Is Aeros still in the cave?

"I don't know," she said, stepping back, but then turned her dark eyes to Ian. "Can you stop him?"

At Ian's hesitation, Rayne glared at him. "Ian, we've got to try."

Ian had spent weeks trying to evade Aeros and save Rayne. It would be insanity to walk into the lion's den when he was so close to completing his mission. He looked in the direction the woman had come.

FORTY-FOUR

Ian and Rayne made their way through the scrambling, frantic crowd heading in the opposite direction. "Go above ground and hide the best you can," they told everyone they passed. "We'll alert you when it's safe to return.

Many of the faces turned from frightened to hopeful when they recognized Ian and Rayne. Several reached out and grabbed their hands, thanking them profusely. Ian struggled to keep a calm façade while Rayne threw her arms around them and urged everyone to keep out of sight.

It was impossible to count how many they passed along the way, but he estimated there were a couple hundred escaping souls.

The shrieks and shouts drew silent and as the crowd thinned, the hallway grew bloodier. The maimed or wounded were supported by other colonists and limped by, or were held upright with dragging feet.

"I wish Dr. Mac were here," Rayne said.

"If we survive this," Ian tossed over his shoulder. "I'll retrieve him."

"You confronted Aeros before, how?" she said when there was a lull in the oncoming crowd.

"I only evaded him," he said and inhaled deep. The guilt at leaving so many others in Stag flooded his chest and filled him with doubt. Was that why he stayed when every fiber of him told him to go? As he hurried down the tunnel, hoping they were headed toward the cave, he recalled how Aeros went after everyone else, but left him unscathed. He paused and turned to Rayne. "I think he wants me alive, but I don't know why. Rayne, you're the one who will be in grave danger. It's not too late. Please go back and hide with the others."

"I can't do that," she said. "These people have risked their lives for me. What does it say about me if I'm not willing to do the same for them?"

Her strength was contagious and in that moment, Ian knew he was capable of anything with her by his side. He continued down the tunnel with determined steps, counting on Aeros to still be in the cave. Ian would need to be near the energy column to have any hope of drawing upon his powers.

When they approached the wood-paneled door, bodies lined their path. Many were facedown while others were slumped over or sitting upright. Most appeared to have suffered core blasts to their heads or chests; a few were missing limbs.

A scream was cut short, just beyond the door. Ian took a deep breath. "I need to face him alone."

"What can I do?" she said.

"I'm going to draw him away from Thrae," Ian said. "And return to Earth. I'll come back for you once he's no longer a threat."

"But he'll go after you," Rayne said.

"On Earth, I can draw upon my powers freely, and there are lots of hiding places." Ian faced the door. "Find Sophenna and my mother. The second he's gone, help them."

She nodded. "Ian, be safe, please."

He opened the door, then hesitated. The scene inside the massive cave was identical to the control room massacre weeks before, yet magnified beyond belief. Body parts strewn everywhere. Some victims hung from the ledges overhead. A few were children still clutched in their parents grasps.

The horror cooled his core. Ian turned a keen ear to the cave, but the pulsing rhythm of the central column made it difficult to hear. He stepped inside and made his way around the outer edge of the cave, circling the column at a distance. He paused in mid-step at coming to Aeros on the opposite side. The megalomaniac had both arms inside the column, up to his elbows, replenishing his core in silence.

"It took you long enough," Aeros said. He glanced over each shoulder as though relishing in his handiwork. "I ran out of cattle."

"They're not cattle," Ian said. "But you slaughter without guilt, don't you?"

"They are lesser beings, no different from the animals they, in turn, kill for food." Aeros removed his arms and strolled around the column, dragging his fingers through the energy. Wherever he touched, sparks and sizzles followed. "The food chain evolves over centuries, why fight what nature dictates?"

"You're not part of a food chain," Ian said, taking one deliberate step after another toward the column. "The chain provides food for nourishment." He spread his arms. "This is for your twisted enjoyment."

"Evolution can't be stopped!" Aeros roared. He turned a furious gaze on Ian with flames for pupils. "I . . . can't be stopped!"

"You've lived too long and can't feel anything?" Ian said. "Not even this gives you pleasure, why else would you mutilate them?" Ian stuck his hand in the column when Aeros passed by. It ignited his core and he absorbed as much power as he could.

"You know nothing about me," Aeros said. His voice came from the opposite side of the column.

"I know evil when I see it," Ian said.

Aeros was upon him in an instant, and leaned in so close his father's breath warmed his cheek. "Evil is necessary." He pulled back with a sneer. "Why else would I exist?"

"There's nothing left for you here," Ian said. "Nothing for either one of us." He looked his father in the eye and withdrew his hand, his core fully charged. "I'm going home."

"There is no home for ones such as us," Aeros said. "Only worlds to conquer."

"You're wrong." Ian turned his back to his father. "Home is where we make it. And mine is on Earth."

A powerful fist of energy gripped Ian's core deep in his chest. "Ugh!" His feet left the ground and he rose into the air, then Aeros twisted him around to face him with his fist raised to Ian.

"I get enough insolence from my other son," he roared. "Like hell I'll take any from you."

"Have you not learned by now that you can't make people do what you want?" Ian snarled as energy seeped from his core and along with it, his warmth. Aeros didn't stop until he sucked what little Ian had left, and he fell to the ground in a slump, shivering.

"But I can, you see," Aeros said. "They'll do anything I ask just to keep their measly, insignificant lives."

"Goading others into submission isn't the same as having devout followers," Ian croaked, struggling to rise to his knees. Aeros had left his core all but drained. "Violence is the only aphrodisiac you have left, and even that isn't enough." Aeros thrust his fist at Ian, and he grabbed his throat, unable to breathe. "You . . . don't . . . dare . . . kill . . ." Ian's last word had no air left to be voiced.

Aeros stepped up as Ian's thoughts blurred. To his horror, Rayne crept into the cave behind his father with a finger at her lips. The irony wasn't wasted on Ian as he suffocated to death on the cave floor.

Jaered appeared a few steps behind Rayne and stood next to her. "Tell me Father, are you taking out your rage with me on my brother?"

Aeros spun around and stared at them with a shocked look on his face. "You . . ." The creases deepened and his skin turned scarlet "I killed you!" he roared at Rayne.

"Even you aren't without error," Sophenna said from the doorway with her arm around Gwynn's waist.

Jaered whipped out his hands and sent a tremendous energy blast at his father. He was lifted off his feet and knocked into the column. A brilliant flash and the room fell silent. "We'll keep him busy, take care of the others," Jaered said and rushed toward Ian, with Rayne close at his heels. Jaered gathered them both in his arms and they fell as one into the sparkling abyss.

Jaered parashyfted them to the northern vortex building at Ian's mansion. Ian collapsed on the floor, shivering while Rayne rubbed her arms, recovering from the parashyft. "Just lie there," Jaered told Ian. "Draw energy from the vortex, and hurry."

Ian mumbled something incoherent. Rayne knelt beside him with worried eyes. "Don't try and talk, Ian, just fill up your core," she said, then stood. "What's to prevent Aeros from parashyfting back to Thrae?"

"He knows we returned to Earth." Jaered opened the door onto the hallway. "And that we're here. We don't have much time before he finds us."

"He can't get into the northern vortex building," Ian said between chattering teeth.

"After everything, you still underestimate him," Jaered said. He took in how pale Ian appeared. Their father had all but drained him by the time Jaered had reached the cave.

A tremendous explosion rocked the building and Jaered was knocked against the doorjamb. The front of the vortex building had collapsed in a pile of rubble.

"Now!" Jaered hurried into the vortex field and shyfted the three of them to the auditorium. When they solidified, Ian remained on the gym floor, and his chest heaved with every breath.

"Why didn't we come straight here?" Rayne asked.

"Because Aeros can sense parashyfting locations, but not common shyfts on Earth." Jaered pushed open the double doors. "We're back!" he announced. Tara's squeal and Patrick's shout followed him back through the swinging doors.

Saxon was the first to burst into the gym, pouncing on Ian, licking his face and whipping its tail so strong that it knocked over Rayne. The wolf turned his attention on her and she fell onto her back, turning her face to avoid getting French-kissed by Saxon.

Tara fell to her knees and scooped up Ian, cradling him. "Oh my god, oh my god, you're all right!" Ian coughed and grabbed her arms in silence. "I should kill you for leaving me behind!" she screamed in his face, but then hugged him tighter than ever. She turned spilt tears to Rayne and reached toward her. Rayne wrapped her arms around Tara from behind.

Ian's coughs subsided and he sat up once the color returned to his face. "Patrick?"

"I'm here," he said, having chosen a seat several rows up from the gym floor. "You look like shit. No picnic, huh?"

"You would have been toast within the first week." Ian got to his feet. "You any better than when I left?"

"You could say that," Patrick said. Ian looked to Jaered for confirmation.

"Our brother's got some punch after all." Jaered gestured toward the picture window.

Ian wandered over and stared at the crumbled glacial wall. Rayne stepped up, then turned toward Patrick in the stands with both arms thrust into the air. "Way to go, Patrick!"

"How can we keep Aeros from going back to Thrae?" Ian said.

"By keeping Aeros's attention on Earth." All eyes fell on Eve, standing in the middle of the gym. She let go of Marcus's shoulder. Milo was with them.

"What changed your mind?" Patrick called out.

"Like you said, I have to trust someone," Milo said.

"He contacted Dr. Mac, yesterday." Eve hugged Ian and Rayne. "Good to have you back."

"Good to be back," they said.

Milo crossed his arms and gave them a scowl. "I leave you alone for a few weeks, and look at how scrawny you've gotten!" He opened his arms, and Tara and Ian fell into his bear hug. Saxon sniffed at his feet with a rotor for a tail. Rayne beamed up at him and Milo gave her a wink and a broad smile. "Hey there, missy."

"Hey, back," Rayne said.

"Now that everyone is finally on the same page, it's going to take teamwork." Eve looked up at Patrick in the stands, then Ian, and her gaze rested on Jaered. "Some of you are better at that than others."

"There's a plan to defeat those two a-holes and take back our home worlds," Marcus announced.

Eve grasped Rayne's shoulders and stared down at her. "But it isn't without grave risk."

"I'm not going anywhere," Rayne said.

"This isn't just about Earth any longer." Ian raised his chin. "I understand that now."

It was his tone that ignited Jaered's core. His brother had faced Aeros, and survived the devastation of Thrae. For the first time, they were kindred spirits indeed. Yet as much as his eyes were opened from what Jaered witnessed in the cave, Ian was as green as ever. Jaered would remedy that.

Milo cleared his throat. "If they're in, I'm in," he said.

"This guy can't tie his shoes without me," Tara said plopping down in the seat next to Patrick.

"How much time do we have?" Patrick asked.

"Not much," Ian said.

Jaered rubbed his hands together and turned a sly eye on Ian. "Foils or sabers?"

"Whichever you're the best at," Ian said from behind a smirk.

"I have two questions," Milo hollered. "Who's hungry . . . and where's the kitchen?

Saxon paused long enough at his sprint up and down the auditorium seat aisles to let out a deafening howl.

GLOSSARY

Book of the Weir: A volume of letters and notes kept by the Ancient Weir Counsel. It is rumored to include secrets to the Sars powers and predicts the coming of the Heir.

boost: A device that draws elements from the planet, such as calcium or proteins, to aid in healing. The boost is fueled by the energy stored in a Sar's core.

Channels: A set of identical Weir twins who share a genetic marker with a Sar. The three are able to communicate telepathically or, when standing close enough together, the Sar may receive visions or eavesdrop on the thoughts of others.

core: Sars are born with a core, deep in the center of their chest. It allows them to control and contain energy drawn from the planet. Not all cores are alike and therefore, it dictates what power they yield. If a core extinguishes, the Sar dies.

core blast: It was known as the Dragon's Breath during the Dark Ages. A core power that enables a Sar to draw and manipulate energy from below the surface of the planet. Many scholars believe that it comes from the center of the Earth.

corona: A colorful gas that's created when a Sar uses a vortex. If a Pur steps into a vortex field and draws energy into their core, the gases turn green. When a Duach uses the field, the gases turn red.

Curse: An unpleasant, often excruciating reaction when a Pur Sar and a Duach Sar come in close proximity to each other. Developed by the Ancients, it prevents the Duach and the Pur from stealing each other's powers, a barbaric practice which often results in death.

Duach: \\dū-ôk\\ A rebellious group of Weir who use their powers for self-gain. They are considered the black sheep of the Weir and are despised by the Pur for their narcissistic ways.

Heir: The Ancients predicted the eventual decline of the Weir race and the coming of the Heir, the last Sar born to the Weir. Prophesy stated that he would be born with the most powerful of cores, and inherit all the combined powers of the Weir Sars that came before him. Since the Weir keep the energies of Earth in harmony, the planet would continue to survive.

mark: In ancient times, known as a Seal. A triangular image of raised skin found on the left breast of Sars. Only the Heir's mark is a triangle that houses a sun. Weir males born without a mark are powerless.

paral: Someone from Earth and someone from Thrae who are the mirror image of each other.

parashyfting: Crossing into an alternate dimension during a shyft. A powerful vortex stream or field is required. Only Sars born with the shyfting power can parashyft.

Primary: The head of the Syndrion.

Pur: *pūr*\\ Thought of as the original and longest practicing of the Weir. They continue to work tirelessly for the good of the planet and to lessen man's impact on the world and other living creatures.

The Rising: A Weir practice, designed to draw a Sar's powers to the surface. Held in the event of a Sar not discovering their powers naturally.

Sar: A firstborn Weir male who's inherited a core, granting them control over a single Earthly power. Most Sars control plants or animals. Sars born with rare powers, such as shyfting or core blast powers, are the most revered and sought after.

shyft/shyfting: *shift*\\ The ability to teleport. The Sar's core allows him to use one of thousands of vortex energy fields or streams found across Earth, and move around the surface of the planet.

shyftor*:* *shif-tor*\\ A Sar born with the shyfting power doesn't need a vortex to shyft over short distances.

Somex: *sôm-ex*\\ A Sar born with the somex power can control neurotransmitters in the brain that affect consciousness.

Syndrion: *sin-drī-un*\ The Weir counsel. Ever since the Duach broke away from traditional practices centuries earlier, the current Syndrion is made up of only Pur Sars. Representatives from each continent serve on the counsel.

Thrae: *thrā*\ Earth's twin planet in an alternate dimension.

vortex: *vor-tex*\ A specific location where energy fields emanate from the planet surface and circulate on invisible gases.

Weir*:* *wē-er*\ Magical stewards of the Earth who have lived quietly among humans for more than two thousand years. Their purpose is to ensure harmony between Earth's various energies and all living creatures. With each generation, there are fewer Weir Sars born with a connection to the Earth. The Weirs' power is dwindling, and along with it, their control of Earth's combined energy. Thus, natural disasters are on the rise in frequency and intensity.

AUTHOR'S NOTE

I hope you enjoyed reading *Stack a Deck, Book Four: The Weir Chronicles*. To get caught up on the series, don't miss *Fade to Black*, book one, *Masks and Mirrors*, book two, and *Sleight of Hand*, book three, all available wherever books are sold.

To receive the latest news about the series, visit my website at www.sueduff.com. Add your name to the fan email list to receive notices about book events, the latest information on upcoming novels in the series, and more.

Check out my blog, A Cook's Guide to Writing, and other musings at www.sueduff.com. Follow me on Facebook at Sue Duff-Writer, Tweet along at https://twitter.com/sueduff55, view my Instagram pics and emoji strips at sueduffauthor, or leave a note at sueduffauthor@gmail.com.

Don't miss the thrilling conclusion to The Weir Chronicles series, *Dim the Lights, Book Five: The Weir Chronicles*, appearing winter, 2018. A suspenseful, epic battle of good-vs-evil that will determine the fate of our heroes, and ultimately, the universe.

OTHER BOOKS BY SUE DUFF

The Weir Chronicles
Fade to Black
Masks and Mirrors
Sleight of Hand
Stack a Deck
Dim the Lights
(available February 2018)

Short Stories
"Duo'vr"
a short story in the anthology
TICK TOCK: Seven Tales of Time

"A Mistake"
a short story in the anthology
OFF BEAT: Nine Spins on Song

ACKNOWLEDGEMENTS

Every writer needs a tribe for support, encouragement, expertise, advice and yes, the crucial critiques. It takes that and more to pull characters, plot and dialogue into a gripping novel that readers will enjoy for years to come.

I adore my publishing tribe and all that they bring to my process. Karri Klawiter @ Art by Karri for her amazing covers, Steve Parolini @ Novel Doctor for his developmental editing, copyeditor Stephanie Viola for catching my grammar snafus, Matthew Woolums for his meticulous Beta reads and Sami Jo Lien at Roger Charlie for spreading the word about the series to eager readers.

As always, thank you to my writers group at the Tattered Cover in Littleton, Colorado for everything you provide each week to make me a better writer. And I can't forget my larger tribe at Rocky Mountain Fiction Writers for everything they do to support writers from a local-to-global scale.

For my friends, but especially my family, who I've dedicated this novel. You are my rock and center of support in all aspects of my life.

A huge thank you to you, the fans. Your enthusiasm for this series is at the heart of encouraging me to be a better writer. I hope to continue to entertain you for years to come.

When not saving the world one page at a time, Sue works as a speech therapist. She enjoys taking her octogenarian dachshund for strolls and stretching her creative juices in the kitchen. A Colorado transplant, she savors the incredible seasons, but appreciates that Mother Nature spares her from shoveling the driveway, too often.

Visit Sue at www.sueduff.com, on Facebook at Sue Duff-Writer and follow her on Twitter @sueduff55.

Book cover designed by Karri Klawiter, Art by Karri,
Author Photo by Liz Garcia

www.ingramcontent.com/pod-product-compliance
Lightning Source LLC
Chambersburg PA
CBHW030700120726
47905CB00001B/294